"When I Saw You Again, All the Years In Between Seemed like Nothing.

"I wanted you so badly I was shaking. When we made love, it was still the same."

"Oh, no, Tonio. Better." Erica's voice was sharp. "You've obviously had a lot of experience since then."

Unexpectedly he chuckled. "Jealous?"

"I don't care enough to be jealous."

His mouth tightened. "But you can't deny what happens when we touch each other. Go ahead, ignore me as long as you can. But remember, I want you in my bed again. And I've changed since the old days. Now I'm used to getting what I want."

KRISTIN JAMES

grew up in a newspaper family, and her dream was always to become a novelist. She took time out to earn a law degree, but she gave up practice to write full time. She shares her Texas home with her husband, who enthusiastically supports her career, and their young daughter.

Dear Reader:

There is an electricity between two people in love that makes everything they do magic, larger than life. This is what we bring you in SILHOUETTE INTIMATE MOMENTS.

SILHOUETTE INTIMATE MOMENTS are longer, more sensuous romance novels filled with adventure, suspense, glamor or melodrama. These books have an element no one else has tapped: excitement.

We are proud to present the very best romance has to offer from the very best romance writers. In the coming months look for some of your favorite authors such as Elizabeth Lowell, Nora Roberts, Erin St. Claire and Brooke Hastings.

SILHOUETTE INTIMATE MOMENTS are for the woman who wants more than she has ever had before. These books are for you.

Karen Solem
Editor-in-Chief
Silhouette Books

Dreams of Evening

Kristin James

Silhouette Intimate Moments

Published by Silhouette Books New York

America's Publisher of Contemporary Romance

Other Silhouette Books by Kristin James

The Amber Sky

SILHOUETTE BOOKS, a Division of Simon & Schuster, Inc.
1230 Avenue of the Americas, New York, N.Y. 10020

ISBN: 0-671-47778-1

First Silhouette Books printing May, 1983

10 9 8 7 6 5 4 3

Chapter 1

ERICA LOGAN STOOD ON THE NARROW BALCONY; watching the gentle blue roll of the waves as they washed into shore. This was her one precious moment alone in the whole day, the few minutes she spent sipping her coffee and looking at the Gulf after Danny dashed to catch his school bus and before she went down to face the multitude of problems that were her lot as manager of the Breezes. She lifted her face, delighting in the caress of the warm, moist air. No matter how many customer complaints she had to face or how many crises arose in the hotel, Erica thought it was worth it all to be back on the Island again. When she was a child, she and her parents had often driven from their citrus farm in the Rio Grande Valley to vacation here on South Padre Island, and she had loved splashing in the gentle surf and running down the sandy beach. It had seemed the answer to a prayer when she was offered this job and could return here to live.

With a sigh Erica drained her coffee mug and stepped back inside her living room. She had dawdled long enough and now must start to work. Going to the mirror, she smoothed her hair and checked her simple green pantsuit to make sure that she looked her efficient best. Then, picking up her key, she strode out the door and down the long hall to the elevator at the far end.

There was a lush, sensual beauty to Erica, which she managed successfully to restrain. She had learned long ago that unusual looks or signs of femininity did not help a woman rise in business. Instead she strove for a neat, pleasant, practical look. Usually she wore an attractive but businesslike suit, with a blazer or jacket to hide the lines of her excellent figure. She pulled her long, rich brown hair, warmed by red highlights, into a sedate knot at the nape of her neck. And though nothing could make her oval face with its classic lines and light gray eyes unlovely, Erica carefully screened from her face the emotions that made it come alive with beauty. Erica had made up her mind long ago to be a career woman, and she ruthlessly molded herself to fit the part.

Downstairs in the lobby Erica walked cautiously across the rust-colored quarry tile, which was still damp from mopping, and made her way to the front desk. The clerk behind the chest-high counter, an attractive but effeminate-looking young man, smiled at her. Dave, always neat and well-dressed himself, approved of her appearance. Erica knew his dislike of Mrs. Berry, who ran the coffee shop, stemmed from her teased blond hair and outdated short skirts.

"Hi, Dave, how's it going?" Erica asked, and he rolled his eyes heavenward. "That bad, huh?"

"Would you like for me to start chronologically or in order of importance?" Dave replied.

"Oh, dear." Erica swung open the half-door and stepped into the area behind the tall counter. Across the back wall of the small room was the telephone complex. To the left lay the semi-enclosed desk of

Rita Escamilla, who acted as Erica's secretary, assistant to the desk clerk and interpreter for many of the Mexican nationals and Mexican-Americans who came to stay. Erica's office was on the right, and she crossed to it to unlock the door.

"Hi, Rita," Erica greeted the pretty, dark-haired girl with a smile.

"Hi. Want a cup of coffee?"

"I'd love one. It looks like I'm going to need it." Erica switched on the light and glanced back at Dave Granger. "Okay, Dave, come on in here and dump it on me."

He followed her lazily and stood leaning in the doorway, where he would be able to see the approach of a customer. "Well, first of all, that new clerk on the evening shift apparently has no conception of what a reservation is. She put people staying more than one night in several rooms that are reserved beginning today."

Erica groaned. "How many?"

"About twenty rooms."

"Are we overbooked?"

"No. I think we have enough leaving today to take care of the reservations. But Room 906 is steamed because 908 should be reserved for a party joining them today, but crazy Connie booked 908 last night to someone else who's staying three days."

"Well, explain it to the guy in 908 and move him. Let the reservation have that room. Any more like that?"

"I don't think so. I can move the reservations to other rooms, I think. It's just a pain. Where is that girl's brain?"

"I don't know. I'll help you with it in a minute, and I'll go over our system of reservations with Connie again this afternoon. What else?"

Rita eased through the door with a cup of coffee and answered for him. "Two maids and one of the maintenance men didn't show up for work today."

That didn't surprise Erica. Absences were far too common, particularly on a Friday or Monday. Personnel was always one of her major problems. The minuscule wage the hotel paid its workers did not attract the steadiest of help.

"Rita, call the maid service in Brownsville and see if you can get a woman for today. I think one should be enough, since it's the off-season. Do you have any idea if the absences are permanent or if they'll be coming back?"

Rita shrugged expressively. "Dolores called and said she was sick, but the others—who knows?"

Her secretary left the room, and Erica looked back at Dave. "More?"

"I saved the best for last."

"Terrific."

"Alan Severn called just before you came, and said he's driving out today to talk to you."

Erica stared at him. "Mr. Severn? But why?"

"As Rita said, 'Who knows?'" Dave replied with a sarcastic smile, and moved back to his desk.

Erica sighed and took a sip of her coffee, her eyes narrowing in thought. What reason could Severn have for coming here today? Although he was the owner of the hotel, he did not take a very active part in the management of it. He spent most of his energies on a shopping center and restaurant he owned in Harlingen, where he lived.

She wondered with a leap of hope if he had decided to renovate the hotel, then reluctantly discarded the idea. Severn had made it clear over a month ago how he felt about making any further repairs.

No doubt it was true that he did not have the money to spend on the Breezes. Business had suffered badly the season before because of an oil spill that had polluted the Texas beaches. Poor economic conditions had hurt all the resorts even further. Then, in August, a hurricane had ripped through, flooding the narrow spit of land that was South Padre Island and damaging the grounds and lobby of the hotel. Whatever money there was to spare had been spent on cleaning and repairing the damage done by the storm. But the Breezes didn't have the financial cushion of chain hotels or those backed by wealthy conglomerates.

It was a pity, Erica thought, for the Breezes, built twelve years before, was a strong and essentially elegant structure. With a little fixing up, it could have been one of the prettiest hotels on the beach. It was a long, thin, white building with elegant black iron-railed balconies off every room, all cunningly slanted so that each had a view of the ocean and none looked into another balcony. But the lobby needed to be refurbished, and the black paint on the balcony railings was chipped and peeling. Years of use by careless tenants had damaged most of the rooms, and nothing more than spot repairs had ever been done. Less noticeable but worse in the long run, much of the original equipment was in poor condition and continually broke done. The breaks were patched up temporarily, and the machinery managed to hobble along, but it didn't stop the accelerating deterioration of the building.

With an effort Erica put aside her musings on the hotel and Mr. Severn's mission and began to open the stack of letters on her desk. When she had finished, she took the two mailed requests for reservations and Dave managed to straighten out the mess Connie Maldonado had made of the reservations the night before. Just as she finished and was about to turn to go back to her office, the front door swung open and Alan Severn hurried in.

"Why, Mr. Severn," Erica greeted him cheerfully, coming from behind the desk to shake his hand.

Severn smiled faintly and took her hand in his dry grasp. He was a thin man whose financial wheelings and dealings had left him with a nervous stomach and a look of perpetual anxiety.

"Mrs. Logan," he returned soberly. "I hope you got my message."

"Oh, yes. Please come into my office. Would you like a cup of coffee?"

"No, no, thank you." He walked past her into the office, and Erica followed him, closing the door firmly against the interested ears of the secretary and desk clerk.

Erica seated herself behind her desk and waited for the man to begin. Severn sat down, adjusted his coat sleeves and glanced around. Finally, with a sigh, he began.

"Mrs. Logan, I guess you know as well as anyone the financial difficulties the Breezes has been having." Erica nodded, wondering with horror if he was going to demand that she cut back expenses. There simply was not anything left to trim off!

Severn cleared his throat and continued, "I don't have the financial capacity to put this old hotel back on its feet. The Breezes has always been my pride and joy, but I've finally decided that I have to give it up. What I'm saying is that I've sold the hotel."

Erica blinked in astonishment. Whatever she had expected Severn to say, it hadn't been this. "Sold?" she repeated. "But . . . who—"

"Cross Corporation," he replied. "It's a resort development company out of Houston."

"Yes, I've heard of them. I saw pictures of a lovely condominium complex they built in Florida."

"They work mainly in Texas and the South. I think they're a rather new company, but very aggressive."

"But, Mr. Severn, what do they want with the Breezes? I thought they built new hotels."

"Oh, yes, usually they do. But they wanted our location; it's one of the best on the island. And they liked the basic structure of the hotel. What they intend to do is renovate the Breezes and add two wings of condominiums and another pool, as I understand it."

"I see." She did see, indeed. She saw that her return to the valley might not be very long-lived. The new owners would probably bring in their own manager to run the hotel. They might even let go many of the other employees in favor of people they had trained themselves.

"I signed the papers yesterday in Houston. The Breezes is no longer mine."

"Will the new owner be contacting me?" Erica asked uncertainly.

"Oh, yes, Cross wants to get on it right away. An architect is coming in tomorrow to examine the hotel. I don't believe you were here then, but he came about four months ago, before we started negotiating. Anyway, I plan to meet him at the airport tomorrow and drive him out to introduce him to you. His plane gets in at one, so we should be here around two or two-thirty."

Severn rose, ending the conversation, and Erica stood up too. Still numbed by his news, she followed him out of the office and to the front door of the hotel. When the glass door closed behind him, she turned to face the curious faces of Rita and Dave.

"What happened?" Rita asked, her voice concerned. "You look like you've had a shock."

"I have, rather," Erica admitted. "Rita, tell all the employees that I want to see them in the dining room at ten-thirty. I have an important announcement to make."

"What?" Dave pressed. "Come on, Erica."

"I guess I might as well tell you now. Severn has sold the hotel to Cross Corporation."

"What!" The two of them gasped almost in unison.

"Yeah, that's what I thought," Erica responded with a little laugh. "Cross Corporation is a resort developer, and they're going to renovate and add on to the Breezes."

"Well, now at least this poor old thing will get a facelift," Rita mused.

Dave threw her a dark glance and gibed, "Yeah, and we may be some of the 'old fixtures' that get thrown out."

"I hadn't thought of that," Rita admitted, the new excitement dying on her face. "Will we get fired, Erica?"

"I don't know. A representative from Cross is flying in tomorrow. Maybe he can give us some answers. By the way, Dave, is there anyone in the top-floor suite?"

"I don't think so," he replied, and flipped through his cards. "No. Want me to reserve it for the big shot from Cross?"

"Yeah."

"What's his name?"

Erica's eyes widened and she said in amazement,

"I don't know. Severn stunned me so much that I never even asked him. Oh, well, just put down Cross Corporation on the card."

Except for the employee meeting, the rest of the day was the usual mishmash of problems, routine and business decisions. At lunch Glynda Berry tried to pump her for information about the sale, but Erica could tell her very little. All the other employees were obviously worried, too, and Erica wished she could reassure them. However, since she had no idea what the new owners would do, she hated to raise what might turn out to be false hopes.

She tried to appear confident and unworried, going about her usual tasks as if nothing had happened, but worry gnawed at her. Where could she go if they fired her? The economy and gas prices had put most of the resort industry into a slump, and a woman with a small boy was not the most attractive prospect for hiring, anyway.

By the time Danny jumped down from the schoolbus and ran into the lobby, Erica felt drained and anxious to get away from the hotel. When he catapulted into her office, she smiled and said, "How goes it? How would you like to drive over to Port Isabel tonight and eat shrimp?"

"Okay," he replied, answering both her questions. "Look, Mom. Mrs. Benitez said I should show you this."

He handed a paper to her; written across the top in bold red numbers was 110. Erica's eyebrows shot up, and she exclaimed, "110! How can you make 110? I thought 100 was perfect."

"She said the test was so hard, she gave us a bonus question to raise the scores. But I got them all right and the bonus question too."

Erica grinned and held out her arms to the boy. "Come here, you mathematical genius, and let me give you a hug."

Danny was a warm, affectionate child, and he came readily into her arms. He had never known his father and, as a consequence, had grown doubly close to Erica. She sometimes worried that the boy was too attached to her, that he should have a father figure in his life. But she hadn't fallen in love again after Tonio, and she couldn't bring herself to marry a man she didn't love, just so Danny could have a father. Her own father might have been a substitute, but Erica had never been close to him, and since Danny's birth, his angry disapproval had caused her to visit him rarely.

Erica gave Danny an extra squeeze, then released him, and he stepped back. "Can I play on the beach until we go eat?"

She smiled fondly at the boy and reached out to brush a stray lock of heavy black hair from his eyes. He was small for his age, a wiry bundle of energy, forever collecting shells on the beach or fishing or just racing along the sand in sheer high animal spirits. All boy, he was a joy and yet a constant mystery to her.

Swallowing the sudden lump in her throat, Erica said, "Sure, but come in by five-thirty. No, never mind. I think I'd like a walk along the beach. I'll come get you."

He was gone in a shot, and Erica returned to her work. At five Rita stuck her head in the door to say she was leaving, and Erica set about clearing the rest of the work off her desk. By five-thirty she had managed to get everything squared away, and she slipped up to her room to change into shorts and a T-shirt. Quickly she pulled the pins from her hair and ran a brush through the heavy brown mass that glowed with red highlights, like fine mahogany. What a relief it was to get out of the restrictive mold work imposed on her. It would be heavenly to walk along the sand and let the sea breeze toss her mane of hair about. After all, she had been raised on a farm, and she missed the outdoors and the freedom.

Erica ran lightly down the stairs that opened on to the back of the hotel and emerged from the service door by the pool. She crossed a brick pathway beside the pool to the steps leading to the beach. The soft sand near the steps soon gave way to the closely packed sand that lined the ocean.

Breathing in deeply, Erica drank in the scene before her. The sun sank low on the horizon behind her, spreading a golden glow across the water. Waves crashed in, foaming white, and she ventured out to let the water swirl around her legs. The water was shallow for a long way out, which was one of the Island's major appeals to tourists. Children and adults frolicked in the surf far beyond Erica, and the water still did not reach their waists.

Erica began to stroll slowly along the beach, shading her eyes to look for Danny. At last she saw him, earnestly engaged in building a sand fort with another child. When she called to him, he glanced up, then rose quickly, dusting off his shorts, and ran to meet her.

"Look what I got!" he shouted, coming to a scrambling halt in front of her; then he proceeded to dig two handfuls of shells out of his pockets. When Erica had suitably admired them, he repocketed his collection and took her hand, and they began to walk alongside the ocean, now and then idly dabbling their feet in the water.

"Something happened at work today," Erica

began, and Danny lifted his face to her inquiringly. "Mr. Severn—you know, the man who owns the hotel—came to see me this morning. And he told me that he had sold the hotel to a company in Houston."

"How come? Doesn't he want it anymore?" Danny asked.

"Oh, I think he still wants it, but he decided he couldn't afford to keep it. It needs a lot of work, and he doesn't have enough money to do it."

"I see. So the new guys are going to fix it all up?"

"Yes, I imagine so. And they're going to build two more wings on to it too."

"Wow! Then I can watch them building! That'll be fun. When are they going to start?"

"I don't know. A man is arriving tomorrow to look at everything. Then I guess he'll draw the plans for the additions, and after that they could start building."

"That'll be neat. Maybe it will be this summer, when I don't have to go to school." He paused and looked at her again. "You don't look very happy. Don't you want them to build on to the hotel and make it look better?"

"Of course I do. I think it could be a fine place. But I am a little worried. Sometimes when a new company comes in, they want to bring in their own people to operate the hotel. They might not want to keep me."

"You mean they'd fire you?" Danny asked in disbelief.

Erica smiled at his tone. "They might. Not because they don't like me, but because they want someone they trained in the job."

"I see," Danny acceded, although to him it still

seemed rather peculiar. "What would we do then? Go to another hotel?"

"I hope so. I would apply to other places here on the Island and in Brownsville and Harlingen. I'd like to stay in the Valley area if we could."

"But what if you couldn't get a job? I mean, here or anywhere else. What would we do?"

"If worse came to worst, we could always go home and live with my father on the farm. How would you like that?"

Danny considered her question. "I'd like to live on the farm, I think. There are all kinds of interesting things to do there. But I'm not sure. We hardly ever go there." He paused. "I don't know if I like Granddaddy."

"Oh, why not?"

"He always looks like this." Danny made a stern face, drawing down the corners of his mouth. "And he talks funny to you, like he's mad about something."

"He probably is. Dad and I never agreed about too many things. I love him, but we don't get along very well." She sighed and looked out at the sea. "He wants us to come home and live, and I want to be independent. Sometimes I wonder if I've done the right thing, refusing to go home. Danny, has it been terribly hard on you, living as we've done? I mean, with me working, and you having to stay with a sitter, and our moving whenever I got a new job."

Her son looked at her in puzzlement. "What do you mean? Would I rather live someplace else?"

"Yes, like on the farm with Granddaddy. Do you wish that we didn't live in a hotel or that we didn't move so often? Do you get lonely?"

"No. I like the farm, but I like it here too. I get to

swim all the time and play on the beach and run around in the hotel. I think it's lots of fun."

She looked down at him, a tiny frown pinching the skin of her forehead, and she wondered, as she so often did, if she had done the right thing for Danny by insisting on raising him on her own. But his open, pleasant face banished the frown and made her smile. Surely she had been right. Danny was so normal, so well adjusted, that it seemed impossible that he should be scarred by his upbringing.

With an affectionate gesture she reached out and ruffled his thick black hair. "Well, that's enough soul-searching for the moment. I think I'm about ready to eat. How about you?"

"Sure. Wanna race home?" he offered hopefully.

With a laugh she agreed, and they set out. Danny was small for a nine-year-old, but quick, and Erica had to run full-tilt to keep up with him. He reached the stairs to the hotel seconds before she arrived, breathless and flushed from the exertion.

"Beat you!" Danny crowed triumphantly. "I'm the fastest boy in my class."

They turned on the outdoor shower head and washed the sand from their feet, then went up to change for dinner. Erica merely exchanged her shorts for a denim skirt and slipped her tanned feet into sandals, for there were few places in this resort town that required anything but casual clothes.

In the blue knit top and with her thick mane of dark hair spreading across her shoulders, Erica attracted several admiring glances as they walked out to their car. However, she paid scant attention to them. She dated occasionally, but between her job and Danny she had little time for, or interest in, men.

They got into her small blue Datsun and drove

over the high bridge that connected South Padre
Island to the Texas mainland.

Padre Island was a narrow spit of land lying
parallel to the South Texas coastline as it curved
south to Mexico. The northern tip of the island was
at Corpus Christi, the southern edge almost at
Brownsville. North Padre and South Padre were two
distinct communities without even a highway con-
necting the two, and in between them lay the empty
beach wilderness of a protected state park. South
Padre, known simply as "the Island" to the nearby
mainland residents, possessed a single main street
running lengthwise straight up the middle of the land
like a backbone. Side streets ran off at right angles,
none more than three or four blocks long. Date
palms stood at each intersection and in front of many
of the hotels, giving the locale a tropical flavor,
enhanced by the pristine white sand of the beaches
and the glittering blue ocean beyond. The industry
of the island was tourism, and the space was dominated by several tall hotels, with shorter motels,
condominiums and a few beach houses squeezed in
between. Except for restaurants, beachware and
supplies stores and realty offices, there was little else
on the island. Most of the people who worked on the
island lived across the narrow bay in Port Isabel,
which provided the island with the normal appurte-
nances of a community, such as grocery stores and
self-service laundries.

Erica and Danny ate boiled Gulf shrimp at a plain
but delicious restaurant in Port Isabel, and after they
returned, there was barely enough time for Danny to
do his homework before he went to bed. They did
not speak again about the sale of the hotel or the
possible consequences to themselves.

Erica tucked her son into bed and sat down to pay

a few bills, but her eyelids quickly grew heavy, and she decided to turn in early. After tying back her hair, she scrubbed her face and put on a simple white nightgown. Before retiring, she slipped into Danny's small room for a final look at him.

He lay on his back, fast asleep, his arms flung wide. As she looked down at him, her eyes misted over, and she smiled. Asleep, there was no hint of the active, sometimes mischievous boy he was during the day. Lovingly her eyes traced the outlines of his tanned face. The cheekbones were wide and high, his mouth firm. His eyebrows were black slashes across his face. Only his hazel eyes were evidence of Erica's parentage; his facial structure and coloring were very much his father's. With his eyes closed, he looked like Tonio, Erica saw with a sudden pang. The older he got, losing the vague lines of babyhood, the more Tonio surfaced in his face.

A lump formed in Erica's throat, and she swallowed and quickly left the room.

The next day, everyone went about their jobs with their eyes half on the entrance to the lobby. They were nervous about the upcoming meeting with the representative of the new owner—Erica as much as anyone, although she managed to hide her nerves beneath a calm mask. She had carefully chosen for this important meeting her most sedate and expensive suit, a chocolate-brown skirt with a matching brown hip-length jacket buttoned over a plain beige blouse. She wore no ornament except for the small gold studs in her ears and a watch.

At about two-thirty, as she sat reading a letter for the third time, her stomach jumping, Rita stepped into her office. "Mr. Severn's here. I just saw him walking to the door. And you should see the guy with him—absolutely gorgeous!"

Erica smiled tightly. "Good, then maybe we'll leave it to you to win him over."

"I wish," Rita said in a fervent undertone.

Erica stepped past her and walked around the counter into the lobby just as the door swung open and Mr. Severn ushered in his guest. The man was of medium height, dark, with straight black brows and thick black hair. His face was angular, his lips firm, almost chiseled. Dark eyes ringed with thick black lashes glanced about the room and came to rest on her, narrowing with surprise as he came to a sudden halt.

Across the room Erica stood stock-still, staring at him, her mind numb with astonishment and disbelief. She heard faintly, as if he were far away, Mr. Severn speak her name. There was a roaring in her ears, and for a moment she was afraid she might faint. It couldn't be—and yet it was. After all these years the man she had thought she would never see again stood before her: Tonio!

Chapter 2

THE ROARING IN HER EARS DIED, AND ERICA STRAIGHT-
ened, pulling herself together, as the two men
advanced toward her. Wetting her lips, she managed
a shaky smile, although her face was paper-white
from the shock.

"Mrs. Logan, this is Anthony Cruz, the architect
from Cross Corporation," Severn introduced him.
"Anthony, this is Erica Logan, the manager of the
Breezes."

Cruz, after his initial amazement, had assumed a
look of careful indifference. "Yes," he said politely,
his glance touching Erica coldly. "I know Erica. We
are from the same town."

Erica held out her hand to shake his, trying to
match his calm unconcern. "Hello, Antonio. I'm
afraid I had no idea it was you who was coming
today."

"Well, isn't that remarkable?" Severn commented. "Strange how you'll accidentally meet people
you know like that. Well, Anthony, I'll leave you in
Mrs. Logan's capable hands. I'm sure she will be
able to help you with anything you need to know.
It's been a pleasure."

The two men shook hands, and Cruz murmured a

polite good-bye. Then he turned back to her, and Erica clasped her hands to hide her nervousness.

"If you would like, I'll take you up to your room now," she offered, although that was the last thing in the world she wanted to do. However, Rita and Dave would think it peculiar and rude if she handed the task over to one of them. She turned toward the desk. "Dave, could I have the key to 1000? Mr. Cruz, allow me to introduce you to my secretary, Rita Escamilla, and our desk clerk, Dave Granger."

Dave handed her the key, and the three strangers exchanged polite greetings. Erica walked to the elevator with Antonio following behind her. She tried desperately to calm her jittering stomach, but the thought of riding up in the elevator with him and walking him to his room was altogether too unsettling. She told herself that no doubt he hardly remembered her. That summer ten years ago had probably been only one in a string of romances to him, even though it had changed her life forever. He would certainly not inject any emotion into this business meeting. There was no reason to feel afraid and sick. It had all happened a long time ago, and she was over the pain as well as the love.

They stepped into the elevator and the door closed behind them. Erica looked down at the floor to avoid his eyes, then forced herself to lift her gaze. She refused to act embarrassed and frightened. She found her companion looking at her expressionlessly, and she braced her shoulders, returning his stare. He was as handsome as ever, she thought, maybe even more so, now that he had matured. However, the sullen, angry good looks had been replaced by a cold hardness. Once he had exuded emotion; now no feeling touched him at all.

"Well, it's been a long time," she commented, to break the oppressive silence, and then cursed herself for sounding so banal. His presence was overwhelming, and she could hardly think or even breathe. Even after all this time, after all he'd done to her, he still set her pulse rolling like a drumbeat and made her nerves quiver.

"Yes," he replied shortly. "I noticed he called you Mrs. Logan."

Her hands turned icy. He must not find out the truth. She gave a brief laugh and said, "Alan Severn isn't known for his memory. For some reason he thinks I'm married. I finally stopped reminding him that it's Miss Logan."

The elevator stopped on his floor, and Erica stepped out gratefully, leading the way down the hall to the large suite at the end. She opened the door and handed the key to Tonio. "If you need anything, just let us know."

"Tomorrow I'd like to inspect the hotel—the lobby, the rooms, the maintenance area, the coffee shop, everything."

"Of course."

"I hope you won't mind taking your free Sunday to show me around."

"Me?" Erica repeated dully, recoiling at the thought of spending the entire day tramping around the hotel with him.

"Of course. You know it better than anyone else."

"Of course," Erica agreed through bloodless lips. "What time shall we start?"

"Nine o'clock?" She nodded, and he continued, "I'll meet you at your office."

"All right."

Erica could feel his eyes on her back as she strode away, and she kept herself stiffly straight. She touched the elevator button, and when the doors slid open, she hurried inside, carefully refraining from glancing around to see if he still watched her. Safe from his gaze, she sagged against the wall, her energy flooding away and leaving her shaking, both inside and out.

Tonio Cruz—after all this time! Why did he have to come here! Why had she accepted this job! She wanted desperately to run upstairs, pull Danny to the car and drive away as quickly as she could. How could she possibly escort that man around the hotel tomorrow as if nothing had ever happened between them?

Once in the lobby Erica walked past the eager, curious faces of the employees and shut herself in her office, where she sat down at her desk and rested her face on her trembling hands. Gradually she calmed down enough to realize that in this state she would not be able to do any of her work. The best thing would be to leave the office and go to her apartment or walk along the beach and think. She had to put her head and her emotions into some semblance of order. Rita stared with surprise when Erica told her she was leaving for the day, but she made no comment. Erica suspected that her face gave away at least some of the turmoil going on inside her. She went to her apartment and changed clothes, glad that Danny was not there but out playing by the pool.

She slipped down the staircase and out the back door, then wandered along the sand for some time, hardly noticing where she was going, her thoughts a jumble. Finally she stopped to glance around her and realized she had walked all the way down the beach.

Erica sighed and sank down to the ground. Pulling

her knees up and circling them with her arms, she stared out at the hypnotic waves. Now that she had worked off her nerves, maybe she could begin to think more clearly. Lulled by the beat of the surf, she relaxed, letting her mind drift. Inexorably her thoughts were pulled backward, past all the years and the barriers she had worked so hard to construct . . . to the time ten years before when she looked out her bedroom window and saw Tonio Cruz in the front yard, talking to her father.

She had been seventeen then, idle, confident and exploding into the full ripeness of her young beauty. Her father was a well-to-do citrus farmer who gave her whatever she wanted in the way of material goods. She spent her summer zipping around in her small sports car or sunning by the pool or gossiping with friends over lunch at the country club. In the evenings she flirted with one or another of the boys who pursued her diligently. It was amazing—and a little heady—this new power she held over the boys she had known all her life, and it was fun to exercise it a little. But her basic generosity prevented her from teasing them to the point of cruelty, and her sense of humor kept the whole thing in perspective.

She herself had never felt the ache of teen-age love that afflicted her swains. Until she saw Antonio. He stood sideways to her as he talked to her father, and she could see his cleanly etched profile, strong and handsome. His head was bare, and the sun glinted off his crow-black hair. His faded jeans clung to his lean, firm thighs, and the sleeves of his blue work shirt were rolled up to reveal corded muscles that belied his slimness. He was lithe and hard, exciting in a way Erica had never known before. Looking at him, she felt a hot, wild explosion in her chest, a strange sizzling along her nerves, and unconsciously she leaned toward him.

She knew him, of course. The town of Santa Clara was much too small for everyone not to know everyone else. Besides, Tonio had worked for her father when he was a teen-ager, before he had gone away to college four years before. But she hadn't seen him for four years, and at thirteen she hadn't experienced the same shattering emotion as when she looked at him now.

She watched as he and her father left the yard and disappeared around the corner of the house. No doubt they were going to the side door that led to Grant Logan's study. Without stopping to analyze her motives, knowing only that she had to speak to Tonio, she darted down the stairs, grabbing a magazine from the hall table as she ran, and went onto the wide veranda that surrounded the house on three sides. She hurried to the wooden swing that hung close to the side door, and flopped down on it; then she opened the magazine and fixed her eyes intently on it as she listened for the sound of her father's study door closing inside the house. As she waited, she fluffed her hair and combed through it with her fingers, wishing she had taken the time to brush it and apply a little lipstick. Her clothes were plain and casual, but she knew how well her tanned legs looked emerging from the short cutoff blue jeans and how nicely she filled out the pale pink halter top.

It seemed forever before she heard the closing of the heavy door inside the hall and then the scrape of Tonio's boot heels on the tile floor. The screen door swung open and he stepped out. Involuntarily Erica sucked in her breath. Tonio was even more handsome close up, more wickedly dangerous-looking.

The chiseled mouth had a surly, almost defiant set to it, and his shadowed dark eyes burned with a cold flame. He looked wild and fiery, pulsing with energy and life. Erica thought that if she touched him, an electrical jolt might pass through him into her. He didn't see her sitting there in the swing, shaded by a large, purple-blooming jacaranda bush, and he started across the porch.

"Hello, Antonio," she called out quickly to stop him. He whirled, startled, and stared at her for a moment. Even his quick, impersonal glance sent shivers down her spine.

"Ma'am," he replied distantly, and started on.

"Tonio, it's me, Erica!" she exclaimed, jumping up. "Don't you recognize me?"

"Sorry, I didn't at first." He swept her with an impassive gaze. "You're quite a bit older."

His words had none of the leer that usually accompanied remarks about her growing up: He sounded matter-of-fact, almost indifferent. Nor did his eyes light up with interest in the woman's face and figure she now possessed. He said nothing more, and Erica felt awkward and foolish, standing across from him in silence. Tonio obviously had nothing to say to her and was simply waiting politely for her to continue the conversation she had forced.

"Welcome back," she murmured lamely.

Something flared then in his dark brown eyes, and he snapped, "I won't be here long."

Erica sank back onto the cushioned seat and buried her face in the magazine, acutely aware of the sound of his boots on the porch and then on the cement walkway. She blinked back hot tears. His cold, brusque manner had hurt, especially since she felt anything but indifferent when she looked at him. Long after she heard his car leave, she remained in the swing, thinking about Tonio and his reaction to her. For a while she was tempted to try to forget all about him, for her vanity had been wounded. But a "So there!" attitude couldn't stand up for long against the burning desire she had to see him again—and, more than that, to fix his interest.

Looking back on it, Erica wondered at her daring and persistence in pursuing Tonio. Nowadays she would never think of making any effort to capture the heart of a man who appeared indifferent to her. But back then she had never lost, never failed to win over any boy's heart. She couldn't really imagine wanting something and not receiving it. And she had wanted Tonio—more than anything in the world she had wanted Tonio. She was caught in the fiery clutches of youthful love and passion. With her usual confidence she was determined to make him fall for her. She began to seize every opportunity to run into Antonio. And for each "accidental" meeting, she made sure her hair and face were at their loveliest and that she wore clothes that set off her excellent figure. She would ride her horse, Morning Star, down to the citrus groves and wander along the borders between the rows of trees. If she was lucky, she would come across Tonio opening the turnout valves along the irrigation pipe and flooding the rows of grapefruit trees with precious water. If Rafael Escobar, her father's foreman, happened to be there, she could stop to say a few words to him, thus placing herself in Tonio's line of vision for a while longer. But if Tonio was by himself, or with one of the other men, Erica could find no excuse to linger. He would scowl and return her greeting shortly, and Erica would be unable to get any sort of conversation going.

One morning, as she left the house in a smart

white tennis skirt and top, on her way to the club to play tennis with Sally Blackburn, she spied Tonio by the barn, working on the engine of the tractor. Quickly Erica tossed her racket into the passenger seat of her car and crossed the yard to the barn.

"Hi!" she called brightly as she drew near, and Tonio glanced at her briefly, then returned to his work. Erica sighed and watched his long, slender fingers turn the wrench. Just the sight of them set up a curious trembling in her stomach. Finally she said, "Tonio, I've been wondering about something. Didn't you graduate from the University of Texas this year?"

"Yeah, got a degree in architecture," he responded laconically.

She went on doggedly, "So why are you back in Santa Clara, working on Daddy's farm? Why aren't you out drawing plans for houses?"

"I plan to design commercial buildings, not residences," he told her gruffly.

"Okay, then, why aren't you drawing big buildings?"

"I've been hired to start work for a firm in September. Until then, I thought I'd come back here and see my mother. Earn a little money."

"I see. Where are you going to work in September?"

He straightened, his brow drawn into a fierce frown. "Don't you have anything better to do with your time than bother me? Aren't you expected somewhere?" He glanced pointedly at her tennis outfit.

A pain pierced her chest at his rough words, and Erica had to force back the tears that sprang into her eyes. "I was just trying to be nice! To be a little friendly! Before you went off to the university, at least you'd stop and talk to me sometimes. At least you were decent. I remember, even if you don't. I remember the time you climbed onto the roof to get the tennis ball I knocked up there. And the time I sprained my ankle out in the groves and you carried me back to the house."

His dark eyes softened a trifle, and he said, "You were a good kid. Besides, you'd done me a favor once."

"A favor?" Erica stared at him wonderingly for a moment, then understanding dawned on her face. "Oh! You mean in the schoolyard when I was in the second grade? When Jim Bob Coulter and Rusty Jansen jumped on you?"

"That's the time." He almost smiled. "You came running over there like a pint-sized tornado, kicking and scratching and screaming."

"Well, they were bigger than you. They were already in junior high. And it wasn't fair, two on one like that."

"Oh, I'm not complaining. I was rather grateful, as I remember. You brought the teachers running. And gave Rusty a nice bruise on his shin."

"So if I helped you so much, why do you dislike me now?" Erica asked bluntly.

His face closed down and he said brusquely, "You aren't a little girl anymore."

Something hot and elemental sparked in his eyes as he said it, and Erica felt a fierce leap of hope. "What does that mean?"

"I think you know." He returned to the engine, plainly ignoring her.

Anger spurted through her, and Erica swung away, striding to her car. All right, then, she told herself. Tonio plainly did not want her, and it was time she got used to the fact. Maybe he was in love with someone else, even engaged to a girl back at the university. Or maybe she was too young in his eyes, too immature and inexperienced; he wanted a girl who had been around. There was obviously no hope for her. It had been idiotic, anyway, to try to fix his interest. Tonio was going away at the end of the summer. Besides, Daddy would have a fit if she started dating one of his workers. It had been silly to try to make him desire her merely because she was stung by his indifference Well. Erica thought grimly, she had learned her lesson now.

One Friday over a week later, late in the afternoon, after the workers had come to the house to get their week's pay, Erica went downstairs and out the side door to the swimming pool. The Logans' house had been built many years before by Erica's grandparents, but the pool was an addition Grant had made a few years earlier for Erica's benefit. Date palm trees and oleander bushes formed a protective wall beyond the pool on two sides, to hide it from the view of the driveway and the front yard. Lounge chairs and a metal table with an umbrella decorated the stone patio beside the rectangular, tile-rimmed pool.

Erica slipped off her terry cover-up and dived cleanly into the water, which glittered in the falling rays of the sun. Quickly she swam laps until her breath was spent, and she had to stop to cling to the side of the pool. The dying sun was warm on her torso, and she slid back into a lazy float.

"Erica." Her father's voice roused her. She brought her feet down and turned toward the house.

Grant Logan exited from the side door and crossed the stone patio to the pool. He was a tall, slender man with a stern, tanned face and fierce blue eyes. His crisp, iron-gray hair was cut short. He loved his daughter, but he disapproved of her generation, and he found it easier to express his disapproval than his love. Erica thought him an unbending man, despite his frequent generosity, and often wondered if he had any real affection for her.

"I'm going to the club to play golf with Fred Barton, and then I'm meeting James Wallace there for dinner. I imagine I'll be gone until fairly late. I sent Cruz over to McAllen for a tractor part, and he hasn't gotten back yet. So when he comes in for his check, you give it to him. It's in my study, in the middle drawer of the desk."

"Okay." Erica's heart began to thud wildly in her chest.

"And for heaven's sake, go upstairs and change into something decent." Logan eyed her turquoise bikini with distaste. "I don't want him seeing you in that."

"Tonio Cruz is the last person you have to worry about," Erica assured him dryly.

Grant gave a snort that indicated his basic distrust of any man, and strode away to the driveway. Erica climbed out and toweled dry, wrapped the white terry-cloth jacket around her, and started for the house to change clothes. Halfway to the door she stopped for a moment, then turned slowly and sauntered back to the patio. Dropping her jacket from her shoulders, she lay down on one of the lounge chairs. She was going to take this one last chance at Tonio. No doubt he would sneer or look right through her with his implacable brown eyes, but she couldn't bear to pass up the opportunity her father had dropped in her lap.

It had been a foolish thing to do, and had Erica been any older or wiser, she would have realized just what her actions might lead to. However, she was young and still rather naive and certain that Tonio's actions had proved his total indifference to her. She wanted something to occur, but she was totally unprepared for what did happen.

Impatiently she waited for Tonio's return, now and then diving into the pool to swim off her excess energy. At last she heard the solid click of his boot heels against the cement walkway, and she forced herself to relax in her chair, her eyes closed, feigning sleep. The steps hesitated as they passed her, then hurried up the steps to the door. He knocked briskly.

Erica opened her eyes and looked at him. Tonio's back was to her, his hands thrust into his back pockets. He wore his usual faded jeans and a white T-shirt. The back of the shirt was damp with sweat, and the short sleeves revealed the bulging muscles of his arms.

"He's not there," Erica called clearly, and rose from the chair.

Tonio swung to face her, turning his head more than his body. The expression on his face was carefully blank, but his eyes flickered over her body involuntarily. Erica felt a warm glow of triumph, no matter how small the victory had been, and she slowly strolled toward the porch.

"Daddy went to play golf and have dinner at the club. He said he wouldn't be back until late and for me to get your check for you."

Tonio stepped away from the door and let Erica pass through before him, then followed her down the hall to her father's study. Erica went to the desk and pulled a white envelope from the middle drawer. The front of the envelope was marked Cruz in Grant's large, precise hand. Erica held the pay envelope out to Tonio and he stretched one arm out to take it from her.

Cruz folded the envelope and stuck it into the back pocket of his trousers as they retraced their steps to the side patio. Erica's hands were cold, despite the summer heat, and the pulse in her throat was throbbing with excitement and hope and fear. She wanted to sit down and let Tonio go his own way, but even more she wanted to make him remain.

"Why don't you stay for a swim?" Erica turned to Tonio and stared him straight in the eyes, a challenge in her unflinching gaze.

Erica could see from Tonio's expression that he was about to refuse, but the dare in her eyes stopped his words. Instead he countered, "I don't have any swimming trunks with me."

Again her eyes flashed a challenge, and an answering flame flared up in his, but she said only, "Oh, Daddy has some extra suits for guests inside. I'm sure we could find one to fit you."

Cruz hesitated for a fraction of a second; then, in one fluid motion, he whipped his T-shirt off over his head, revealing a hard, brown chest, smooth and muscled, a small gold medal on a chain bright against his skin. Erica faltered, suddenly shy and amazed at her boldness, fighting the breathless surge of feeling that swelled in her throat. Quickly she skirted Tonio and returned to the house, and Tonio followed her more slowly. The swimsuits were in the downstairs bathroom, and Erica left Tonio there to change. She returned to the pool, a blush staining her cheeks with red.

Erica dived into the pool and swam to the end, then turned, holding on to the rim with one hand, and waited for Tonio to emerge from the house. He came out a few moments later, bright red trunks a slash of color against his tanned skin. His legs were slender but well muscled, his stomach flat and spare. Without glancing at her, Tonio dived into the pool and swam to her end, his strokes smooth and economical. He surfaced in front of her, treading water lazily, the water streaming from his face and thick hair. Impatiently he pushed his hair from his eyes, and his hands sent droplets of water flying.

"You swim well," Erica complimented him.

His smile was thin and bitter. "For a boy who never saw the inside of a country club? Fortunately, U.T. forces you to learn to swim, and I enjoyed it, so I used the pool all the time I was there."

"You don't accept compliments very gracefully," Erica pointed out. "I didn't mean anything nasty by it."

"Sorry. My mistake. I forgot you were the defender of the underprivileged." Suddenly he moved closer, his eyes bright, almost menacing, and grasped the edge of the pool beside her with one sinewy hand. "Tell me, Miss Logan"—his tone mocked her name—"is that why you flaunt yourself in front of your daddy's workers? Riding down to inspect the work in jeans as tight as your skin and a T-shirt that clings to your breasts? Handing out the paychecks in a bikini? What's that for? To give the poor peons a little lift in their day?" His other hand went to the rim of the pool on the other side of her, hemming her in, trapping her between his arms. He sneered as he spoke, white teeth flashing against his tan skin. "Or is it to tantalize them, to give them just the tiniest taste of what they'll never have, what they'd be killed for touching? Damn, you're a little tease, Erica. Doesn't torturing the rich boys down at the club give you enough of a thrill? Isn't their blood hot enough for you?"

"No!" Erica stared at him, her eyes wide with horror. "No, I didn't—I don't do that. I mean, I never intended to—"

"No?" One black eyebrow arched in disbelief.

Wildly Erica searched for something to say to make him believe her, but she couldn't tell him that her actions had been meant to entice only him, to spur him to notice her, want her, ask her out, kiss her. . . . Erica could only stare at him, unable to defend herself, and shake her head helplessly.

Cruz moved closer to her, and his hands slid along the rim until they touched the bare skin of her shoulders. Erica could hardly breathe or think; Tonio's nearness overwhelmed her senses. His fiery, glittering eyes mesmerized her, held her motionless before him.

Thickly he muttered, "Somebody ought to teach you a lesson, Erica Logan. Not to tease and torment a man until he almost explodes from wanting you." Then his lips were upon hers, pressing fiercely against her mouth, opening her lips to his hot, savage tongue, and one iron arm went around her shoulders, imprisoning her against the tough bone and muscle of his chest. Erica's dismay and resentment fled at his touch, and she was conscious of nothing except the wild roaring in her ears, the sweet delight of his mouth and the hard metal circle of the medallion pressing into the tender flesh of her chest.

Her arms went up to encircle his neck, and her inexperienced lips responded eagerly to his kiss. Erica felt a shudder pass through Tonio's body, and his free hand cupped her breast, gently kneading it through the wet fabric of the swimsuit until the nipple thrust out against the cloth, firm and proud. Tonio lifted Erica, bracing her against the cement edge of the pool, to bury his face against her chest, his tongue and mouth exploring the creamy, quivering tops of her breasts. The rim bit into her back, but Erica hardly noticed the discomfort, so aware was she of the touch of his lips on her skin.

Now his hands were beneath her buttocks, digging hungrily into the soft flesh, pressing her against his lean, hard length. She gasped as a fiery pinwheel burst inside her, a wild and wanton thing she had never experienced before. Suddenly frightened by her own response, she stiffened. No! This was not what she had intended when she had set out to lure Tonio to remain with her by the pool. She had meant only to dazzle him and make him admire her, to sow the seeds of love such as she felt for him. She hadn't meant to bring about this wild, abandoned lovemaking.

Erica reached out behind her and struggled onto the cement that surrounded the pool. He let her go easily, but before she could gather her thoughts enough to wonder about that, Tonio was heaving himself out of the pool with his strong arms, and she realized it had suited him to have them both out of the water. Quickly Tonio stood and pulled her up with him, running his hands over her slick, wet body. His eyes were black and molten with desire, and his fingers trembled slightly on her skin.

He murmured something softly in Spanish, words Erica did not know, but whose meaning was torridly, pulsatingly clear, and his hands fumbled at the thick knot tying her bikini top until it fell from her, revealing her lush breasts, a pale contrast to the rest of her carefully tanned skin. Tonio swallowed hard, his eyes hungrily roaming the naked globes, lingering over the soft pink aureoles of the nipples, with their desire-pointed centers. Erica did not move, her body aflame with the fire he had created. Quickly he stood and in one swift motion pulled the swimming trunks off. Erica swallowed, her throat dry, filled with eagerness and yet also touched faintly by fear.

"Tonio," Erica said softly, holding up her arms to him, and the steady flame in his eyes exploded into something more fevered. She meant to ask him to go slowly with her and be gentle, but the words never reached her lips. He covered her with the full weight of his body, pressing her against the cloth slats of the chair, and his knee parted her legs. Erica stiffened at the brief moment of pain, and he paused, his breath searing her neck. Slowly he began to move within her, building to the white-hot pitch of pleasure that shook him and made Erica arch feverishly against him.

"Tonio," she breathed again as he sagged against her, and her arms went around him, clasping him to her fiercely. "Tonio."

Chapter 3

ERICA ROSE FROM THE BEACH WITH A SIGH, DUSTED the sand off her bare legs and began to trudge back toward her hotel. It had been ten years, yet she remembered that day by the pool as clearly as if it were only a week ago. She could still feel the dying heat of the sun enveloping them, Tonio's muscled body relaxed against her, his breath warm and uneven on her neck. Tonio had made a funny half-groan, half-laugh and sat up, plunging his hands into his thick, dark hair. "Well, I guess that cuts it. Of all the stupid things to do . . ."

Erica, awash in the aftermath of passion, frowned faintly and reached up a hand to touch his corded brown back. "What's the matter?"

He swiveled and shot her an unreadable glance. "I—I'm sorry. I didn't know you were a virgin. Oh, hell, I didn't even think about it, any more than I considered the consequences." He looked away, staring at the hot-pink oleander blossoms on the opposite side of the pool. "What do you intend to do now?"

"What do you mean?" His voice chilled her glow, and Erica was suddenly very aware of her nakedness.

"Are you going to send the posse after me for defiling your fresh young Anglo body?"

"No!" She sat up indignantly. "Do you honestly think I would tell anyone?"

"Your father."

"Him least of all." Hurt and embarrassed, Erica turned away to retrieve the pieces of her swimsuit. It was a struggle to get into the wet bikini, and by the time she finished, her face was aflame.

Tonio left his swimming trunks where they lay and pulled on his jeans and T-shirt. Leaning back in the lounge chair, he clasped his hands behind his head and studied her coolly. "So your game isn't to lure the poor dumb Mexican into bed and then claim rape. What is it?"

"Damn you," Erica muttered through clenched teeth. He was destroying all the beauty and warmth of what had happened. "I wasn't playing any game! Why do you have such a chip on your shoulder? You must realize you're devastatingly handsome. You have a degree from U.T. and you're an architect. Why do you insist on pretending you're some poor migrant worker who just sneaked across the border? Why *shouldn't* I be interested in you? Is it a crime?"

"No crime. But hard to believe. I've seen too many like you who love to tease."

"Was that teasing?" Erica gestured toward the chair where they had lain, tears sparkling in her eyes. "Do you think I'd do that with just anyone? For your information, I never—*never*—threw myself at anyone like I did at you. I wasn't trying to show off to the workers. I wanted *you* to notice me, to talk to me. How can you—didn't it mean anything to you? I mean—oh, why did you have to go and ruin it?" With a choked cry, she broke and ran for the house, slamming the door behind her.

On the patio Tonio Cruz rose and gazed at the still-vibrating screen door, his usually arrogant posture replaced by uncertainty, his dark eyes troubled. Finally he shook his head and whispered to himself, "No. Don't be an idiot, Cruz." Shoving his hands in his pockets, he walked away.

Erica passed the following two days in a haze of misery, shame and remembered delight. She recalled the electric excitement that had flared between her and Tonio. How could he have gone through that experience and felt nothing? She knew she would never be the same again. With teen-age naiveté she had thought she had fallen in love with him at first sight, thought that what she had felt for him up until then was the most wondrous thing on earth. Now she knew differently. Her earlier love wasn't a tenth of what she felt for him now. In the brief moment that they had come together, they had seemed perfectly united. She understood what people meant when they said a husband and wife were one. She had been one person with Tonio and had believed that he shared the feeling. Then he had shattered her illusion by telling her he believed her to be a sly, vindictive bitch who had merely been playing a game with him. Recalling the things he had accused her of, she shriveled inside with embarrassment. To make it even worse, in her anger and hurt she had exposed her own feelings for him. Had he dismissed her with contempt? Or had he gone home and bragged about the easy conquest he had made of his boss's daughter? Her cheeks flamed at that thought. How could it have meant so little to Tonio?

Yet, she loved him, wanted him with all her heart. She could not forget the bursting joy of their lovemaking, and she prayed he would return and pull her into his arms again to show her all the hot, yearning mysteries of a man and a woman. Later she would realize how foolish her hopes were, for the love and pain she experienced at that time were small compared to what she would feel for Tonio later.

One evening, when she had all but given up her eager hopes, she sat at her bedroom window, staring out into the night. There was a movement on the lawn, a shifting of shadows that drew her attention, and she leaned forward.

The yard was washed in moonlight, the pale gleam shimmering on the leaves of the date palms and turning the century plants silvery. The tall white oleander bushes along the side of the yard quivered, and she saw a shadow separate itself from the bush and stroll to the cover of a palm. Her nerves leaped in excitement. The man moved quietly, as if he had no desire to be noticed, but without the furtiveness of someone afraid. His face turned up and he gazed at her window intently. Erica's breath caught in her throat. It was Tonio.

Without stopping to think, she darted from her room on tiptoe, carefully edging past her father's room and down the back stairs. Grant was already in bed and probably asleep, although it was barely ten o'clock. He kept farmer's hours, rising and retiring early. Erica silently turned the lock of the kitchen door and slipped out, hurrying across the moonlit lawn to the palm tree where Tonio stood waiting. He did not move from his position, simply watched her, his face betraying none of the tingling that swept him at the sight of Erica in brief denim shorts and a clinging pink top. Erica halted a few steps from him, suddenly uncertain. Why did she act so boldly around him? He already thought her a heartless, brazen vixen. Finally he moved, reaching out to pull

her beneath the cover of the palm tree with him. He
didn't kiss her or touch anything but her hand,
although his smoldering black eyes roamed her
body. Finally she whispered, "What are you doing
here?"

"Probably risking my neck," he responded dryly.
He moved deeper into the shadows, and Erica
followed him without a murmur. Soon they were
past the oleanders and out of sight on the driveway.
They strolled, hands still clasped, the only sound the
quiet crunch of the gravel beneath their feet. Tonio
broke the silence at last, although his voice was low
in the hushed night: "I parked down by the old
house."

Erica glanced at him, but did not question his
decision. She knew instinctively, as he did, that the
less Grant Logan knew about them, the better. He
wouldn't take kindly to his daughter slipping out of
the house at night to meet one of the Cruz boys,
college graduate or not. "I didn't think you'd come
back."

His fingers tightened around hers briefly. "You're
hard to forget."

"You mean there was something more to last time
than punishing a flirt?"

He halted abruptly and pulled her into his arms.
His mouth sought hers, lips scorching, tongue flickering and bold. He slipped his hands down her back
and dug his fingers into the soft flesh of her buttocks,
pressing her into him. Instinctively Erica moved her
hips, and he breathed in sharply, his mouth widening
as if to consume her. At last Tonio drew away. His
voice was shaky when he spoke. "Where can we
go?"

Erica didn't hesitate, caution and good sense
thrown to the wind as they always were with him.

"How about the old house? I know where the key is."

"All right."

They continued along the driveway, his arm around her shoulders, pausing now and then to touch or kiss or hold each other, driving themselves into a frenzy of frustrated desire, knowing how deliciously it would be eased when they reached the house. The "old house" stood near the gate where the driveway met the main road. It was the original structure built by Erica's grandparents when they had settled the land many years before. Her father had grown up in it until he was a teen-ager, when they had built the "big house" where Grant and Erica now lived. For the first few years of her life, Erica and her parents had lived in the old house. Then her grandparents died when she was six, and the family moved into the larger, newer house, closing up the old one. Now and then it had been opened and rented on her mother's whim until she had died a few years ago. After her death Grant locked it up. It was a sturdily built wooden structure, with three bedrooms, a modernized kitchen, high ceilings and wooden floors.

When they reached the house, Erica slipped around to the side door and found the key in its usual hiding place beneath the tiny stoop. She opened the door and they stepped into utter gloom. The hurricane shutters had been closed to seal the house tightly, and no stray light entered. Erica fumbled in a drawer and drew out candles and a match. She lit one of the candles. Her face shone eerily in the dark. "You seem pretty familiar with this routine," Cruz commented suspiciously, and she giggled.

"I don't meet my boyfriends here, if that's what you mean. But when my friends and I were feeling really daring, we used to sneak over here during a slumber party, to scare ourselves and prove how adventurous we were." She held out a hand and he took it, following her up the stairs to the second floor. What little furniture he could glimpse was shrouded in dust covers, misshapen and anonymous. "Isn't it spooky?" she whispered, a bit of the thirteen-year-old lingering in her voice. He had to agree.

Erica opened a door on the second floor, and they entered a bedroom. She pulled the covers from the massive four-poster bed, exposing a clean, bare mattress. Suddenly the dim candle and strange surroundings didn't seem strange or frightening, but cozily sealed off from the world for the private use of lovers. Desire flared in Tonio's eyes, and he reached out to slide his hands across the thin pink top, caressing her breasts until the tips thrust boldly against the cloth. "Damn, you're beautiful." His fingertips drifted lower, easing down the taut expanse of her shorts and slipping between her long, tanned legs. Erica closed her eyes, trembling beneath his touch. She stroked the hard muscles of his arms as he explored her body, until finally she could stand it no more and moved away to pull off her clothes.

Tonio watched the pale gleam of her body in the candlelight, desire pounding and swelling in him so that he could hardly breathe. He slipped out of his tight jeans and light shirt and pulled Erica to him, molding her flesh to his and branding her mouth with a deep kiss. They fell quickly into the bed, their hands and mouths wild upon each other, frantically aching for the final sublime moment, but eager, too, to taste each delight along the way. At last they could stand the sensual torture no longer, and they came together, hot and young, soaring swiftly to the heights of love.

Afterward they lay together, her head nestling in the hollow of his shoulder, his thumb lazily, rhythmically, running up and down her arm. Erica tensed, afraid that Tonio would turn sarcastic and hurting, as he had before, but he did not. When at last he spoke, his voice was soft, almost friendly. "What is this old place, anyway?"

"My grandparents' house, the one they built before the main house. We lived in it when I was a little girl. When my grandparents died, we moved into the big house."

"When I started working for your dad, I wondered why he had two houses. Seemed the height of luxury to me."

Erica laughed. "Believe me, this house is hardly luxurious."

"But it's sturdy. I kind of like it." He smiled. "Particularly now." Erica hardly breathed, her hopes rising at his last words. Did he have some feeling for her after all? Besides lust, that was, which he obviously had in plenty. But he did not pursue the subject. "You don't have much family, do you?"

"No. I'm an only child. Mama died five years ago, so there's just Daddy and me."

"No grandparents, no cousins, no aunts and uncles?"

"I have one aunt."

"Yeah? Who?"

"She lives in San Antonio."

"Oh. It must be nice, having everything to yourself."

Erica shrugged. "I guess. I envy people with brothers and sisters. I mean, they fight and everything, but they seem to have more fun. They always have a built-in friend, somebody to stick up for them. Don't you enjoy your brothers?"

"Sure, when I'm not having to get them out of trouble."

Erica didn't have to ask what trouble. Lucio had been in her grade at school, and she knew he'd been expelled or suspended several times. Jorge, the youngest, was said to be even worse. "You don't sound as if you mind too much."

"Oh, Lucio's not a bad kid. His main problem is me."

"You! Why?"

"Because his teachers always ask him why he isn't like me, why he doesn't make good grades. That kind of thing. But that's not Lucio's personality. He's easygoing and fun-loving, like our father. He doesn't feel any drive to get ahead in life. He'd rather flirt or drink beer. Lucio doesn't have anything to prove."

"And you do?"

He shrugged. "Sure. I had to make people realize I was better than they thought. Just because Mama's a maid and Papa's a sometime gardener, I've always been treated like dirt. My father isn't filled with drive. So when he couldn't get a job except gardening, and often not even that, he accepted it. He isn't the kind to beat his head against the wall. So people say he's lazy. Anglos chuckle and shake their heads. 'Typical Mexican,' they say, 'lazy and happy.' He's a smart man. With a little opportunity, a little education, he could have done all kinds of things. But he was trapped in his role."

"You got out of it," Erica pointed out.

"Did I? I'm still a Cruz, still less than nothing."

"That's not true!"

"Then why are we meeting like this? Why not tell your father you have a date with Tonio Cruz?"

Erica bit her lower lip. She didn't have an answer for that. He was right. They both knew Grant wouldn't want her to date him. Finally she countered, "Daddy doesn't want me doing this with any boy."

He shot her a sardonic glance. "Think you can slip out of it that easily?"

"Why not?" she retorted impishly.

He grinned and trailed a hand down her smooth hair. "Pretty clever, aren't you?"

He nipped gently at her earlobe. "You know what happens to girls who are too clever, don't you?" Now his lips were nuzzling her neck, sending pleasant shivers through her.

She laughed. "No, what?"

"I'll show you." He rose up on one elbow beside her, his dark eyes feasting on her body. "They have to pay."

"You're just trying to change the subject."

Tonio bent to take her nipple between his lips, toying with it until Erica shoved her hands into his thick black hair and arched upward, moaning softly. All thoughts of any other subject fled both their minds as his mouth captured hers in a deep kiss.

For the next two or three weeks, they met almost every night. Erica would wait until after ten, when she was sure her father was asleep, then slip out the side door. She hurried across the yard and down the driveway toward the old house, where Tonio sometimes waited for her, seated on the steps of the side stoop, lithely rising when he saw her. Other times he stood just beyond the oleander hedge and swept her into his arms as soon as she passed it, then walked with her to their meeting place. He brought an old oil lamp to provide better light than the flickering candles, which burned out all too soon and left them the option of either being in the dark or parting. Erica went to the old house during the day and cleaned the upstairs bedroom, dispelling the faintly musty smell of the unused room with scented candles. She covered the mattress with fresh, clean sheets, swept the floors, and dusted, even though she and Tonio rarely noticed their surroundings. She wanted the setting of their lovemaking to be as beautiful as the act.

Nightly it became more beautiful. Erica would not have believed such a thing possible, and she had worried that Tonio would soon tire of her and move on to another girl. But each time they came together was better than before. Smiling, he taught her pleasures she had never dreamed existed, new ways to send his own passion spiraling. He couldn't seem to get enough of her body, and he took his time with her, sometimes vaulting Erica to ecstacy several times before he succumbed himself. They no longer met and instantly tumbled into bed, consumed with passion. They talked and joked, before and after, often lying together, content to caress each other and simply be together.

Gradually, as the days passed, Tonio's bitter, suspicious resistance fell. He stopped questioning her motives and accusing her of using him. He accepted her, teased her with laughing eyes, kissed her until she was breathless, murmured endearments in her ears. They talked of their childhoods, their families, of Erica's stiff, uneasy relationship with her father and Tonio's far happier one with his own lackadaisical father.

"Papa was always good to us, willing to listen, to take time to help us with things. Sometimes he drank too much—mostly to soothe his pain over not being able to provide for us as well as he wanted. He had a bad leg from a childhood accident, which made it impossible to work as a picker. He couldn't stand on the ladders for a long time. It was always a sore point with him that he couldn't work in the winter, picking fruit to bring in some extra money. And it hurt his pride that Mama had to work. He kept it all inside, though. He never took it out on us. He was always laughing and loving with us."

Erica smoothed her hand gently over his arm. She knew Tonio's father had died a couple of years earlier, and she would have liked to offer comfort, but she didn't know what to say.

"Sometimes I wish I were more like him—and the others. But I can't let things slide and take whatever comes, without thought or fear, getting by on a sweet disposition, like Olivia, or the face of an angel, like Lucio. I have to take things and make them into something, control my life." He paused and sighed. "Though, God knows, I haven't had any control where you're concerned."

Erica smiled. "No? That's nice."

He studied her, his usually grave mouth curving upward. "So you enjoy that, do you? You like to drive me out of my mind?" She nodded. "Well, you've succeeded. I can hardly work anymore for thinking about you. It was bad enough before, when you'd ride into the groves and flaunt yourself in front of me. God, I'd ache to pull you off your horse and take you right there on the ground."

"Did you honestly think I was merely a flirt? A tease who wanted all the men to desire her?"

"What else could I think? I couldn't believe you

did it only for me, that you wanted me to take you. I thought you must do it for your ego, for a cheap thrill, to see me and the others suffer."

"And now?"

"Now I don't know." He ran a hand down her slender arm to her hand, outlining each finger in turn. "Now I work in the groves and wish you'd come out so that I could see you again. Yet, I pray you don't, because I know I couldn't control the way I'd look at you. I'm not sure I could even refrain from touching you and kissing you in front of the men. And I think I'd kill you if you came around the others in your skimpy shorts and tops."

"Don't worry. I won't come. I don't think I could trust myself around you, either, not with other people there." She lifted his hand to her mouth and kissed his palm, softly nibbling at his fingertips.

"What do you get out of this?"

She glanced at him in surprise. His face and tone were serious, open. She saw none of the hostility and suspicion that had been there in the past. "Don't you know? Tonio, it's so obvious—I love you."

He cupped her neck and pulled her head down to kiss her fiercely. His lips burned against hers, and his arms imprisoned her like steel. "Erica, Erica." His words were a hot groan against her neck and cheek. "I love you, too, *querida*. It's insane, but I love you too."

When at last he released her, Tonio reached behind his head to unfasten the chain of the golden medallion he constantly wore around his throat. Taking it off, he reached to clasp it at the nape of her neck. Erica's hand flew upward to touch it. "Tonio," she whispered, "what are you doing? You always wear this."

"Now it's yours. It's the only thing I have that I

value, not that it's worth anything in monetary terms. But Olivia, my sister, gave it to me six years ago. She bought it with the first money she ever made. It's a medal of St. Anthony."

"But it's too precious to you. I can't take it," she protested.

His eyes were warm, glowing coals. "You are a part of me. If I lost you, it would be like tearing my heart out. This is all I own that's of any importance to me, that expresses even a fraction of what you mean to me. I'll never be without it because you will be with me always. It binds you to me, and me to you."

Erica hugged his avowal to herself in an ecstasy of happiness, just as she pressed the cold medal against her warm skin. She had no reservations, being young and unused to denial or failure. Her father was distant but usually indulgent, and she was accustomed to obtaining whatever she wanted. She couldn't conceive of not having what she wanted more than anything else in her life: Tonio Cruz. Grant would balk and be troublesome, but once Tonio was established as an architect, he would get used to the idea. After all, Tonio would then be a young professional with a good life ahead of him, not one of Grant's workers. And even if her father didn't like it, he would simply have to accept it. There was the problem of her having another year in high school, of course, but there would be holidays when she and Tonio could visit one another. And next year she could go to college in Houston, and they would be together once more. Before, the only real problem had been whether Tonio cared for her, and now that he had admitted he loved her, Erica was certain her future was sunny.

She did not see Tonio the next night. There was a

big dance at the country club, one of the two really important, grand affairs for the teen-agers that were held there every year. Jeff Roberts had asked her to it weeks earlier, before she had become involved with Tonio. She would have preferred not to attend, but it would have been unfair and unkind to Jeff to call off the date at the last minute. It didn't mean anything, but it was really a question of good manners. So she told Tonio that she couldn't see him Friday. She saw the small, instantaneous spark of resentment in his eyes, and she thought it wise not to mention that Jeff Roberts would be taking her to a dance. Tonio's jealousy made her warm with pleasure, but she'd just as soon not be treated to a full rendition of it, particularly over something as trifling as a date with Jeff Roberts that she couldn't break.

She and Tonio had agreed to meet again Saturday evening, but when Erica slipped down the hushed driveway to the old house, she did not meet Tonio along the way. His car wasn't parked beside the house, so she sat down on the porch to wait. When time passed and he still didn't come, Erica went to the side door to make sure he hadn't already arrived and entered. The key was in place and the door solidly locked. Sighing, she resumed her vigil on the porch. Soon her eyelids grew heavy, and she leaned against a column and dozed off. She awoke with a start sometime later and stared at her surroundings, at a momentary loss. Then she remembered where she was and why, and she glanced at her watch. It was almost two o'clock! Tonio hadn't come. With an irritated twitch of her lips, she stood up and walked back to the house, strangely frightened in the familiar surroundings without Tonio's presence.

Sunday evening was a repetition of the previous night, and Erica wavered between anger and worry.

Had something happened to Tonio? Why hadn't he shown up? Why did he leave her sitting there, waiting for him? He could have called to say he couldn't make it. He wouldn't have wanted to ask for her, of course, but if her father had answered, he could simply have hung up. On Monday she rose early and placed herself conspicuously on the front porch, so that Tonio could innocently stop to say good morning and explain his absence. However, either he had arrived already or he didn't come to work that day. He didn't appear at their meeting place on the following two nights, nor did she see him at work. Sizzling with resentment yet stung by worry, she waited for word from him, debating in her mind whether to go riding in the groves and find him as she had earlier in the summer. One minute she was positive he was being callous and cruel, and her pride would not allow her to seek him out. The next instant, she dreamed up hundreds of dreadful things that had kept him from calling her. He could have been in an accident or caught some awful disease and even now might be lying unconscious, near death, unable to reach out to her. Tears would fill her eyes and she would dash for the stables. But the mood never lasted long enough for her to reach the groves before pride won out and she would turn back.

She visited her friends more than before, hoping to hear some stray bit of gossip that would explain Tonio's absence. She drove around town, hoping to see a sign of him or his car. Once she saw the car, and her heart leaped within her, but then Lucio walked out of a store and hopped into it, and she plunged back into despair. When the local weekly newspaper came out on Wednesday, Erica grabbed it and searched in vain for a story of a wreck or any other event that might make sense of it all. Finally she was driven to question her father.

At supper she began casually, "I haven't seen Tonio Cruz around lately." Her father's only reply was a grunt as he dished peas onto his plate. Suppressing a sigh of irritation, Erica continued. "Doesn't he work for you anymore?"

"No," Grant Logan replied briefly, his attention on the meat he was cutting. "Quit last Saturday."

Erica stared, glad Grant hadn't looked up from his food and seen the shock on her face. She wet her lips and struggled to control her voice. "Why? I thought he was working here all summer."

He shrugged. "I don't know. He told me he'd decided to quit early and go to Houston to find an apartment. His job there begins in a few weeks."

Houston! "You—you mean, he's already left town?"

"That's what I understood him to say. Well, you know the Cruzes. They're a shiftless, unreliable lot."

Erica didn't reply, numbly returning to her food. She took a few more bites, the food as tasteless as cardboard in her mouth. Houston. Tonio had left town without seeing her, without saying good-bye. She swallowed hard to force down the roast, her fingers trembling on her fork. She laid it down and pushed back her chair. She could no longer sit there pretending to eat while the tears beat at the backs of her eyes, no matter what her father might think of her leaving the table early. Let him wonder. She didn't care anymore. Tonio had left her without so much as a farewell.

She stumbled up the stairs to her room and shut the door, collapsing on her bed in tears. False! It had all been false. Tonio hadn't meant what he'd said.

He didn't love her. It had been a lie, just as his lovemaking had been. He'd wanted a summer's fling, and once she revealed she was getting serious about him, Tonio had fled. She gripped the medallion and yanked at it furiously. The chain bit into her neck, then snapped. Erica hurled it against the wall. Damn him! Pain knifed through her heart.

The last days of summer passed slowly, and Erica walked through them like a zombie. She had never imagined feeling like this: empty, hurt, churning with anger and yet throbbingly in love. In dismay she realized the full meaning of a broken heart. She knew she loved Tonio even as she hated him for deceiving her. She also knew that it was something she would never get over. The rest of her life would be spent in misery.

School started, and Erica returned to the familiar classrooms and hallways. She was thinner and strangely silent. Her friends found her distracted and morose, uninterested in their conversations and in her normal activities. She quit the cheerleading squad and began to shun club meetings. A new fear welled in her, adding to the turmoil of emotions already battling inside her chest. At first she thought she was off schedule because of her upset state, but after a whole month had gone by, she knew that was not the case. It had been too long. She couldn't continue to pretend to herself that everything was all right. And yet, she couldn't bear to face the implications. She finally gathered up her courage and made an appointment with a doctor in McAllen. The following Monday she drove to his office after school. He examined her and made the necessary test. Erica nervously clasped her hands together, folding her right hand over the telltale emptiness of

her left ring finger. Why hadn't she thought to get
out her grandmother's old diamond ring? Afterward, she went home, still on pins and needles,
anxious yet dreading the answer. The following
afternoon the doctor called and confirmed her worst
fears. She was pregnant.

Chapter 4

IT TOOK HER TWO MORE DAYS OF SOUL-SHAKING fear before she finally told her father. She thought desperately of running away rather than facing him, but she knew of no place to go, nothing she could do to take care of herself and the baby. One of those awful homes for unwed mothers? A backstreet abortionist in McAllen or Harlingen? No, that was unthinkable. She couldn't kill the baby. Tonio's baby. Besides, she had been indoctrinated with Grant Logan's strict moral code. She must face the consequences. She had been silly and headstrong, as always, completely under the control of her desires and Tonio's animal magnetism. The punishment would be facing her stern, puritanical father.

She followed him into the den one evening after supper. He looked up questioningly, surprised at her presence, and Erica swallowed hard. Her father was a difficult man to approach, his gray eyes hard and his square, tanned face unreadable. Clearing her throat and lacing her shaking hands together, Erica bluntly informed him that she was pregnant. Her father's face drained of color as he stared at her. Slowly he rose from his chair and asked her to repeat herself. She did so, her voice barely audible. To her surprise he did not rant and rave, did not even question her about the identity of the father. Not once did he tell her that she would have to marry the boy. Later she realized he would have assumed it was one of the local Anglo boys, the son of a man he probably knew and dealt with all the time. Grant obviously didn't want to have to face the knowledge of who it was.

Calmly, his face ashen, he began to formulate plans. He decided to send her to his sister Rachel, who lived in San Antonio. They waited until the Christmas break, and Grant arranged with the school system to allow her to take her semester exams early, as she planned to move to San Antonio for the rest of the year. Because she had lost so much weight, the slight thickening around her middle was not noticed. She felt sure her sudden, mysterious move to her aunt's, as well as her strange behavior that fall, would cause many to guess what had befallen her. But, her father reassured her, no one would know for certain. Erica knew the reassurance was more for himself than for her. Frankly she no longer cared what the people of Santa Clara thought. She was too deep in her misery.

Her Aunt Rachel, a successful businesswoman and unmarried, welcomed her niece's company, and Erica found her life much more bearable there than at home, where everything had seemed to remind her of Tonio. As the time passed, she grew to despise Antonio Cruz. He had lied to her and abandoned her, and she built up a fierce hatred of him and all men. They were either callous, careless creatures like him or self-righteous condemners like her father, and she was determined to live without either kind. She made a firm decision to be like her aunt, a dedicated career woman, able to support herself and her child.

Danny was born late in May, small, squalling and utterly beautiful to Erica. Whatever she felt for his father, she loved him completely the moment she saw him—had loved him even before that. Her father urged her to give up Danny, claiming she would never have the sort of life a young girl should have if she were burdened with a child. But Erica was determined to keep him and she stood fast against her father. Whenever he visited her in San Antonio, they argued fiercely over the matter and parted in anger. Finally Erica cried at him that she would never embarrass him by bringing her illegitimate child home for a visit. Grant left the house in a huff, and though he continued to send her money, he didn't visit her again for over a year.

Erica finished high school and went on to college, living with her aunt and hiring a baby-sitter to take care of Danny while she was gone. Her aunt doted on both of them, and though Erica was often overworked, her life maintained a steady, pleasant course. She enjoyed school, and Danny was a constant delight to her. She decided to enter the field of hotel management and finished her schooling at the University of Houston. Several times, while she and Danny lived there, she thought of Tonio and wondered whether, in such a huge city, she might ever run into him again. She even looked up his name in the telephone directory, although she never called him. She thought about him and what he might be doing, how he would feel if he knew he had a son, how he might react if one day she ran into him by accident. She wasn't sure whether she dreaded the thought or longed for it to happen. Whatever her feelings, the occasion never arose. After she finished college, she obtained a job as the assistant manager of a motel in Austin, then moved to one in San Antonio. Over the years she learned to tame her vibrant good looks into a sober, genteel attractiveness, striving above all else to appear mature and competent. She worked hard at her job, proving her abilities at every opportunity, and she had done well. She took pride in her work and her achievements, and the rest of her life was her son. There was little left over for other involvements, and though she gradually lost her resentment of men and began to date again, she kept carefully free of any entanglements that might interfere with her career or Danny. It hadn't been difficult, since none of the men she dated inspired the kind of wild, overwhelming love and desire she had once felt with Tonio. Feelings like that, she reasoned, occurred only once in a lifetime, when one was young—and really she was glad she had too much control of herself for it to happen again. It had been as frightening as it was delightful.

She and her father mended their rift to some extent. Though he was obviously never very pleased about Danny, he did come to see her infrequently, and once or twice she went home for a brief visit. In recent years he had begun to urge her to return home and live with him, reasoning that the mother of a young boy should not have to spend her time working. Erica quietly, firmly refused. She wasn't about to live under her father's—or any man's—power again.

She had achieved the independence she sought and even a sort of quiet contentment that she had once thought she would never experience again. In fact, she had been doing very well—at least until

Tonio Cruz showed up. Damn him! Why did he have to return to her life? And why did she have to react like a schoolgirl, going shaky in the knees, her stomach twitching, surging with all the old bitterness and pain and—yes, admit it—attraction to his strong male beauty!

Erica shook off the thought. That was crazy. She was no longer an impressionable schoolgirl. Tonio was facing an entirely different woman now. She was calm, mature, and now that she had thought over her past and faced her emotions, she was certain she could face him coolly tomorrow. She would be able to deal with him as one professional to another. Erica lifted her chin determinedly. She refused to be intimidated in any way. She would handle the situation, just as she always handled the tough times in her life: alone.

Erica was at her office well before nine o'clock the next morning. Although she dreaded the meeting, she wasn't about to let Tonio accuse her of inefficiency or tardiness. As she walked through the lobby, she caught sight of Tonio sitting at a small table in the coffee shop. He sipped at a cup of coffee, absorbed in a stack of papers on the table beside his empty plate. Involuntarily Erica stopped and studied him. She had been too nervous really to look at him the day before. He had aged. It showed in the squint lines around his eyes and the sharp creases beside his nose and mouth. How old was he now? Thirty-two? Thirty-three? Tonio was in his prime, and he looked it. The thick, crow-black hair was well cut and shorter, stopping at his ears. The tanned face was sculptured and expressionless, only the full underlip hinting at the sensuality and passion that had once blazed within him. Straight black brows, dark brown

eyes ringed with lashes so long and thick it was unfair
for a man to have them, prominent cheekbones—the
same face, hardened into maturity, the promise of
youth fulfilled. He was still slender, and the arms
below the short sleeves of his shirt bulged with
muscle. Erica's eyes followed the line of his arm
down the forearm, lightly covered with black hair, to
the slender, well-manicured hands. His fingers were
sensually long and slender, graceful, but saved from
delicacy by the thick sinews running across the back.
Erica wondered if his palms and fingertips were still
calloused. Color sprang into her cheeks at the
thought, and she quickly jerked her mind away,
instead noting his clothes. He was dressed informally
in brown slacks and a white terry-cloth shirt that
opened in a V at his neck, exposing the smooth
tanned skin of his throat. No gold medal glinted at
his neck now, she noticed, her mind going back for a
fleeting moment. Though Tonio's clothes were casual, they were obviously expensive, as were the gold
watch on his wrist and the simple gold ring on his
right hand. Obviously he had done well for himself.

Erica glanced down at her neat, cream-colored
pantsuit. What would Tonio think of her appearance
now? Would he wonder how the pretty girl with the
thick mane of hair and ripe figure, carefully revealed
in halter tops and shorts, had changed into this sober
woman of business suits and tight chignon? Had her
face aged and bittered in the intervening ten years
until it was dry and unappealing? Other men told
her she was lovely, but Tonio had known her when
she was young and flush with love and life. Erica
turned away and strode into her office, telling herself
not to be foolish. What did it matter what Tonio
thought of her? She had no need to be beautiful for
him. Yet, she shrugged out of her suit jacket and

tossed it on her desk, knowing guiltily that she did so because the creamy, soft blouse emphasized her swelling breasts and trim waist.

She sat down behind the desk and pulled out a file of correspondence left over from the day before. She didn't want Tonio to find her waiting idly for him. However, she could not keep her mind on the material and kept glancing at her watch. He was ten minutes late; was he purposely being rude to put her in her place? No doubt he enjoyed having the upper hand, just as he had taken pleasure in seducing the daughter of a well-to-do Anglo farmer. Her bitter thoughts were interrupted by a noise at the door, and she forced herself to wait a moment before she looked up.

Tonio stood framed in the doorway, the light from the sunny, glass-walled lobby behind him outlining his figure but leaving his face dark and unreadable. Suddenly Erica's office seemed too small and enclosed, dominated by his masculinity. "I'm late. Sorry," he began curtly. "I hadn't expected you to be on time. You never—" He bit off the words, which Erica knew would have been that she had often been late to their rendezvous spot ten years ago. For an instant the air quivered with an unspoken intimacy.

Erica rose briskly, breaking the moment. "That's quite all right. I managed to catch up on some work." Deftly she shoved the letters back into the file and dropped it on her desk. Unlocking the middle drawer, she pulled out a large ring of keys. "Now, where would you like to begin?"

"Let's take the inner workings first. Pipes, air conditioning . . ."

"Of course." Erica left her desk, and he stepped back slightly to let her pass through the doorway.

However, she was too close to him for comfort, and had to drop her eyes to avoid making contact. He followed her through the swinging door into the lobby, and she half turned to hold the door open until he took it. As she did so, she saw his eyes upon her, dark and smoldering, sweeping the length of her body and lingering over her hips and thighs. Quickly his eyes went blank, and she wondered if she had imagined the expression.

They turned into the back hallway of the first floor and entered the maintenance men's lair, full of huge pipes and noisy, clattering machines. Erica didn't understand their workings, but she knew enough to understand that everything was in shabby shape, patched but not completely fixed. Tonio examined the area minutely, his mouth tightening with disapproval as he jotted notes on a yellow pad. Next they inspected the lobby, where he poked and pried into every corner, then followed the same routine in the now-empty coffee shop. They walked together silently, Tonio busy with his notes and Erica saying no more than was necessary to answer his questions or point out something he had asked to see.

From the coffee shop they went out the front door of the hotel, and Tonio walked to the street for a better view. Slowly his eyes traveled over the face of the building, studying the peeling rails of the balconies and pausing on the iron script sign proclaiming "The Breezes." "It's shabby," he stated, his mouth grim. "How could they let it get into this condition?"

Erica bristled as if he had criticized her, although she had had nothing to do with the hotel's downward slide. "Mr. Severn didn't have the funds to maintain it properly. I understand it was all he could do to repair the hurricane damage last year."

His eyebrows rose lazily, and the corners of his

mouth quirked in amusement. Erica knew she had been overly defensive and could have bitten her tongue for her quick retort. "Hotels aren't meant to be hobbies," Cruz said. "Severn should have sold it years ago. He has neither the capital nor the knowledge to run it."

"Hardly any hotel can survive now if it's not part of a chain."

"And that annoys you. Why? Simply the love of the old guard for their fast-dying world?"

"Old guard? I hardly think I qualify. You sound as if I were a Russian aristocrat after the Revolution. I'm simply a modern working woman. You were always more aware of class divisions than I."

"Was I?" His face was cold, his mouth curled in a sneer. Abruptly he turned away and started around the side of the building. Erica grimaced and followed him. He toured the patio and swimming pool, as well as the huge air conditioning unit hidden behind the building. Afterward they returned to the inside and began a floor-by-floor inspection. Strolling side by side along the halls, it was more awkward maintaining their stiff silence. Finally Tonio commented, "I was surprised to see you yesterday. I didn't think you'd still be single or have a career."

"Oh? And what did you envision for me?" Erica was coolly sarcastic.

"I thought you'd marry somebody like Jeff Roberts, spend your time at the country club."

"And no doubt have two and a half children and drive a station wagon?"

"Something like that."

"You don't know me very well, then, do you?"

He shot her a sideways glance. "No, I guess I never did."

"I, on the other hand, was sure you'd be successful, although I didn't know you were the Cross Corporation architect."

They had reached the end of the hall, and he punched the button for the elevator. His dark eyes swept over her and he added dryly, "And owner."

"What?"

A thin smile stretched his lips. "I take it you couldn't picture me being quite that successful. An architect is one thing, but for a Mexican to be the president of a corporation—that's unheard of, isn't it?"

"I see you still have the same chip on your shoulder," Erica replied heatedly. "Obviously you think I'm prejudiced because I'm surprised a man in his early thirties owns a multimillion-dollar hotel construction company! I'd be amazed at anyone who rose that far that quickly."

"I worked at it. After I left the Valley, it was the only thing that mattered to me."

"Of course. It was all that ever did." For a moment their eyes locked, resentment shimmering between them. Then the elevator arrived, breaking the tension, and Tonio stepped into it. Erica didn't follow. "You won't need me for the rest of the tour, will you? There's nothing to be unlocked or explained on the other floors, as far as I know."

"No, it will be routine, I'm sure," he replied in a clipped voice.

"Then I'll leave you here."

"Yes. Thank you for your help."

"You're welcome."

The doors slid shut, and Erica leaned against the wall, her throat burning with suppressed tears. It had been as awful as she had feared. Tonio was arrogant and hateful, and she had been awash in turbulent emotions the whole time they were together. She hated him. She would have liked to slap his arrogant, handsome face and tell him exactly what she thought of him for leaving a vulnerable seventeen-year-old girl in the lurch. She wanted to scream out the pain she'd suffered from his lies and desertion. It shouldn't have surprised her at all that he owned Cross Corporation. He had all the qualities necessary for a ruthless business tycoon.

Erica turned to walk down the stairwell instead of waiting for the elevator. She needed the extra moments alone to gain control of her emotions. It had been difficult trying to maintain a calm, indifferent mask around Tonio, as if they were no more to each other than casual acquaintances. No doubt that was all she was to him, but he had been an earthquake in her life, tearing open her placid existence and leaving everything broken and changed. However, she had too much pride and hatred to let him know how much he had hurt her, and too much fear to let him learn of Danny's existence. She had had to pretend an indifference to equal his, when all the time she was very aware of the familiar scent of his body mixed with the musky fragrance of his aftershave, aware of the strength of his hard brown arms, aware of the long, sinewy fingers that had once drifted over her body, bringing her untold pleasure. She was anything but indifferent to him, and the playacting had been wearing on her. Thank heavens she wouldn't have to endure him any longer. Whatever else he needed he could obtain on his own, and soon he would leave. Then she would seek another job. She wanted to make sure there was no chance of running into him again. She wanted Tonio out of her life forever.

Erica opened the door of her apartment, and Danny bounced up from the floor, where he had been lying as he watched TV. He launched into his usual set of questions, punctuated periodically by the desperate statement that he was starving to death. Erica made them a quick meal of sandwiches, then escaped to the bathroom, where she took a long, leisurely shower. The steady beat of the hot water on her skin soothed her and helped take away some of the tensions of the day. Stepping out, she toweled herself dry and put on a short blue terrycloth robe. Belting the sash, she picked up a comb and combed through her wet, tangled hair. When she returned to the living room, she found that Danny had given up the television set and had retired to his room to play. He stormed around his room, chasing imaginary monsters, and Erica closed the door against the noise he created. With a sigh she sank down onto the couch and put her feet up casually on the coffee table.

A knock sounded imperiously on the front door, and Erica grimaced. Her employees often brought their work problems to her, even during her free hours. They seemed to think she was always on duty because she lived in the hotel. She rose and went to answer the knock, not bothering to change from her robe, since she expected to find Connie at the door. Instead she opened it to a well-dressed, assured Tonio Cruz. Erica's stomach plummeted to the floor. Dear heaven, she wasn't prepared to deal with him again.

Tonio's eyes flickered over her assessingly, taking in the short robe, its only fastening the casually knotted sash around her slender waist. Erica swallowed, suddenly very conscious of the fact that she wore nothing beneath the robe. Tonio's eyes darkened, and she knew that he, too, realized she was naked underneath the skimpy garment. Erica's hand went instinctively to the neck of her garment and pulled the two sides of the V closer together. She cleared her throat and demanded with as much force as she could muster, "What do you want?"

Unexpectedly a grin slashed his face, and she was reminded heartbreakingly of a younger Tonio. "That's an open-ended question," he commented. "Do you really want me to answer?"

Erica stiffened at the implied sexuality of his remark. Surely, with their past, he couldn't be so at-ease as to make lewd jokes! "I beg your pardon," she countered.

His smile vanished and he extended his hand. "I'm returning your keys."

"Oh." Erica looked down stupidly at the key ring in his outstretched palm. Why did she feel this absurd disappointment that he had sought her out only to return the keys? "Thank you."

She didn't want to have to take the keys from his hand, but there was no way she could gracefully keep from doing it, so she reached out and picked them up lightly. Even so, her fingertips grazed his rough, warm skin, and the contact sent a shock up her arm and into her chest. Dear God, how could he still affect her this way? It was impossible. Unfair.

She clutched the keys tightly in her fist, hardly noticing the cruel bite of the metal into her palm as they faced each other, silent and awkward. Finally Erica said, "You didn't have to bring them back to me. You could have left them at the desk."

"I wanted to see you."

"What?" Erica gaped. He couldn't have said anything that surprised her more.

"I wanted to explain to you the changes I plan to make to the hotel. It's always a good idea to clear away any misconceptions the present staff might have about our takeover. I want you and your employees to be fully aware of what Cross Corporation intends to do with the Breezes and to be certain that your jobs aren't endangered."

"I'm sure your word will be sufficient on that score," Erica put in quickly. She couldn't, simply couldn't, spend any time alone with Tonio, casually discussing his plans for the hotel.

"Nevertheless I'd like you to be fully informed. I thought we could discuss it over dinner."

"I've already eaten." Erica felt as if she were suffocating.

"Then let's have a drink together."

"Tonio, really, I don't think it would be a—"

"Look, may I come in?" he interrupted.

"No!" she blurted out in horror, then stopped, blushing. She was behaving like an idiot. Tonio would think she was still in love with him. She wasn't acting at all indifferent or professional. A couple left their room and walked past them toward the elevator, staring at Erica's brief attire. "Really," she continued in a shaky voice, "I must go back inside. People are staring."

"There's a lot to stare at," he remarked genially. "Your robe isn't exactly meant for public display, you know."

"It wouldn't be on public display if you'd leave."

His eyebrows rose questioningly. "Why the coy virgin act, Erica? Don't you think it's a little late for that?"

Tears burned behind Erica's eyes. How could he be so cruel as to remind her of the unrequited love she had felt for him so long ago? "People change."

"It doesn't seem as if you've changed at all," he retorted. "You're just as spoiled and blind as you ever were."

"Well, thank you very much! Just because I don't go along with your plan to ruin my evening off, I'm spoiled. Excuse me, but I'm going back inside now." She swung the door to, but he caught it with his arm and held it back.

"Not quite so fast, Erica. I *have* changed. I am now your employer, in case you've forgotten, and I intend for us to have a little discussion." He grasped her arm firmly and almost shoved her inside the apartment, closing the door behind them.

Erica whirled and tore her arm from his grasp, frustrated anger shaking her voice. "Sorry to disappoint you, *boss,* but I intend to submit my resignation Monday."

"What?" He frowned. "Why?"

"Why?" she echoed. "You can't be serious. Surely even you can see what an awkward situation this would be."

His eyes went to the top of her robe, and she realized suddenly that when she had jerked away from him, the sash had loosened, and the robe gaped open, revealing a wide swath of her bare white skin almost down to her waist. Tonio's eyes were black as night, unreadable, but telltale moisture dotted his upper lip and his hands knotted into fists. "Good Lord, Erica, can't you put on some clothes? Or are you expecting some other male visitor?"

She stared, too insulted by the sneer in his words to even speak. Pulling the top of the robe together, she turned away, retying the sash with shaking hands as she walked toward the balcony door. "Tonio, please go," she said in a low voice. "What's the point of this?"

"I'm sorry for the crack. I had promised myself I'd be civil, but I find it's damned difficult to do that around you."

"I think it's 'damned difficult' for you around anyone."

He smiled faintly. "Oh, you'd be surprised, Erica. I've become downright diplomatic the past few years."

"Then you really *have* changed." She looked through the glass door to the beach and drew a deep breath, then turned. "Tonio, couldn't we talk about this matter tomorrow? I really am very tired tonight." Her eyes flickered toward the closed door to Danny's room. What if he heard a stranger's voice and came out to investigate? Tonio would be certain to guess that Danny was his child the instant he saw him. There was so much of his father in Danny: the dark hair and olive skin, the angular shape of his childish face. Erica didn't know what would happen if Tonio found out—and she didn't want to know. Her pride couldn't bear for him to learn the humiliation and pain he had caused her. Far better for him to think she had sailed through their affair unscarred and uncaring. She would hate to be the object of his casual pity. Even worse, what if he was amused, or even pleased? She refused to swell his masculine ego with the knowledge that he had fathered a child at her expense. And if he happened to be intrigued by Danny, demanded to see him like a father—well, it didn't bear even thinking of. It would be disastrous.

Tonio caught her surreptitious glance at the closed door, and his eyes narrowed. "Is there a lover in your bedroom? Is that the reason for your nervousness? Is that why you didn't want to let me in?"

Erica's eyes widened at his tone. "Of course not! Not that it's any of your business," she added hastily. After all, she didn't have to answer to him. The spark that had flared momentarily in his eyes died. "Then why the reluctance? It seems a fairly simple request to me."

"Because I'm tired!" she snapped. "Now, would you please get out?" She flinched at the sound of her own raised voice and guiltily clapped her hand over her mouth. Her eyes went involuntarily toward Danny's room. A muscle jumped in Tonio's jaw, and he started purposefully for the door. Erica leaped after him, grabbing his arm frantically. "No! Please don't go in there. I swear—"

The door opened, and Danny peered out, a worried frown on his forehead. "Mama? What's the matter?"

Tonio stopped abruptly, surprise, then relief, chasing across his face. "A child? That's who was in there?"

"Yes, and I didn't want you disturbing him," Erica retorted, amazed to find that she had succeeded in sounding cross rather than fearful. Even more amazing was the fact that Tonio had not recognized Danny as his son. How could he not see it as soon as he set eyes upon him? The thick dark hair, the sharp little face, the creamed coffee skin—wasn't the resemblance obvious to anyone but her? Perhaps it was Danny's size that fooled Tonio. He was smaller than most nine-year-olds and could easily pass for seven or eight. Whatever the reason for his lack of recognition, Tonio was studying Danny now, and unless she got him away quickly, it surely wouldn't be long before he made the connection. She stepped forward, blocking Tonio's view of Danny, and took her son by the shoulder to propel him back to his room. "It's okay, sweetheart. Mr. Cruz and I were discussing something, and I'm afraid we got a little loud. There's nothing wrong. You go back and we'll go upstairs to Mr. Cruz's room to discuss it. You'll be all right by yourself?"

"Sure," Danny replied scornfully. "I'm not a baby."

"I know, I know." Erica had to smile at his indignant tone. She bent and placed a quick peck on his cheek. "If you need me just telephone, okay?"

"Okay."

Erica turned to face Tonio, her face set and expressionless. "Just a second. Let me put on some clothes." She hurried into her bedroom and thrust on underwear, jeans and a top. She didn't want to leave him waiting long, in case Danny decided to return to keep their visitor company. She was back in the living room in seconds. Tonio rose from the couch, surprised at her quick change. His eyes flickered to the softness of her breasts, and Erica blushed. He had noticed that she hadn't slipped on a brassiere. Under his survey, her nipples hardened involuntarily, making it even more obvious that she wore nothing beneath her blouse. Erica wished she had taken the time to don the flimsy bit of lace and satin.

Quickly turning from his gaze, she swept her key from the table and walked to the door. Tonio followed quietly. Why, oh, why had she told Danny they were going to Tonio's room? It had been the first way to get Tonio away from Danny that popped into her head. But she could have agreed to talk to Tonio in the coffee shop downstairs or in her office— anywhere but his room, with the bed looming beside them. That was the last place she wanted to be with Tonio. What did he think about her suggesting his room? Would he decide that she was hinting that she wanted to return to his bed? Her face flushed with embarrassment.

When she reached the elevator, she swung to face Tonio. "Shall we go to the coffee shop or my office instead? Danny can reach me at either of those places too."

He smiled derisively. "Why? Are you afraid the temptation would be too much for me if we were in my room?"

Erica blushed again. Now she felt even more foolish. Of course, there was no danger of his seducing her. That had all ended for him years ago. She was the one who was affected by his proximity, not the other way around. "Of course not. I simply thought it might be more comfortable."

"My room is fine. Your office is a box, and the restaurant is rather public for discussing business. So if you have no objections . . . ?" He trailed off questioningly as the elevator door opened and he stepped inside. Erica shook her head and he punched the button for the top floor. As the elevator climbed, Erica was aware of a sinking feeling in the pit of her stomach that wasn't caused by the ascent of the rather slow elevator. What a mess this was. Why couldn't Tonio have been content to leave things as they were? Why did he insist on talking to her? And why did she have to be so blasted nervous and self-consciously aware of a man she thought she had gotten over years ago?

As they rode up, Tonio watched her, his arms folded across his chest. Finally he said, "Is that why you were so against our talking—because of the child?"

"Yes," Erica replied a little sullenly. What else could she say? She couldn't admit to him that being around him reawakened her senses and reminded her far too vividly of the passion and hurt she had once known with him.

"Why didn't you tell me?" He seemed puzzled. Erica shrugged and made no reply. He went on, "But your name's still Logan. Did you take it back even though you had a child?"

Erica hesitated. She ought to say yes. It would be an unusual thing to do, but he would probably accept it, and that would be the end of his questions about Danny. But even as she opened her mouth to agree, her moment of indecision gave her away. Tonio's face darkened. "Poor little guy."

"Don't you dare say anything about Danny," Erica warned, her voice shaking with anger.

"I wouldn't," he snapped back. "I know how he feels. I've been on the outside too." The elevator opened, and Tonio stepped out. "So you wouldn't marry his father, either," he mused.

Erica, following him, wasn't sure she had heard him correctly. Had he said *either?* What did that mean? Well, whatever he'd said, the best idea was to get him off this subject as quickly as possible before he began to put too much together. "He left me," she stated flatly.

"Left you?" His brows rose slightly. "So someone finally took you down a peg."

Erica swallowed, embarrassed that her lips trembled at the deadly slash of his words. "You're a cruel man."

For an instant his expression softened. "You loved him?" he asked, reaching for her elbow.

Erica averted her face, afraid he would see the truth in her eyes. "Yes."

A faint tremor ran through Tonio's fingers and into her arm. Erica glanced up into his hard, set face. His voice was calm, almost impersonal. "Damn you."

"I seem to choose the wrong kind of guy." She

strove for a light cynicism, meeting his eyes defiantly, chin thrust up and out. "What business is it of yours, anyway?"

"None. Obviously." He strode ahead of her and unlocked the door to his suite. Erica followed him hesitantly into the room.

The suite was large and the most luxurious in the hotel. The balcony provided a magnificent view of the Gulf and beach, and there was a sitting area of couch, table and two comfortable chairs set slightly apart from the rest of the room by a waist-high wall topped by a wooden railing. Although it was attractive and afforded some privacy to the sitting area, the wall did not entirely separate the sitting area from the rest of the room. The couch could be reached only by passing the king-size bed. It seemed to fill the room. Erica walked past it, trying to keep her eyes from straying to the bed. Tonio strolled behind her to the table at the far end, where several rolls of paper and his drawing utensils lay. "These are my plans for the Breezes—a rough sketch, of course."

Erica looked down at the table as he unrolled one sketch after another. He stood so close beside her that she could feel the heat of his body, and her heart began to thud in her chest. He extended a hand to point out something on the drawing, and his fingers grazed the skin of her arm like a breath of fire. "As you can see, I intend to add two three-story structures running out in a V from the beach side of the building. They'll be condominiums. Here's a view from the front." He unrolled another drawing and explained the general facelift the old hotel would receive, then went into his plans for rearranging the top floor to include an elegant dining facility and bar. "We'll enlarge the ground floor, beautify the lobby, maybe put in some small shops. I'll add a

couple of tennis courts outside. I'm also considering
a second pool. We'll pretty-up the rooms as well,
though I haven't yet thought out a floor-by-floor
renovation."

"You seem to have done an awful lot already,
considering the short amount of time you've been
here."

"Oh, I came earlier in the year—before you were
here, I guess. These sketches are primarily from
what I saw then. I wouldn't have bought the place if
I didn't have some notion what to do with it. Now
I'm getting into the details. By the time I leave, I
hope to have enough concrete ideas that I can draw
the final plans." He paused, and when she didn't say
anything, he prodded, "Well, what do you think?"

"Very nice. It'll hardly be the same place."

"Which you, naturally, disapprove of."

"I didn't say that!" Erica flared. "You make a lot
of erroneous assumptions. As a matter of fact, it's
everything I could have wished for the place. I've
wanted to fix it up since I started here. I didn't
envision anything on such a grand scale, but . . ."

"It'll do? Well, thank you. I'm glad it meets with
your approval."

"Why are you so sarcastic? You asked me to look
at the plans! You wanted my opinion, didn't you?
Are you sorry I liked it? Would I have fit your
stereotype better if I had hated it?"

"I don't think of you as a stereotype. Believe me,
you're one of a kind." His face was drawn and bitter.
Strangely, Erica felt a stirring of something akin to
pity. Pity Tonio? How absurd. Pity the man who had
left her? The man who had clawed his way to the
top, using who knew what kind of ruthless means?
Who had wealth and status and all the things he'd
yearned for? Yet, there was something lonely and

sad in his dark eyes, and it was only with effort that she refrained from reaching out to him.

"Tonio . . ." she began hesitantly, but he interrupted her, his voice low and fraught with tension.

"Damn, Erica, how can you be even lovelier? All these years I told myself you'd gotten older, fat, lost the luster in your hair and the color in your cheeks." He raised a hand to run his fingers along her clean jawline, and she felt the little tremor in them. "But I don't have the satisfaction. You still turn my knees to water."

Erica swallowed, unable to move, trapped by his eyes and husky voice. The crazy, tingling excitement she had thought lost forever once again shot through her veins. She struggled to control the fiery pulsation his touch aroused in her. This was the man who had broken her heart, who had left her without a word, not caring whether she was pregnant. He was callous and cruel, and she was not about to be trapped by his honeyed words again. She jerked away. "Did you think I'd wither and die without you? Grow pale and languish away like some tubercular heroine out of an old novel? Sorry to disappoint you, but I think you overrate your importance."

She moved to walk past him, but Tonio's hand lashed out to clamp around her wrist like a steel manacle. "No, I knew exactly how important I am to you. I was good for a roll in the hay. I provided a little hot Chicano passion your Anglo boys couldn't. You didn't care about me, wouldn't have dared to be seen with me, but you enjoyed our stolen moments in the sack. One thing I know you never lied about: your body's response to my touch."

His harsh words stabbed Erica. She ached inside for all her old crushed dreams. There couldn't have been a clearer statement of how little their nights of love had meant to Tonio. Her pride held her straight, formed her lips into a sneer, although she wanted nothing but to break into tears. "You're crude. You always were."

"No more so than you, lady. I just say it straight out. I don't hide it in sweet smiles and silken words. You were always as hot for me as I—"

Erica cut off his words, crying out incoherently in rage at his taunts. Every boastful word he said about her love for him pierced her anew, reminded her of her old pain and humiliation until she couldn't bear it. She lashed out, slapping his cheek with all her strength. His head jerked under the force of her blow, and the mark of her hand flamed red against his tanned skin. Choking back a sob, Erica turned and ran. But, lithe and silent as a panther, Tonio caught up with her before she reached the door. One hand clamped down on her shoulder and spun her around. Tonio pulled her forward against his hard chest, his arm imprisoning her. She twisted her head, but his fingers turned her face to his and forced up her chin. His eyes blazed down at her, hot and black as coal. His mouth was a tight line of fury. Erica quailed before his anger, but she kept her back rigid and faced him defiantly. His hand went behind her head, fingers digging into the nape of her neck. His eyes bored into hers for a moment before the hard mouth swooped down to take her lips in an endless kiss. Erica struggled to escape his burning mouth, to quell her responding surge of passion, but the touch of his lips was an electric shock, sealing her to him as surely as his strong arms.

When at last Tonio lifted his head, she sagged weakly against him, averting her face so he wouldn't see her longing. "No," she groaned softly, tears rising in her throat at the realization of what he could do to her. In ten years she had not responded to any man's kiss this way, had not felt yearning flood through her like molten iron.

"Oh, yes," he murmured, his lips nibbling at her earlobe. Impatiently he tugged at the pins holding up her hair, and when it tumbled free, he sank his hands into the sweet-scented mass and dragged it against his cheek, burying his face in it. "God, your hair. I never forgot the way it smelled. I picked up a girl in a bar one evening because her hair looked like yours. But when we got home I found the scent was wrong. I didn't want her anymore."

He bent and kissed her again, his tongue roaming her mouth, rediscovering the honeyed warmth. A wordless moan sounded deep in his throat, evoking in Erica a feeling equally primitive. She wanted him, wanted nothing in the world *but* him. His touch, his kiss, his searing breath upon her skin, were so familiar she thought she might weep. She knew him as well as if they had parted only yesterday, yet she ached for him with the hunger of over nine years. Like a woman trapped in the desert, she drank him up, the taste all the sweeter for its familiarity.

Tonio kissed her eyes, cheeks and throat, running his lips downward until stopped by her blouse. He tore at the buttons and shoved the garment back from her shoulders, sending it to the floor. The soft flesh of her neck and chest was exposed to his voracious mouth, and he explored eagerly, his tongue working at one nipple while his fingertips caressed the other. Like a master musician with his favorite instrument, his mouth played her breasts, sucking and squeezing, rousing her nipples into hardened peaks. Erica leaned back in surrender against the steel band of his arm, awash in her passion, hardly knowing whether she was in the present or reliving that day at her swimming pool when she and Tonio had made love for the first time.

She dug her fingers into his shoulders, almost moaning in frustration at the cloth of his shirt, which impeded her. Erica tugged at the top buttons, her fingers clumsy with haste, and his roaming hands left her body long enough to yank his shirt free of the waistband of his trousers and undo the remaining buttons. Erica slid her hands beneath the cloth and caressed his chest, moving over his ribs and up to his shoulders, her fingertips digging into the hard muscle encased by smooth, warm skin. He bent his head, leaning it against hers as he stood still under her ministrations. His breath was quick and uneven, his body rigid and almost quivering. "Erica." Her name seemed torn from him. "Oh, Erica, it's been so long."

He wrapped his arms around her and pulled her backward with him and down onto the bed. His legs encircled hers tightly, and he rolled over, pinning her beneath him. Slowly, hypnotically, he rubbed against her, arousing her breasts to tingling, pointed fullness. A steady, aching throb started low in her abdomen, building and building until she thought she would explode from the force of it. Tonio cupped her breasts and rose on his elbows to gaze down on her. His eyes were dark fire as they roamed over her, quickening her desire almost as much as his hands. Erica moved against the tight prison of his legs, wordlessly urging him on. A sound that was almost a growl escaped his lips, and Tonio bent to take one nipple in his mouth, sucking at the dark pink aureole. His tongue laved the engorged peak as the soft suction of his cheeks tugged at it, creating a fierce pleasure in her that was almost painful.

He moved to the other nipple to work the same

magic on it, and his hands slid behind her and down, digging into the soft flesh of her hips, pressing her even more tightly against him. Erica felt lost, engulfed, sinking down into a dark, endless abyss of pleasure and desire. She caressed his arms and chest and back, her hands moving in a ceaseless pattern of passionate exploration, digging her fingertips into him whenever he caused a spasm of even more intense yearning. Her nails scratched his skin, but he was as heedless of the pain as she was of causing it. She turned her head, kissing the salty, moist skin of his shoulder, just as his tongue started to create a fresh delight, and she nipped him. Tonio shuddered, and suddenly his mouth was wild and frantic over her skin, as if he yearned to consume her. Erica twisted helplessly, caught up in the maelstrom of passion. She sank her fingers into his thick, black hair, kneading, tugging painfully. He tore at the rest of their clothing, almost ripping her slacks from her and undressing himself with equal haste. Then he separated her legs with his knee, and she arched up eagerly to meet him. Clenching his teeth, he battled the force of his desire and moved slowly. Savoring each moment of joyful torment, he drove them higher and further until they were beyond thought or words, aware of nothing but their wild rush to fulfillment, building to their final burst of glory. Together they slid into sleep, exhausted by the earthquake of their lovemaking.

Chapter 5

WHEN ERICA AWOKE, SHE WAS AT FIRST BEWILDERED by the hard brown body sprawling beside her, one arm and leg thrown intimately over her. Then with a flash of shame she recalled what had just occurred. Tonio had kissed her, and she had yielded to him with disgusting alacrity. For almost ten years she had hated him from the depths of her soul, yet his expert hands and mouth had brought her to abject surrender within minutes. She blushed, recalling the way she had writhed beneath him. She would have begged him to take her if she had been capable of speech.

With a soft moan she sat up, covering her face with her hands. No doubt it would give Tonio a good laugh to know how swiftly he had brought her under his control again. How could she have done this? She seemed to have no pride or control around him. He had boasted of his onetime power over her, her eagerness to bed him, and then he had proved that he could handle her just as easily today. Despite all the pain he had given her, despite her hatred for him, despite everything, she had received him willingly, even eagerly. He must think she was a weak, mindless slut, so ruled by her passions that he could treat her like dirt and she would still want him.

Never had she felt so humiliated and ashamed of herself.

Shuddering, she reached for her clothes and began to pull them on. Behind her on the bed, she heard Tonio stir and mumble sleepily, "Erica?" He reached out and touched her shoulder with his hand and she pulled away violently.

"Don't you touch me!" she spat, whirling to face him, her self-disgust clear in her eyes. "God, don't you ever touch me again."

His relaxed face went suddenly taut, and the dark eyes, warm before, turned blank and cold as slate. Almost wearily he sighed, "Oh, so now we're going to go into an outraged virgin routine, huh? Don't you think that's a little bit outdated now?"

He was mocking her, just as she had feared, reminding her of the fact that he had taken her virginity long ago and was making fun of her present lack of self-control. Hot tears bit at the back of her eyes, and her voice shook with emotion as she whispered fiercely, "I loathe you!"

There was a moment of pure, still silence. Then Tonio pulled his face into a look of wry mockery. "You have a peculiar way of showing it."

He was right, of course. That was what was so awful about it. As much as she hated him, she had acted as if just the opposite were true. "Damn you." She buttoned her blouse with shaking fingers. "No matter what you think, I will not fall into bed with you whenever you get the urge." She didn't know why he had taken her, what strange titillation he got from proving she still wanted him no matter how he had mistreated her, but from now on she wasn't going to provide his entertainment. He wouldn't get past her guard again, she'd see to that. Tonio might want a weekend's amusement while he was away from home, but she wasn't about to be left bruised and bleeding a second time. Let some other woman hurt over Tonio Cruz. She was tired of it. "Tonight should never have happened. God knows, I wish it hadn't." Erica summoned up the tough girl smile she had learned years ago when Tonio had first left her. She was determined not to let him know how he had crushed her again. "Just chalk it up to too many months of 'all work and no play.' "

He regarded her woodenly, saying nothing. Erica was sure her pasted-on grin was about to melt into sobs. "Of course, I'd forgotten." When he finally spoke, Tonio's voice was smooth and soft, containing none of her frantic emotion. "You must be well versed in men now. I thought I detected a bit more expertise."

His contemptuous words lacerated her already bruised pride, and she lashed back, "Well, you won't have another chance to test it. I don't want to see you again. I'll type up a letter of resignation tomorrow, and I'll be leaving here in two weeks."

"Don't do it on my account," he retorted icily. "I think I can withstand the temptation of your body next time I'm here."

"I can't bear to have to work for you. I would have resigned anyway."

He shrugged. "Then don't let me stop you. Make your fine gesture."

Erica whirled and stalked away, her back stiff with unspent anger. She hated him, hated him. The words beat like an incantation in her brain all the way to the door. She shut it with a speaking softness. Once outside she ran to the stairway, unable to stand in the hall and wait for the elevator. Tears spilled over onto her cheeks as she clattered down flight after flight of stairs until finally she stopped, exhausted, blinded by tears, and sank onto the cold cement steps. Folding her arms across her knees and sinking her head onto them, she gave way to the sobs storming inside her.

By the time Erica returned to her apartment, Danny was fast asleep, a fact for which she was very grateful. She was able to slip into her darkened bedroom, crawl into bed and go to sleep without suffering the barrage of questions that would have come had Danny seen her blotched face and red-rimmed eyes. She was tired and miserable, and sleep came as a blessed relief.

However, the next morning she had to face the same painful reality she had left the night before. She had gone to bed with Tonio Cruz, a man she had hated for years, and had reawakened feelings she had thought long dead. Once again she was in an emotional turmoil, angry, hurting, yet pulsing with desire for him. No matter how much she regretted what she had done the night before, she was too honest not to admit that she had enjoyed it and that at this very moment she wanted Tonio.

She didn't still love him, of course. How could she? She despised him! She had gotten over her foolish love ten years ago when he had left her. It had been nothing but an adolescent crush. And love didn't survive that long without nurturing except in corny old books and movies. No, love didn't enter into what she felt. But she did desire him. He made exquisite love. No other man's most ardent kisses could melt her like Tonio's mere glance could. And when he stroked her body and rained kisses over her face and neck, when he whispered love words against her skin and patterned her breasts with his tongue, he transported her to a kind of ecstasy she had found in nothing else. Erica thought dismally that she was a slave to her passions. She had believed herself to be controlled and aloof all these years, when in reality it had simply been that she hadn't had to face the temptation of Tonio's love-making. It was easy to be calm around other men. Tonio was her weakness. He seemed to be able to make her mindless and shameless.

And that was why she had to get away from here. Tonio was bound to return to the Breezes to work on his plans and then later to check on the construction of the new wings and renovation of the main build-ing. If she was around when he was there and if he put out any effort to get her into his bed . . . well, she wasn't sure she could resist. She had to quit.

Erica stayed in her office all day, cowardly avoid-ing any chance of seeing Tonio. Every time her telephone rang her stomach quivered with the fear that it would be Tonio's voice on the other end of the line. Fortunately it was not, and she made it through the day without once seeing or hearing him. Late in the afternoon, Rita casually mentioned that Mr. Cruz had checked out about twelve and taken the hotel's van to the Harlingen airport. Erica breathed a sigh of relief. Good. Surely he wouldn't come back anytime in the next two weeks, and she'd be gone after that. Another shattering episode of her life was over.

That evening she updated her resume, wrote a form letter of inquiry and began making a list of hotels and motels to which she could apply for work. She had already written her letter of resignation and mailed it to Cross Corporation in Houston. That had been the first item on her agenda that morning. Now she just had to find another job somewhere to support herself and Danny.

Her list of possibles grew slowly. She found herself reluctant to leave South Padre Island. The view of the blue Gulf from her window grew more inviting daily, the squat date palm trees more appealing, the wide, white beach more beautiful. Resentfully she wished Tonio hadn't thrust himself into her life again. The odds were against her getting another job on the Island. He was forcing her to leave this sunny, balmy place. But however much she might dislike it, she had to do it. So each evening and the weekend were spent typing up letters and sending them out to various hotels, first in the Rio Grande Valley area, then in the San Antonio–Austin area.

Danny noticed her evening occupation and inevitably began to question her about it. Reluctantly she admitted that they would soon be moving again. Although he was obviously disappointed, he stoutly maintained that he would enjoy living somewhere else just as much as he enjoyed it here. Not for the first time, Erica thanked her lucky stars for a son like Danny, then immediately worried that it wasn't good for a child to be so adult. He needed a father. He needed a more normal life-style. He shouldn't have to be so responsible and considerate, so grown-up and understanding. Yet, how would she manage if he were not the way he was?

She accepted a date with Joe Westfield on Friday. She had dated him on and off since coming to the Island. A pleasant man in his mid-thirties, he was divorced and had two little girls whom he kept every weekend. Their dates seemed easy and natural, affording them an opportunity to take their children along, with no great commitment or feeling on either side. Nor was there any excitement, Erica thought to herself as she and Danny left Joe at the elevator in the lobby after she had given her date a platonic kiss

on the cheek. Nothing could create a safer relationship than three children in the backseat. Everytime
they went out, they ate at a fast-food place favored
by the children and then went to see a G-rated movie
or partook of some other family-type entertainment.
It seemed deadly dull, particularly after the fire-
works of Tonio's presence the weekend before. But
then, she reminded herself, at least it didn't tear her
apart. After all, life was a matter of compromise.

Erica told her employees that she had submitted
her resignation and would be leaving at the end of
the week. Their shock and dismay were gratifying.
Rita Escamilla even cried. She reassured them that it
was a personal matter and that her resignation had
not been forced by Cross Corporation. From her
conversation with Mr. Cruz, she was sure Cross
would retain the Breezes' present employees. Although they accepted her statement, the rest of the
week was spent under a cloud of gloom. Erica
expected Cross to send a new manager, but none had
arrived by the weekend. Shrugging, she told herself
that it wasn't her problem. Rita and Dave could
keep the place running smoothly even if the manager
didn't show up for another week or so. Anyway, it
was no longer her responsibility.

All week, in every spare moment, Danny and
Erica were busy packing their belongings. They had
done it often enough that they were experts. They
had learned to live with a minimum of possessions,
which was made easier by the fact that they usually
lived in furnished apartments in the motels Erica
managed. And what belongings they had were port-
able and had been packed, unpacked and repacked
so often that they could almost go through the
process blindfolded. By Saturday they were ready to
leave. A couple of the hotel staff helped them load

the small rental trailer attached to the rear of Erica's little gas-saving car, and they set off, waving a cheerful good-bye to the employees who gathered to see them off.

Erica had decided to spend some time at her father's house. She had not been to visit him since she had moved to the island a few months ago, and she felt a little guilty about it. She and Grant had never been close, and their distance had been aggravated by his attitude toward Danny. Erica had felt a definite reluctance to take Danny to her father's farm. However, Grant had asked her often in the past two or three years to come back home to live, and she knew he must want to be closer to her as he grew older. When she got the job at the Breezes, she had promised herself that she would go to see Grant more often. However, the problems of settling into a new job, as well as the usual catastrophes that a hotel manager had to deal with, had kept her so busy that she had let the time slip away from her. She realized in dismay that she hadn't seen her father in over six months and had talked to him only once or twice over the phone.

Her quitting had presented her with the perfect opportunity to visit him. She knew it would be awhile before she got a response from any of her letters of inquiry to other hotels. She had little to do and no particular place to go until then. She could go home and let Grant get better acquainted with Danny. Maybe a better father-daughter relationship would grow out of it. After all, she was too old and should be too mature to let the rift of ten years ago still stand between them.

So she drove west through Port Isabel and on to Highway 77 leading from Brownsville to Harlingen. As elsewhere in the Valley, the road was lined on either side by towering Washingtonian palms, bare all the way up their enormously tall trunks to the cluster of leaves at the top. Looking out across the flat land, one could see the various lines of Washingtonians that marked distant roads. The land on either side of the highway was arid, almost a desert, dotted with scrubby mesquite and various other cacti: Spanish dagger, with its sharp, thrusting points; prickly pear; aloe vera; yucca; the wide, spreading century plant. The beautiful flowered plants of the Valley—the royal poinciana, the purple-flowered jacaranda, the bright scarlet and pink bougainvillaea, the oleanders ranging from pristine white to pink to deep crimson—grew only where there was water to be lavished on them.

Erica turned right onto oleander-lined Highway 77 to Harlingen, then headed west toward McAllen. She exited from the highway before she reached McAllen and took the county road to the small town of Santa Clara. A warm eagerness crept through her as she drove through the dusty, somnolent town. Santa Clara had changed somewhat in appearance since she had lived there—a new storefront here and there, a new supermarket on the edge of town—but the basic quality of the place was unchanging. There was still the central town square with a squat stone municipal building in the middle. The businesses clustered around the square, and the residential areas ran out from the business center. Old men sat on benches outside City Hall, and shoppers strolled along the sidewalks, mingling with businessmen and teen-agers looking for something to do. There was little going on, and the few people who were out moved slowly or not at all, part of the slow, lazy, small-town scene. Erica smiled. There was something about her hometown that brought forth all her

sentimentality, no matter how much she had disliked
it when she had lived there.

Past Santa Clara she stepped on the accelerator,
eager to reach the house. After a few miles she
slowed, searching for the gravel driveway of her
father's farm. "There it is," she exclaimed, turning
off. "Danny, that's the old house where I lived when
I was a girl and where my grandparents lived later."
Where Tonio and I used to meet, she added silently.

Danny shot her a scornful look. "I know. You
showed me when we were here before."

Erica grinned. Clearly Danny had little use for her
sudden heart-tugging nostalgia. They drove past the
row of date palms, noticing a gap here and there
where weather or disease had taken one out of the
line. Then she glimpsed the roof of the house and
the cascade of crimson bougainvillaea down the side.
She drove past the sheltering hedge of oleander and
pulled to a stop in front, then climbed out of the car
and looked around, taking stock. The hedges and
bushes had grown shaggy, and the cream-colored
house needed a paint job. One of the two lemon
trees was clearly dead, but hadn't been removed.
Several of the overlapping brick-red Spanish tiles
were missing.

Danny raced to the porch, then turned questioningly. "What's the matter, Mom?"

"Nothing," she replied with false brightness,
though inside she was dismayed at the changes in her
home. "Just looking around."

The front door was locked for the first time she
could remember, and she had to ring the doorbell
for admittance. The house looked so different, so
untended and careworn, that she half expected a
stranger to open the door. It was a relief when the
heavy wooden door was opened a few moments later

by Lupe, the housekeeper who had worked for Grant ever since Erica's mother died. She was a small woman, fragile-looking, although Erica had seen her moving couches single-handedly, and her thin, usually reserved face was quiet, almost sad.

After an initial surprised stare Lupe burst into a wide grin. "Señorita!" she exclaimed, reaching out to pull Erica into the foyer. *"Gracias a Dios!* God has answered my prayers. Come in, come in."

Erica followed her, startled by her unusually enthusiastic greeting. "Lupe? What's the matter?"

Lupe shook her head sorrowfully. "Come into the kitchen with me. I have to talk to you before you see Señor Grant."

Erica frowned and turned to Danny behind her. "Sweetheart, why don't you go outside and play? There are all kinds of interesting things around here."

"Sure," Danny agreed, glad to get out of listening to grown-ups talk, and took off at a run. Erica strode rapidly down the hall to the spacious kitchen.

"Now, what is all this, Lupe? Is there something wrong with Daddy?"

"Oh, señorita, I wanted to call you, but Señor Grant wouldn't let me. He said I was being a silly old woman, but it's not true. He is very sick."

Erica's heart began to hammer wildly. Her father ill? But that was impossible. Grant was like the rocks, the cactus, the soil—indestructible. Logically she knew that was a silly idea. Grant was human, like everyone else, and he was getting older. It wasn't unlikely that he might be ill. But emotionally she couldn't conceive of it. Erica drew a calming breath. "How sick?"

Lupe looked away. "I think he is dying."

"No!" Unconsciously Erica stepped back. "You're wrong. He never said a word . . ."

Lupe shrugged. "He wouldn't. You know him. He wouldn't even tell me what is wrong. But he has a death face."

"Lupe!"

"It's true," Lupe assured her with placid acceptance. "My Uncle Emilio looked that way when he came home from the hospital to die in his own bed."

"But what—why—" Erica stammered to a halt, too stunned to think. Slowly she turned, one hand going to her head as if to still the turmoil inside. "I . . . guess I better see him myself. Where is he?"

"In his room. He's been in bed the past two days, hardly gets up. It's worse than before." She paused, then added, "Just remember, he will not look the same. He is smaller, older. Don't be too shocked."

Erica nodded and walked slowly to the staircase and up the curving stairs. The upstairs hall floor was made of tile and covered by a runner of Mexican design. Its bright colors had dimmed with age, and it was thinning and worn through in spots. Erica knocked at her father's door and opened it cautiously when she received no response. Her father lay propped on his pillows in bed, half sitting, half lying. His eyes were shut in sleep. Erica drew in her breath sharply, and the fear in her swelled. Grant Logan had aged since she had seen him last. He had lost weight and seemed almost to have shrunk. His face was deeply lined and the texture of his skin was papery and thin. The hands, which lay loosely clasped on the bedcovers, once so strong and sinewy, were an old man's hands, knotted and splotched.

Erica's knees began to tremble, and for one wild

moment she wanted to run away—down the stairs and out of the house. But, biting her lip, she waited. Grant seemed to sense her presence, and his eyelids fluttered open. At first his gaze was puzzled, almost unfocused, then his eyes brightened and his lips formed a narrow smile. "Erica? What are you doing here?"

"I came to see you, Daddy," Erica responded, amazed at how normal and cheery she managed to sound. "Business is slacking off, so I was able to take the time off." No point in letting him know she had quit her job. That would worry him needlessly. "How are you?"

"Fine, fine," he lied and pushed himself up straighter against the pillows. Erica pulled a chair to his bedside and sat down. An awkward silence fell upon them. She could not ask the questions which simmered in her. Grant was too private, too reticent a person, for her to intrude upon him with personal questions. It seemed a violation to ask him about his health—and, yes, admit it, she was afraid of his answer. Oh, dear God, what was she to do?

Pasting a weak smile on her face, she began to talk about the hotel and its sale. "You'll never guess who bought it!" she added brightly. "Antonio Cruz! Remember? He used to work for you. He went to the University of Texas and became an architect."

A shadow touched his eyes. "Yes, I remember."

"He's quite a success now, runs a big corporation."

"Did you meet him? Talk to him?"

"Yes." Erica glanced at her father's face, surprised at his interest. "I showed him around the hotel."

"What did he say?"

"Uh . . . not much. We didn't talk about the past. It was purely business."

"Good." He lay back against the pillows, his face weary and pained.

"I'm tiring you, aren't I?" Erica asked quickly and stood up. "You go back to sleep and have a good nap. I really need to see what Danny's up to, anyway."

"Yes, that's fine," he agreed, his eyes already closing. "We'll talk later. We—need to talk."

"Of course, Daddy." Erica stepped into the hallway and closed his door behind her. Away from his gaze, she stopped and pressed her palms to her temples. Tears swam at the edge of her vision, and she blinked them away, breathing deeply to stem the flood of fear rising in her. Grant was terribly sick. Dying? No, she would not think that way. It was simply that he needed someone to take care of him. Maybe that was why he had been urging her to come home to live the past year or so. She had regarded it as an attempt to control her, but now she wondered. Perhaps he had wanted her with him because he needed her. That possibility had never occurred to her. She realized that for too long now she had continued to look at her father with a child's eyes, not an adult's.

Slowly she made her way downstairs to the kitchen. Lupe turned at her entrance and silently studied her. "Would you like a cup of coffee?"

"Yes, please." Erica sank into one of the heavy wooden chairs around the plain kitchen table.

Lupe poured a cup of coffee and set the steaming black liquid before Erica. She waited for Erica to take a steadying sip, then asked, "So? Now you've seen him."

"Yes. Lupe, there's something terribly wrong with him. What is it?"

Lupe shrugged. "I don't know. He won't talk."

"Is he going to Dr. Marsden?"

"No. Old Dr. Marsden's gone. He retired and went to live with his daughter in Brownsville."

"Then where does he go? He has been to a doctor, hasn't he?"

"Sí. My brother Rudi drives him. A few months ago he got sick. In his stomach, you know. He thought it was ulcers or appendicitis or something. He went to McAllen. He was in the hospital a week. After that, he went to the hospital all the time, then once a week for a while. He got Rudi to drive him because he always felt sick when he came back."

Erica ran a shaky hand through her hair. Chemotherapy? Radiation treatment? It sounded as if that could be it. Cancer? Did her father have cancer? "Why didn't he tell me? I could have helped. I could have come home earlier. I didn't know . . ." But an insistent voice at the back of her brain reminded her that she hadn't asked, hadn't visited even though she lived only a couple of hours away. If she had visited him, she would have known far earlier that something was wrong with him. Erica rose, leaving her half-finished coffee on the table. "I think I'll take a walk around."

Aimlessly she wandered about outside the house, half looking for Danny. She strolled to the barn, her head sunk in thought. The door to the equipment shed stood open, and instinctively Erica went to shut it. It had been engrained in her all her life to keep the equipment protected. Glancing inside the shed, she stopped, shocked. Tools and pipes lay scattered about carelessly, some rusting in pools of water that had collected beneath leaks in the roof. Erica gaped.

No self-respecting farmer would allow things to get in this condition. If she had needed any proof that Grant was desperately ill, this was enough. He obviously hadn't inspected the farm in weeks, possibly months, and that would never have happened if he hadn't been extremely sick.

Erica bit her lower lip and turned away from the barn. She couldn't afford to dither around here like a frightened child. Grant needed her help. She had to find out what was the matter with her father and what she could do to heal him. She wouldn't let herself consider the possibility that perhaps healing was not possible. Hurrying toward the house, she saw Danny playing by the swimming pool. Her father had had it drained long ago, and the gaping hole wasn't a very safe place. Her mind registered the danger, but she reminded herself that Danny was a good, cautious boy. Waving a hand, she called, "Be careful!"

"Oh, Mom" was his scornful retort. Erica wondered when a person lost his youthful certainty that all bad things could be held at bay forever.

She strode down the hall to the kitchen, willing her mind to think rationally despite the knotting of her stomach and the pounding of her heart. "Lupe? Do you have any idea of the name of the doctor Grant sees in McAllen?"

Lupe shrugged. "He's at the hospital. I don't know if he sees just one."

"Would Rudi know?"

"Maybe. I'll call him."

Five minutes and several phone calls later, Lupe returned with the triumphant news that her brother had been tracked down at his sister-in-law's house and that he had remembered the name of the doctor. It was Blaisdell. Erica quickly dialed information and obtained his home phone number in McAllen. His wife answered the phone and was reluctant to call him to the phone on business, but finally Erica's persistence won out, and the woman set down the receiver with a sigh. After a moment a man's rich baritone came on the phone. "Yes? This is Dr. Blaisdell."

"Doctor, I'm sorry to disturb you at home. But my father, Grant Logan, is one of your patients, I believe, and I'm rather worried about him."

"Yes?" His voice turned sharp and quick. "What is it?"

"Then he is your patient?"

"Yes, of course. I've been seeing him since June. What's the matter?"

Tears of relief clogged Erica's voice. At least she had found someone who could help her. "I don't know. I didn't know there was *anything* wrong with him until I came for a visit today. He looks awful." Stumblingly she related her story.

When she finally came to a halt, there was a long pause on the other end of the line. "Miss Logan, I don't discuss my patients over the phone, even with close relatives. I think it would be a good idea if you brought him to the hospital and let me look at him. From your description it sounds as if his condition has deteriorated since I saw him last. After that I'll discuss his situation with you. I think it would be better face-to-face. Can you bring him in?"

Erica's fingers clenched around the phone. "Yes, yes, of course." Even after he hung up, she remained staring at the blank kitchen wall, the receiver still clutched in her hand. It couldn't be good if he felt he had to tell her face-to-face. Deteriorated. His condition had deteriorated. Mechanically her hand moved to hang up the phone, and she began the long walk down the hall and up the stairs to her father's room.

This time she did not knock, just walked into the quiet room. Her father's face was waxy, his eyes closed. Erica swallowed and bent down to touch his arm. "Daddy? Daddy? It's time to wake up. I've talked to your doctor, and he— Daddy?" Panic entered her voice. Why wouldn't he wake up? For a moment the thought that he was dead jolted through her like an electric shock. She bent even closer. No. She could hear his shallow breathing. Erica sought the pulse in his wrist and finally found a weak beating. "Daddy!" she demanded more loudly, but received no more response. "Lupe!" Erica took a few swift steps to the open door and called at the top of her voice. "Lupe! Quick! Come here! I need your help."

Within seconds the wiry woman was racing up the stairs to help her. But even Lupe's deceptive strength could not help her get Logan's unconscious weight out of the bed. "There's no way," Erica said, panting from the effort of trying to lift him. Panicky sobs were beginning to rise in her throat. "We could never get him down the stairs, even if we did manage to get him out of bed. I'll—I'll have to call an ambulance." She started for the door, then stopped. "But it'll take ages to get here. Oh, Lupe, he could die by then. What am I going to do?"

Chapter 6

A SLEEK TOBACCO-BROWN MERCEDES SEDAN EASED into the town of Santa Clara and pulled to a stop at the town's single red light. Shoving up his sunglasses, the driver rubbed his eyes. Antonio Cruz was tired from more than the long drive from Houston to his hometown in the Rio Grande Valley. He had spent a hard two weeks, working like a driven man on the plans for his new hotel. Today, finished with the preliminary drawings, he had decided to take a break. For some reason he had been drawn to Santa Clara and his family.

He rolled his shoulders to get out the kinks, then on impulse turned right instead of proceeding directly to his mother's house. After two blocks he turned into the parking lot of Cruz Chevrolet. Four years earlier Tonio had bought out the former owner of the town's only car dealership and given it to his brother Lucio to run. To everyone's amazement except Tonio's, his happy-go-lucky younger brother had made a success of the business. The charm that had enabled him to breeze through school without opening a book, coupled with a native shrewdness that he had done his utmost to hide all his life, had enabled Lucio to wheedle almost anyone into buying a new car. Within two years he had offered to buy

Tonio out of the dealership, and Tonio had willingly agreed. Nothing could have been more to his liking than his brother's success and ultimate independence.

Tonio slid out of his low car and strode into the glass-fronted building. Since Lucio had taken over he had repainted the fading exterior of the auto dealership and added bank after bank of tinted glass. In business, as in everything, Lucio believed in flaunting it. The showroom was deserted, so Tonio climbed the wrought-iron staircase to the loft offices overlooking the lobby. There were three offices, each with a window on to the showroom below. Lucio's, the largest, was on the end. Lucio glanced up, saw his brother and immediately jumped from his chair to greet him. "Hey, Tonio! *Qué pasa?*"

Tonio's younger brother resembled him in the face, although Lucio's was more delicate, more perfectly handsome, without the sober lines around his mouth and eyes. However, at twenty-seven, there was a slackening in the firm lines of his face, and a small paunch now protruded above his belt. Lucio was beginning to show his years of rich, easy living, but he was still an arresting-looking man in his smart blue pin-striped suit, a diamond ring flashing on one finger.

"I think I'm doing better than you," Tonio retorted, indicating the room below with a flick of his head.

Lucio grimaced and enfolded his brother in an affectionate hug. "Don't rub it in. The car business, *mi hermano,* is not exactly in a boom period."

Tonio began to play an imaginary violin, his mouth drawing down in mocking pity. "Think you'll have to sell out?"

"Naaa . . . who'd be crazy enough to buy it?

Come on inside." He motioned toward his office. "Want some coffee? A soft drink?"

"I'd rather have a straight shot of whiskey."

Lucio's brows rose expressively. "Rough day?" He pulled open a door of his low credenza and extracted a black-labeled bottle and two short, heavy glasses. He splashed a healthy portion of liquor into one, handed it to Tonio, then poured himself a drink.

"Rough week," Tonio answered, then amended it. "Rough two weeks." He grinned. "Always trust you executive types to have a bottle hidden away."

Lucio turned his hands palm up. "So what's the problem at the top?"

Tonio rubbed a hand wearily across his brow. "You wouldn't believe me if I told you."

"Try me."

"A woman."

Lucio stared. "You're right, I don't believe you. Antonio Cruz, the celebrated Hispanic without a heart? Come on. Well, at least you've come to the right place with your problems. Who is it? Anyone I've met?"

"Oh, you've met her all right." Tonio's mouth twisted into the semblance of a grin. "Erica Logan."

Lucio's mouth literally fell open as he stared at his older brother. *"Qué!* B–but, Tonio, where? Why?"

Tonio chuckled grimly. "Would you believe she's an employee of mine?"

Lucio laughed. "How rich. A Logan working for a Cruz. That's a switch. So tell me, what happened?"

"It's a long story, longer than you think. Do you remember the summer after I graduated from U.T.? When I came back here to work before I went to Houston?"

"Sure. That was the summer you kept stealing my

car and sneaking off someplace, but you'd never tell me where— Wait a minute. You're not telling me—you were meeting Erica back then?"

Tonio nodded, his face etched in grim lines. "Yeah, I was meeting Erica."

"I'll be . . . well, go on."

"It was crazy. She was bored and restless, and I guess I piqued her interest because I didn't fall at her feet like every other guy. I wasn't a total idiot, so I tried to resist her, but let me tell you, it was difficult. Anyway, we started meeting at the old abandoned house on her property. To her I was handy, a safe subject for her sexual experimentation. But I loved her. I really loved her." He paused, swallowing, memories flooding in on him. He remembered the hot sun beating down on his back in the groves, and a vision of Erica pulsing in his brain and body. Every day had been torture until they met at the old house and made wild, sweet love. He had lived for nothing but the taste and smell and feel of her in his arms. Blindly he had entrusted his heart to her keeping, even dreaming she would marry him, making plans to take her away when she finished high school. "I thought she loved me too. She took away all my bitterness. The past didn't matter with her. Who I was didn't matter. I was proud, happy."

"I remember," Lucio put in softly. "I've never seen you like that, before or since."

"Then I discovered I was building castles in the air. She didn't really love me. One night I admitted how much I loved her, and I suppose it was what she'd been aiming at all along. The next day her father came to 'talk' to me. He was really blowing smoke, said he'd found out Erica was sneaking out to meet me. He wanted me to leave town. 'Course, I was really cocky and replied that I'd take Erica with me. He laughed in my face and asked me how I thought he knew about us. Erica had told him and asked him to get rid of me for her. She didn't want to see me again. I said he was lying. Erica loved me. So Logan revealed that all the time Erica was meeting me, she was dating other guys—'boys of her own class,' as he put it. I was okay for a thrill, but not for the public. I knew he was right. It had been too good to be true. But I still tried to pretend I didn't believe it. He told me I could see for myself. Erica had a date that night with Jeff Roberts. I went there that evening and hid by the driveway behind the oleander hedge. Sure enough, about seven-thirty Jeff picked her up." He closed his eyes, seeing her again, her hair swept up in a grown-up hairdo, her lush body wrapped in a floating, pale-green chiffon dress that lay like sea foam against her creamy skin. And again Tonio experienced the piercing ache in his gut that he had felt then. "I watched them drive away, and the next day I left for Houston."

There was a hushed pause. Finally Lucio said, "I'm sorry. I never knew. . . ."

Tonio shrugged. "It was a long time ago. And I have her to thank for my success. When I went to Houston I decided to work my tail off and become somebody, just to spite her." He smiled, minimizing the almost ten years of driven work, the obsessive need to succeed, the sterile, contemptuous relationships with women. It had taken him several years to get over Erica, and every step on his upward climb had been stained by bitterness.

"Well, you certainly managed that," his brother agreed. "And now she's working for you."

"Yeah. She's the manager of the Breezes, an old hotel I bought on the Island. Isn't it ironic? When I stepped through the front door and saw her walking toward me, I thought I'd slipped back in time."

"And?"

"And what?"

"What happened? How'd she act? What did she look like?"

"She hasn't gotten her just rewards, if that's what you mean. I was hoping she'd grown fat and was beginning to age, but no such luck. If anything, she's even prettier." Tonio had once thought he would never see a woman more beautiful than the teen-age Erica, bursting with health and life. But now he knew he had been wrong. The mature Erica was far more lovely. The luxuriant mane was tied back in a repressive knot, but the warm color glowed, tantalizing in its restrained lushness. The naive wonder was gone from her face. Time and experience had stamped it, but they had served only to bring out the promise of her youthful countenance, melting the roundness of cheeks and chin and leaving stark, fine-boned beauty. Even the hint of sadness that darkened her eyes made them more mesmerizing. "And she was cool as a cucumber, kept it on a purely business level."

"Uh-huh," Lucio agreed, disbelief tinging his voice. "And you've been upset for two weeks because she was just business to you?"

"Oh, no. I said *she* kept it on a business level. I couldn't. I started telling her some drivel about liking my employees to be aware of the changes I'd be making, so I wanted to take her out to dinner."

"And did you?"

"No. Even worse, we went back to my room to talk. She has a kid. Can you imagine that?"

"I'd heard rumors. No husband, though."

"No. No husband." His eyes turned remote and blank.

"So? What happened? Did you . . . ?" Lucio's voice trailed off delicately.

"Oh, yeah." Tonio laughed shortly. "I made as big a fool of myself as ever. It was—God, there's no other woman like her. I felt like a green kid again." He ran a hand distractedly through his hair and stared at his feet, unable to meet his brother's gaze. "Oh, Lucio, when am I going to learn? Afterward she looked at me with such disgust, such loathing in her eyes. She told me she hated me and never wanted to see me again. Then she left. The sex is great between us, it always was. But anything more than that—uh-uh, she wouldn't stand for it."

"Women." Lucio shook his head in an eternally male gesture of bewilderment at the opposite sex.

"Especially Anglo women."

"So what are you going to do?"

"Do? What can I do? She wants nothing to do with me, and believe me, I'm better off without her. She submitted her resignation the next day. I don't know where she's moving. It'll be easier this way."

"Is that why you've been working so hard for two weeks? To convince yourself of that?"

"I don't care for her anymore!" Tonio insisted, standing up to pace the thick carpeting. "There's nothing between us. But that one night haunts me. When I went home I took out a girl I've been dating recently. A knockout. Holly Blakely. Not much for brains, but a gorgeous figure. Young, sexy. I felt about as much desire for her as I do for that chair. Couldn't even touch her."

"Tonio, Tonio, what am I going to do with you?" Lucio exclaimed in mock exasperation. "You're too serious, too involved. Just because you still have the hots for Erica Logan doesn't mean you can't enjoy the rest of the feminine half of this world."

Tonio shot him an amused glance. "Not to you, obviously. Like you said, I'm too serious. But I can't get her off my mind."

Lucio shook his head. "I am going to have to take you in hand." He paused. "You know, it's strange, your saying all this about the Logans. I have a kid who works for me who's one of Lupe Delgado's innumerable nephews. He told me the other day that Logan's real sick. Dying, in fact."

"Dying?"

"Yeah, Rudi's been driving him over to McAllen since June to take some kind of treatments. Cancer, I guess."

"Poor Erica," Tonio murmured. The phone rang shrilly and they both jumped.

"Excuse me, I'm the only one here. I have to get this." Lucio punched one of the buttons at the bottom of his phone and raised the receiver. "Cruz Chevrolet." He frowned in silence as a voice rattled off something in Spanish. "Wait, wait, he's not here." There was another spate of words and Lucio covered the mouthpiece, raising his eyebrows expressively. "Speak of the devil," he stage-whispered. "This is Lupe. She's going crazy. I can hardly understand what she's saying." He spoke into the receiver, "No, Lupe, Johnny's not here. Everybody's left for the day. Wait! What's the matter?"

Across from him, Tonio went taut. "What is it?"

Lucio held up a hand. "Look, Lupe, I'll be right out, okay? No problem." He hung up and rose. "Lupe says Erica's there and wants to take Logan into McAllen to the doctor. Apparently he's lapsed into a coma or something. They can't lift him, and she was trying to get her nephew to come help them. I told her I'd go, but you don't have to—"

Tonio was already out the door and running swiftly down the stairs. "Come on!" he called back over his shoulder. "We'll take my car."

"Lucio said Johnny wasn't there, but he would come himself," Lupe announced, rejoining Erica in her father's bedroom. "It'll take awhile, but not as long as an ambulance from the hospital."

Erica clenched her hands tightly together. "Oh, God, Lupe, I feel so helpless. If only I'd come home sooner."

"Shhh. There's no sense to that kind of talk. You didn't know."

"I should have." Erica walked to the window and looked out. "I'd better go tell Danny. Will you stay here with him? I'd hate for him to have to sit and wait for me in a hospital."

"Of course. I can spend the whole night if you need me."

"Thank you." Erica smiled faintly and went downstairs to explain her departure to her son. She found him in the barn, and when he saw her, he began to chatter about all the wonders he had found. Erica nodded absently and took his hand to tell him about her father's illness. When she told him she was taking Grant to the hospital and that Danny would stay there with Lupe, her usually pliable child turned suddenly stubborn, insisting mulishly that he come with her. Erica sighed. Why on earth did he have to choose this moment to be recalcitrant? "It's out of the question, Danny," she began, then looked at his thin face. She saw fear in his wide brown eyes, and she realized that he was afraid to remain with Lupe in this strange house. The move, the new house, the unexpected illness of his grandfather, had combined to throw him out of his usual equanimity. Of course he was unsettled and wanted to remain by her familiar side. "Okay," she reversed herself. "You can come, but I warn you, you'll get tired and bored."

"That's okay."

She took his hand, and they strolled back to the house together. When they reached the front porch Erica turned to glance down the long driveway. Had she heard a car? Moments later an elegant Mercedes came into view. Erica opened the front door and yelled up the stairs, "Lupe, I think Lucio's here." Eagerly she ran down the shallow steps of the porch and across the yard to meet the car.

To her amazement it was Tonio's trim form that slid out of the driver's seat. "Erica? Are you all right? What happened?"

Strangely Erica was swept with relief. Hardly thinking what she was doing, she stepped forward and reached out to take the hand Tonio offered. "Oh, thank God, Tonio! Daddy's so sick. He's dying and I can't wake him. I have to get him to the hospital."

Tonio strode into the house, still holding Erica's hand in his comforting grip. Lucio and Danny followed them, eyeing each other curiously. "Where is he?" Tonio asked, and Erica wordlessly pulled him upstairs to her father's bedroom.

Lupe stared at Tonio's entrance, but wasted no time with questions. She stepped aside and Tonio went to the bed. Erica watched, her hands knotting nervously together, while Tonio pulled her father to a sitting position. With Lucio's help he lifted him from the bed, and the two began the slow, treacherous descent of the stairs with their heavy burden. Lupe followed with a blanket, and Erica and Danny came on her heels. They carried Grant to the back seat of the car and gently laid him inside, where Lupe covered him with the blanket, before they buckled him in. Despite the warmth of the September day Grant's skin was cold and damp.

Erica grabbed her purse from the kitchen table and hurried out to slide into the front seat, Danny jumping in after her. Tonio turned to his brother and said tersely, "I'll take them into McAllen. Can Lupe drive you back?"

"Sure."

Tonio slid behind the wheel, turned the key and took off with a roar. Erica, seated close beside him with Danny on the other side of her, for once was not unnerved by Tonio's presence. Somehow, in the stress and anxiety of the moment, it didn't seem peculiar that he had appeared when she needed help or unnatural that she should turn to him. There was a calm, cool air about Tonio, the air of a man accustomed to taking command. And that was what she wanted. Her mind whirling with fears and guilt, she didn't want to have to make any decisions.

"It'll be okay," Tonio assured her, his free hand sliding with feather softness over her hair. "We'll get him there."

"I know."

The trip seemed endless, although Tonio blatantly outstripped the speed limit in the powerful car. He drove with one hand, the other holding Erica's. Erica clung to it, grateful for the reassurance in his quiet, steel-hard body beside her. When they pulled up outside the emergency entrance, Tonio calmly took charge, going inside to summon two white-clad orderlies to bring Grant Logan inside. Tonio led Erica and Danny to chairs in the small waiting room, then went to the waiting nurse to relay the necessary information.

Erica sat numbly, watching Tonio talk to the nurse as the orderlies whisked her father into a small curtained-off cubicle. Moments later a tall, bearded doctor appeared in the emergency room. After a brief consultation with the nurse and Tonio, he, too, disappeared into the cubicle. The nurse followed, and Tonio came back to sit beside Erica. "That was Dr. Blaisdell," he explained. "He said he'd know more later. We'll just have to wait until he's examined him."

Time dragged by. Tonio offered to bring her coffee or a soda, but she refused both. Danny, however, was quick to accept the offer of a soft drink and went charging off in search of a machine. While he was gone the nurse emerged and told them that the orderlies were taking Mr. Logan to the lab for tests and then up to his room. "Would you like me to show you to his room now?" she asked gently.

"Yes, I—I guess so. Oh—Danny . . ."

"Don't worry. Go on. I'll stay here and bring him when he gets back," Tonio said quietly.

"All right." Erica didn't spare a second thought for the danger of Tonio spending time with Danny, which had so bothered her two weeks before. Now she had no concern except for her father.

Tonio waited for the boy, his mind on Erica. No matter what had passed between them, he had jumped to help her. One look at her wide gray eyes filled with fright and he had felt as if he would fight dragons to take away that fear. He had no more stopped to think than she had, reacting with the swift, sure movements of a strong man protecting his woman. His woman. Tonio sighed. Did he still love her? Had he been fooling himself all these years? He had thought himself wise and cold, immune to women because he had learned. Could it be that he simply hadn't wanted anyone else because his heart still belonged to Erica?

"Hey, aren't you the man from the hotel?" Danny's return interrupted his thoughts. Tonio looked up at the boy, studying him. He was a good-looking child, Tonio thought. He could see Erica's elegant bone structure in his face, and Danny had her wide eyes, although the color was different. Small, tan and wiry, Tonio judged him to be about seven or eight years old. What man after him had given Erica a son? She had told Tonio that she loved him, then left him so soon for another. His insides twisted at the thought.

"Yes, I am," he replied calmly, long used to hiding the ache inside him.

"Why're you here?" Danny asked bluntly.

"Lupe, your grandfather's housekeeper, called my brother Lucio, and I happened to be there with him. So I came to help Erica."

"Why?"

Tonio stared at him, puzzled. "Why wouldn't I? She needed help."

"Yeah, but you made her leave the hotel, didn't you? That means you don't like her, doesn't it?"

"Did she tell you that?"

"Naaa," the boy replied. "She'd think I'd worry about it. She told me she wanted to go someplace else, but I know that's not true. She liked living on the island. She'd always wanted to be there. So I know she wouldn't have left unless you forced her to."

"I didn't. I promise you. But, you see, your

mother knows me from a long time ago. We grew up in the same town."

"Santa Clara," Danny supplied knowledgeably.

"Yeah. Anyway, your mother has some bad feelings from when we knew each other before. I—uh, she just didn't want to work for me. But I never asked her to leave."

Danny tilted his head, considering. "You seem okay," he admitted finally.

"Well, thank you." A grin flickered across Tonio's face. "You seem okay too. You're pretty protective of your mother, aren't you?"

"What does that mean?"

"You take care of her."

"Sure. I have to. My dad's dead, you see."

"He is?"

"Yeah. He was a real great guy, always helping people and everything. Everybody loved him."

A lump grew in Tonio's throat. "Including your mother?"

Danny flashed him a scornful look. "Sure! Mom loved him most of all. That's why she had me— 'cause she loved him so much. I'm part of my dad, see, and that way she'd always have him."

Jealousy pierced Tonio's heart. Erica had loved the man who had gotten her pregnant and not married her. Had he really died and was that the sorrow Erica carried in her eyes? Or was the sadness because he had deserted her?

"I never knew him, but Mom told me all about him," Danny continued, going on to relate a few stories about his father, who seemed to be a kind of hero who rescued people from one misfortune or another. They suspiciously resembled the tales of Robin Hood, which convinced Tonio they were stories learned from Erica rather than boyish imaginings. Obviously what she had told Danny about his father bore no likeness to the truth, but equally obviously she had tried to foster the boy's love for his absent parent. She must have loved the man to picture him so for her child.

Despite his gnawing jealousy of the boy's father, Tonio couldn't help but like Danny. He had a frank, open charm, and an almost adult sense of humor twinkled in his eyes. For the first time Tonio experienced a twinge of regret that he had never loved anyone but Erica. There was something to be said for marriage and children.

Tonio laid a tentative hand on Danny's head, and the boy didn't seem to mind. As he was used to doing with Lucio's and Olivia's children, Tonio ruffled Danny's hair and received a grin in return. "You're quite a boy. I think we'd better go upstairs and join Erica. All right?"

When they stepped off the elevator Tonio guided Danny to the waiting room. It was furnished with a comfortable couch and chairs and had a small television set. Before long Danny was happily ensconced in the room, watching TV and sipping at his soft drink.

When Tonio stepped into Grant's room there was no one in the bed, but Erica was sitting in the lone chair, staring out the window. She turned at his entrance and smiled, her lips trembling. "Hello, Tonio. I'm sorry. I haven't thanked you for helping me."

"Don't worry. There's no need."

"I—somehow didn't seem to be able to cope. This has all been such a shock to me. I didn't know Daddy was even ill. He—I—the doctor came in to talk to me."

"What did he say?"

"A lot of words I didn't understand. Basically what it boils down to is that Daddy is dying. He's been dying for over three months now. He has stomach cancer, and the treatments haven't helped him. He stopped taking them almost a month ago." She stopped and drew a shaky breath. Tonio put his hand on her head, then slid it down to her shoulder. Tears sparkled in her eyes. "I—I'm so glad you're here."

Tonio pulled her up into his arms and held her comfortingly. She leaned her head against his chest and absorbed the hard strength of his body. "I'll be here as long as you need me. I promise." He rubbed his cheek softly against her hair. Funny how after all these years without it, giving could bring as much pleasure as receiving.

Chapter 7

Two attendants wheeled Grant into the room moments later and transferred him to the bed. "He's been regaining consciousness on and off," one of the men told Erica. "He might be able to speak to you."

"All right." Almost timidly Erica approached the side of the metal bed and picked up her father's cool, flaccid hand. "Daddy, can you hear me? It's Erica."

He made a faint movement, rolling his head on his pillow, but did not open his eyes or speak. Tonio came up behind her. "Would you like me to leave you alone with him? I'll check on Danny."

"Thank you." Tears stung Erica's eyes. After Tonio left, Erica talked to Grant for a time, speaking of any inconsequential thing that came to her mind. Finally, after receiving no response from him, she abandoned the effort, replacing his limp hand on the bed sheet. She sank down into the large easy chair nearby and watched him. Night crept in through the window, and gradually the room dimmed. Sitting there in the dark, Erica tried to make her peace with the father she had never known well.

Tonio brought her a meal from the cafeteria, but she could hardly touch the food. Around midnight she strolled down the hall to the waiting room to check on Danny. He lay stretched out on the couch, his head in Tonio's lap. A considerate nurse had covered him with a light blanket. Beside him Tonio, too, was asleep, one arm stretched along the top of the couch and his head resting on it. The picture of the two of them together brought unshed tears to Erica's throat, adding to the warm ache there.

She returned silently to Grant's room and continued to sit with him, marking time by the comings and goings of the nurses. Now and then Grant grew restless, twisting his head and moaning. Once he called out Erica's name, but by the time she reached him, he was quiet again. She fell into a shallow sleep, waking often, until Grant's voice disturbed her. "Erica? Erica, is that you?"

"Yes, Daddy." She was on her feet and beside him in an instant. "I'm here."

"For a minute I thought it was your mother. Where is she?"

"Mama?" she repeated, momentarily stunned. "Why—why, I'm not sure, Daddy." Obviously his mind was wandering.

He turned his head away, then back, and asked about his crop. Erica assured him that the crop and farm were in fine condition, though if the state of the house was any measure, she doubted she was speaking the truth. Grant was quiet for a moment, then began, "Tonio Cruz . . ."

"Yes? He drove us here. Did you see him?"

Grant seemed to have lost interest in whatever he had been about to say about Tonio. He frowned. "Baby, I—I'm sorry. I didn't know."

Didn't know what? Was he still talking about Tonio? Or something else altogether? "It's okay, Daddy, don't worry about it."

He slid into a shallow sleep. About thirty minutes later he awoke and struggled to sit up. "I was wrong." The words burst out of him in short, panting gasps. "I thought you'd be happier without him."

"It's all right," she reassured him earnestly, assuming that he was now referring to his demand that she give up Danny for adoption. "I understand. You wanted what was best for me." Grant nodded weakly. "That's all any child can ask. I was hurt then, but not anymore. Since I'm a parent, I can understand your concern for me."

"Forgive me."

Tears coursed down Erica's cheeks unheeded. "Of course, of course, I forgive you—if you'll forgive me for the worry I gave you. It must have been hard to raise a daughter alone after Mama died. I didn't think about you, just me and my problems. I'm sorry I didn't come back when you wanted. I never realized." Tears choked her into silence. Grant seemed calmer. He fell into a deeper sleep, no longer moving his head, his breathing shallow and irregular.

Erica sat down and wiped away her tears. She continued her vigil through the night, dozing, then awakening with a start. Grant did not move or speak again as dawn gradually lightened the sky. His breath began to come in fits and starts, sometimes stopping for a moment, then resuming with a long shudder. It reminded her of Danny's breathing when he was a baby. At about eight o'clock Tonio came in, tousled and sleepy-looking. He convinced Erica to go to the cafeteria for breakfast with Danny and him. Erica hated to leave Grant for even a few minutes, but eventually Tonio's reasoning won out.

She would feel a little better, she knew, if she escaped from this bleak room for a while.

She picked at breakfast, consuming little but her coffee. It seemed strange that it should be Tonio who sat through this with her. He was the last man she would have dreamed would help her. But it felt too comforting to quibble about it. Her mind and emotions had more than enough to handle trying to deal with what was happening to her father.

When they returned to Grant's floor, they saw Dr. Blaisdell stepping out of Grant's room. Catching sight of Erica, he motioned to her. Erica hurried toward him, a tight band of fear suddenly cinching her heart. His news was bad. She could see it on his face. "Miss Logan," he began gravely, "your father's breathing has slowed considerably. I think he's near the end. Do you want to be with him?"

"Yes." Erica walked past the doctor to Grant's bedside and took his hand in both of hers. He was barely breathing. She stood motionless, her hand as icy as his, as his breath gradually shuddered to a stop. It was a moment before Erica realized what had happened. Then the nurse was beside her, gently opening her hand and releasing Grant's. Numbly, Erica allowed the nurse to propel her into the hall. She glanced around, not knowing what to do. Tonio. Tonio would deal with it.

She walked to the waiting room on leaden feet. Tonio stood against the wall beside the door. When she turned the corner and he saw her, he straightened. She knew Grant's death must be written on her face, for Tonio came forward without a word, his face filled with compassion. He held out his arms to her, saying only "Erica." She went to him, leaning her head against the solidity of his chest. The steady thud of his heartbeat was reassuring, the warmth soothing. She was too numbed to cry and could only stand, clinging to Tonio.

Tonio took care of everything for her. He drove Erica and Danny home and firmly instructed Lupe to put Erica to bed. Lupe, weeping, led her to her old room and guided her into bed. Erica didn't resist. She was too weary to do anything but sleep. It seemed a heavenly comfort at the moment.

It was the middle of the afternoon before Erica awoke. She found that Tonio had notified her Aunt Rachel in San Antonio, who was flying to Harlingen immediately. Tonio would pick her up there. Erica was overwhelmed by his support. He had seen to all the details, so that she was required to do no more than visit the funeral home and pick out a casket for her father. Tonio even helped her do that, a strengthening arm around her waist.

Erica was silent on the drive from the funeral home to the farm, lost in a haze of stunned sorrow. Tonio glanced at her. "Erica, have you looked around your farm?"

Erica shook her head. "No, just the house," she replied absently. "It looks awful. Daddy really let it go. I guess it was too much for him." She left unspoken her next guilty thought: *I should have been there to do it for him*.

"Well, the rest of the place is in the same condition. Oh, not quite as bad. Mr. Logan's been letting the house deteriorate for years. He was much more interested in the groves. But he'd begun to slip there too. After I brought you home this morning, Danny and I walked in the groves. He wanted to learn about citrus farming. Anyway, I noticed that several of the trees are in bad condition. Some irrigation ditches have caved in, or close to it. There were weeds sprouting around the trunks. There were quite a few dead trees that should have been cleared out and some others with gummosis. They should have been taken away, too, to keep the rest of the groves from getting infected."

Tears welled in Erica's eyes. "Poor Daddy. It must have killed him, knowing he couldn't keep everything going." She paused, then frowned, her brain beginning to function through its haze. "But wait, Rafael wouldn't have let those things happen, even if Daddy wasn't there looking over his shoulder."

"Rafael Escobar is no longer his foreman," Tonio told her grimly. "I wondered about that, too, so I asked Lupe a few questions. Believe me, she was more than eager to tell me what had happened. Apparently your father had been sick for some time before he went to the hospital. He realized he was no longer capable of keeping the farm up, so he hired a manager."

"Daddy? I can't imagine that. He would have hated anyone else having control of his land!"

"I'm sure he must have been feeling pretty desperate. Anyway, he hired a manager named Goodson, whom Lupe described as something barely short of the Devil. He's been careless and incompetent. But more than that, I think he's cheated Mr. Logan. He must have been cutting corners to let the farm go so, and I'm sure the excess money went into his own pocket. No one knows for sure. I called your father's attorney, Bill Matson, and Rafael. Rafael quit because he couldn't continue to work with Goodson, seeing what he was doing to the farm. Matson was very suspicious of Goodson, too, but he could do nothing without dragging Grant into it, and he thought that was out of the question, with Grant being so ill."

Erica sighed. "How awful. How could anyone do that to a dying man? He must have known how sick Daddy was, yet he cheated him and ruined the one thing Daddy loved most. I'm glad Daddy didn't know what was happening. It would have crushed him."

"I agree. It made me furious to see those ruined trees and neglected ditches. I know how your father felt about his land. I was going to confront Goodson, but Lupe told me he took off this morning. Just went into the office and got a few things, then left. He must have known it was close to being over. He was renting a duplex on Lamar Street, but when I checked there, he'd vanished. Cleaned everything out, so I'm sure he's skipped town. If you don't object, Erica, Bill Matson and I want to go over your father's books to find out how badly Goodson was cheating him."

"No, I don't object. Why should I? It's very kind of you to want to help."

He glanced at her again but said nothing. Erica lapsed into her fog again, the distressing facts that Tonio had related sliding away before the onslaught of her grief. When they reached the house, Erica went in to see Danny. Several visitors were waiting in the formal living room to express their condolences, so she straightened her shoulders and went to thank them, although she wanted nothing but to be left alone. Visitors continued to arrive all afternoon and evening. Her father had been a well-known and respected member of the small community. By the time Tonio returned with her aunt, Erica was ragged and worn. Rachel held out her arms in an unusually affectionate gesture, and Erica went to hug her. Then, although it was growing late, Bill Matson arrived. After offering his sympathy, he disappeared with Tonio into Grant's study. Erica left her aunt to greet any guests who might come so late and went upstairs to be alone.

She sat in her room, in the one uncomfortable chair that was there. When she had been living at home, she had never sat in a chair, only on the bed, with her legs folded under her, Indian fashion. Funny how the room she had lived in for so much of her life didn't seem to fit her any longer. She sighed and left the chair to stand by the window, gazing out into the black night. Nothing was the same anymore. Nothing.

The funeral was the next afternoon. Erica moved through it dry-eyed and seemingly calm. Inside she was shaking and scared. What was she to do now? she kept thinking, not quite sure what she meant, but certain that the question terrified her. Emotion was seeping back in around the block of numbness. Her aunt sat on one side of her and a quiet Danny on the other, and Tonio was never far away. It occurred to Erica that he probably ought to return to Houston, that he must have business he needed to attend to. But she didn't suggest it to him. Nor did she think about the situation between them and the strangely warm relationship that had blossomed over the past two or three days. She needed Tonio too much right then to question it.

After the funeral and the brief ceremony at the cemetery, Tonio drove Erica, Danny and Rachel back to the rambling farmhouse. Erica contemplated how few people the Logan family had shrunk down to in the past few years. Rachel would die childless, and Erica felt certain she would never marry and produce more children. The future of the Logans rested entirely in Danny, a small child to constitute a whole family.

She pulled her mind away from her gloomy thoughts and summoned up a fairly cheerful smile for the others. She offered to throw together a little dinner from the mountains of food that neighbors and friends had brought to them. Rachel helped her, and somehow the familiar routines of the kitchen were soothing. Erica even managed a small joke about the shiny, expensive microwave Grant had bought a couple of years ago, which Lupe refused to operate.

After eating, she even felt strong enough to help Rachel dig through some of the old photographs and memorabilia stored away in a spare bedroom. She smiled over pictures of herself as a child and exclaimed when Rachel found an album from her own childhood. When Rachel left late in the evening to go to bed, Erica continued for a little while, then set aside the box she was exploring and wandered downstairs. The coffeepot was still half-full, and she poured herself a cup before she strolled into the den. Tonio was the only person there. He looked up and smiled at her entrance. "Hi. How are you doing?"

"Okay. Better. At least I was able to get something done instead of just sitting and staring." Erica walked over to sit on the couch beside him. She gazed at her hands. It was hard to describe the process occurring inside her, the gradual thawing of her frozen emotions and consequent realization of the extent of her loss. She was emerging from her foggy state, only to find herself lost and frightened, not knowing what to do. "You've been awfully good to me the past few days," she murmured.

"I wanted to help you."

"I've needed it." The feelings that had been awakening in her during the day suddenly pressed in upon her, filling her heart with a piercing, frightening agony. "Oh, Tonio, I feel so helpless. I couldn't do a thing to help him. He wanted me to come home to live, and I wouldn't. Even after I moved to the island four months ago, I didn't come for a visit. I said I had too much work to do. Can you imagine that? Too much work. I don't remember even a third of what I did. Anyone else could have done it as easily. Yet, I wouldn't let any of it slide in order to see my father. And now I'll never see him again." Her voice turned raspy with tears.

Gently Tonio laid a hand on her head, sliding it down the smooth length of her hair. "Don't think like that. It wasn't your fault. Grant didn't tell you he was sick, and he wouldn't let anyone else tell you, either. How could you have known he was dying? You wanted to do well at your new job, so you put it before a visit home. That's only natural, considering the fact that you thought your father would live for years yet. There's no reason to feel guilty."

"But that's not all there was to it. Daddy and I hadn't gotten along well since—well, for several years. I avoided coming home. I didn't want to face the hassle we usually had. It wasn't only that I had work to do. I didn't want to see him!"

"Erica, please, don't do this to yourself."

"Oh, Tonio." Erica turned to him, huge tears shimmering in her clear gray eyes. She was beautiful, vulnerable, and suddenly he wanted her more than he ever had before, wanted to hold and comfort her, to take away her pain with the balm of his lovemaking and turn her aching sorrow into joy. It was with a great effort that he restrained himself from pulling her close to kiss her. Now was not the time. He must put her before his own desires. "Tonio, I'm so scared." She gave a shaky little laugh. "Isn't that ridiculous? I'm twenty-seven years old and have a son, and I've been supporting us both for years. But suddenly I'm scared to face the world without my daddy. Like a little girl. Oh!" A tremendous sob racked her body. "Oh, what am I going to do? He's gone, and I never even told him I loved him!"

"He knew," Tonio assured her. "He knew."

He pulled her against him, and she laid her head on his firm chest. The tears that had been dammed up in her throughout her father's death and funeral burst their barriers. She wept in loud, painful sobs, pouring out her loss to the man she had loved—and hated—more than anyone else in the world. And he accepted it, holding her and rocking her gently as he murmured unintelligible, soothing words.

Erica awoke the next morning with a tremendous headache from crying. She padded to her dresser and peered into the mirror above it. Her hair was wild and tangled, her face puffy, her eyes swollen and red-rimmed. She looked, she thought, like the wrath of God. But she found she couldn't care very much about it. The numbness of the past few days was gone, washed away by the night before in her flood of tears. Her brain had finally begun to accept the awful truth that Grant was dead, and her emotions were coming painfully alive again.

She showered and dressed in drab brown slacks and a plain matching blouse. She had never liked the outfit much, but it was the first thing she found when she reached into the closet where Lupe had hung up her clothes. It really didn't matter what she looked like. Downstairs she poured a cup of coffee from the percolator and sat down at the kitchen table. She sipped at the hot liquid and stared listlessly out the window.

Now that she was beginning to think again, it seemed incredible that she had cried her heart out on Tonio Cruz's chest the previous night. Why was he doing all this—comforting her, protecting her, taking care of all the painful tasks for her? He was acting like her husband, when actually he cared so little for her that he had run out on her years before. On the surface he seemed to be acting out of the purest human kindness, but Erica couldn't help but be suspicious. He had hurt her too badly for her to truly trust him. Perhaps she had wounded his ego a couple of weeks earlier when she told him she would not return to his bed and he was determined to prove he could win her back, no matter what. It was the only thing she could think of to explain his attitude. There couldn't possibly be any monetary benefit to him or his company in helping her.

No, it had to be that she had sparked his desire when he saw her, and he had decided to seduce her all over again. He had done it with humiliating speed, but then she had informed him that she wouldn't hop into bed with him again, had in effect refused him in advance and told him she despised him. Doubtless that had made her quite a challenge to him, and he hoped to lure her back by moving in when she was at her weakest point.

Erica grimaced. Well, she had certainly fallen in with his plans once again. She had been so bruised and stunned that she had turned everything, including herself, over to him, letting him do things for her, be with her, comfort her. Why, she had even left him with Danny for long periods of time, when that was the thing she had feared most! With her father's death she had reverted to a helpless female, clinging to Tonio as if to a rock. It was discouraging to realize that she wanted to continue in the role. She quaked inside, lacerated by guilt and left vulnerable by the death of the parent who had protected her all her life. Erica remembered that she had felt a similar panic and remorse when her mother had died. But then she had been only twelve years old! And the feeling had not been as strong. She had had her strong father to take care of her. Nor had she been expected to behave as an adult or look after a child of her own, as she did now.

She wondered if everyone felt this way at their parents' deaths, or was it only women who reverted to childhood no matter what their former independent state? Or was it only her?

Erica was awakened from her thoughts by the muffled purr of a car—no, two. She rose and went to the window to peer outside, where she could glimpse the distinctive grill of a Mercedes. Tonio. Firmly she pushed down the instinctive surge of relief. She had to stop behaving like a child and letting Tonio make all her decisions. No matter how frightening the future seemed, she must be a responsible adult. There was no one to help her anymore. She was all alone and she had to take care of Danny. The best way to start was to get Tonio Cruz out of her life. Whatever he wanted from her in return for his help, she was sure she would be foolish to give it. She couldn't let him run her life or pull her back into the seductive circle of his charm. She had to protect Danny and herself. Erica knew she couldn't bear the ultimate pain that would come from falling in love with him all over again.

Straightening her shoulders and wetting her lips, she strode purposefully down the hall toward the front door. She opened it almost immediately after the sharp ring of the bell and stepped back a little in surprise at finding not only Tonio on the front porch but also her father's attorney, Bill Matson. "Oh. Hello, Mr. Matson. Tonio."

Tonio smiled, his dark brown eyes holding hers warmly. She felt as if he had touched her, and something pulled at her; she wanted to step into his arms and abandon all her problems once more. Firmly she turned away from him toward the older man. Matson was slightly younger than her father, a hearty man with a shock of pure white hair that gave him a kind, avuncular air. "Erica, I hope you don't mind our barging in this way, but there are some matters of importance that we need to discuss."

"Of course. Come in." She showed them into the formal living room, which seemed appropriate for a call by the family attorney. They settled into the heavy Spanish-style furniture, and Bill Matson opened his briefcase. Erica could feel Tonio's gaze on her, slightly puzzled by her sudden coldness, but she stubbornly refused to look at him, keeping her eyes fixed on Bill.

"Now, Erica, we have to talk a little business. I know this is an unpleasant time to do so. People think it's mercenary, disrespectful, but with a farm you can't just sit around waiting for a few months until you feel better able to cope with it. Unfortunately *we* have to fit into Nature's timetable, not the other way around. It'll be October in a couple of days. The first shipments of oranges are already going out. Next it'll be the grapefruit. You know as well as I do that the crops from this farm will be growing and maturing from now until April. Somebody has to have the authority to hire and pay workers, oversee the growing and make contracts

with the shippers. And since you're the executor
named in your father's will, I'm afraid the burden
will fall on you."

"Yes, of course." At least the work would give her
something to occupy her time and mind.

Matson went on, handing her a copy of Grant's
will and explaining the various clauses that left the
farm and all his possessions to her, as well as naming
her the executor. He also enumerated the duties of
an executor, assuring her that he would take care of
all the legal work. Erica nodded uninterestedly.
What he was saying held very little appeal. At the
moment she could summon up no motivation except
the drive of duty and responsibility. Someone had to
run the farm. Someone had to take care of Danny.
Someone had to keep life going on an even keel. On
that sort of thing she would move day to day. But
she couldn't work up any eagerness.

"The big problem, of course, is money."

"Money?" Erica repeated almost stupidly. "What
do you mean?"

"Erica." Tonio leaned forward earnestly, reaching
across the gap between their chairs to take one of her
hands. His was warm and strong, and she was
conscious of a treacherous longing to leave hers
there. However, she forced herself to pull it away
and folded her hands together in her lap. Tonio
frowned, but continued, "Look, I know your father
has always had plenty of money. Of course, you
know farmers have suffered economically the past
few years. There simply hasn't been as much profit.
Still, there would be plenty if not for Goodson."

"Who?"

"The manager your father hired. You remember
my telling you about it."

"Yes, he was incompetent."

"More like crooked. Mr. Matson and I checked the farm accounts, and it's obvious that he's been robbing your father blind. The ledgers and bank statements show payments for which there are no bills, and many of the bills in the file were for much less than what was recorded in the ledger. Several pieces of equipment were supposedly bought from a nonexistent firm in McAllen. I'm positive Goodson was endorsing and cashing the checks. He's skipped town, of course, but if you're willing, we can bring a criminal charge against him."

"Provided he's caught."

"Yes."

"Does it really matter now?" Erica asked lethargically. "It won't bring Daddy back. It won't restore the farm. I mean, even if he's caught and tried, I'm sure he wouldn't still have the money."

"No," Tonio admitted. "You're probably right. But, sweetheart, you can't just let him get away with that, can you?"

Erica stiffened at his use of an endearment. For the first time she looked at him. His dark eyes gleamed, and his whole body was taut. He wanted vengeance, Erica thought, and wondered why. Was it the successful businessman in him, horrified that another business had been embezzled from? Or was it the compulsive achiever who would never let anything slip from his grasp? Or was it just another way to put her in his debt, to suck her further down into the whirlpool of helplessness and gratitude? Deliberately she turned to Matson. "What do you think? Is it that important?"

"Well, Erica, I'm devoted to upholding the law. You must know that. And I'd hate to see some swindler get away with taking a dying man to the cleaners, wouldn't you?"

"Yes, well, I have no objections, certainly. It just seems a futile exercise, but if the police want to look for him . . ."

"Good. However, you brought up the salient point when you said it wouldn't help the farm. Grant's estate is not very large, except for the cash value of the farm. Grant's treatment wasn't inexpensive, and with Goodson's skimming and the cash bequest Grant left to your aunt, well, the estate isn't very liquid. We'll know more for sure after we've collected the assets, but I suspect we're looking at selling the farm. No doubt that's what you'd want to do anyway, since you won't be living here. Mr. Cruz has come up with a very generous solution."

Again Tonio took over. "Erica, I want to buy the farm from you. I'll offer you top dollar. I've considered getting a place around Santa Clara for some time now. I have to return to Houston today, and I'll have my lawyers get started on the deal."

"Perfect, isn't it?" Matson chimed in like the other end of a song and dance team.

"Wait!" Erica grated out. "Just a minute. I think I'm the one who's involved in all this, not you two." She rose, her eyes flashing fire. "You've got everything worked out to your satisfaction, haven't you, and of course 'the little woman' will go along with whatever her protectors tell her is best, right? Well, I'm sorry if I've given you the wrong impression the past few days. I was dazed by Daddy's death, but I'm not mindless or incompetent."

"Now, Erica," Matson began soothingly, while Tonio leaned back with a sigh, his dark eyes regarding her impassively.

"Don't you 'Now, Erica' me," she retorted. She swung on Tonio. "Is that the goal you've been after?

The Logan farm? I knew you must have some ulterior motive."

Tonio's tanned face tightened, turning as chilly as Erica's voice. "Naturally you'd think of something like that."

Matson blinked at the sudden animosity, finding himself inexplicably in the midst of a fight when he had envisioned nothing but grateful acceptance of his plan. He glanced at Tonio, who returned his gaze with a wry lifting of one eyebrow. Matson swung back to Erica. "Now, honey, I think you're being unfair to Mr. Cruz. He's making a very generous offer, much more than this farm is worth in its present condition, to be quite candid."

"Oh, please, let's do be candid for once," Erica thrust. "Mr. Matson, you knew my father as well as anyone, I think. I'm sure you know that this is not what he would want done with his property."

Matson sighed. "I'll admit Grant had a certain old-fashioned allegiance to his land . . ."

"He loved it!"

"Yes, but, Erica, it simply isn't feasible for you to operate the farm. Even Grant was aware of that. He knew you'd probably sell."

"Well, I won't. Grant Logan looked upon this land as a sacred trust given him by his parents, something that he would hand down to me and I would someday give to Danny. I've heard him say so many times. He didn't build one of the finest citrus farms in the valley just for his own aggrandizement! He did it for me, for his posterity. It meant something to him, and I can't just throw it all away because keeping it might be a little difficult."

"But, Erica, surely you don't intend to run the farm yourself?" Matson expostulated.

"Why not?" Erica thrust out her chin stubbornly. "I *am* familiar with the business, after all. I've already quit my job, as Mr. Cruz can tell you. So there's nothing to stop me."

"But this is a tough operation, even for a man."

Erica bristled. "You think I'm not capable of doing it because I'm a woman?"

Hastily Matson tried to soothe her ruffled feathers. Tonio made an exasperated noise and stood up. "This is pointless. Erica, you're obviously in too emotional a state to make any rational decision. We'll discuss it some other time."

"My answer will be the same then."

Matson quickly stuffed his papers back into his case, seizing the opportunity to salvage the situation. "Yes, yes, of course. We'll talk again in a few weeks, Erica. I'm sure that once you really get involved in running the farm, you'll see that it would be an impossible task."

Erica escorted them to the door. She and Tonio didn't exchange a word until he opened the door and turned. "Erica, I . . ."

"Thank you for all your assistance, Tonio. I'm sorry I haven't been properly grateful."

A muscle in his jaw jumped, and he swung away, eating up the distance to his car in lithe, easy strides. Watching him go, the terror of being alone swelled inside Erica, and she longed to call after him, to beg him not to go. But she held still, managing not to give in to her weakness.

Chapter 8

ERICA'S ANTAGONISM TO TONIO'S OFFER SERVED TO snap her from her lethargy. Running the farm gave her a goal to work for, a purpose. Instead of sitting aimlessly and wallowing in her sorrow, she called Rafael Escobar, her father's foreman before the advent of Mr. Goodson. He was ecstatic to hear from her, although his voice lowered in regret as he told her how sorry he was about Grant's death. When Erica revealed that she planned to run the farm and asked him to return to help her, he agreed quickly.

She and Rafael toured the groves, and he pointed out the weakened irrigation ditches and diseased trees, recommending that she hire a good crew to make repairs and cut down the trees. Everything she saw of what Goodson's crooked management had done to her father's beloved farm made her more and more determined to stay on the farm and build it back into something Grant would have been proud of.

In general Erica knew the process of selling and marketing a citrus crop. The fruit was usually bought by a shipper, who then transported and sold it to grocers or processors, or gift-packaged it in boxes for the holiday season. It could also be bought by a processing firm that canned the inferior fruit. The shipper or a buyer for the processor would inspect a farm and offer a cash price for the fruit on the trees. Then the buyer would hire a contractor to furnish a crew to pick the fruit and load it into trucks. However, Erica knew none of the buyers or their reputations, and she was happy to rely on Rafael's recommendations as to what buyers to deal with and what price to accept.

She put Danny into the public school in Santa Clara and plunged into learning her business. Daily she listened to Rafael's advice, and every evening after Danny went to bed she dug out all her father's pamphlets and books from the A & M Agricultural Extension Service, which contained information about raising citrus crops. She hired a crew who, under Rafael's direction, set about getting the groves in order. Lupe volunteered the services of her brother and several nephews to shape up the house and grounds. Erica took pride in the fact that before two weeks had passed, the house and yard, at least, looked decent.

She enjoyed her work. It was challenging and a good release for her energies. It gave her something to concentrate on besides the loss of her father and her brief but painful reinvolvement with Tonio Cruz. She was glad she hadn't yielded to Matson's urgings. This was where she belonged, what she needed to do. It provided the contact with her dead parent that she had not had earlier.

As the days passed she grew more certain that Tonio's kindness had been a ruse to satisfy some selfish motive of his own. She remembered how he had hurt her before and how she hated him. Even if he had been sincere in his efforts to make her father's death easier for her to bear, it couldn't make up for the past. No, she had to get along on her own, as she always had. Maybe Tonio had been there for her this time, but she knew it wouldn't happen again. This farm, Danny and herself: That was all she had in life.

Between the farm and her father's estate, Erica kept very busy. Although she managed to run the farm on the money she received from the buyers of her grapefruit and orange crops, she knew that before long it would not be enough. There were enormous estate taxes to be paid because of the high value of the land, even though there was little cash in the estate. Also, she had to buy new heaters for the trees to replace several of the old ones, which had been damaged by neglect. She needed to buy new seedlings to ensure the future of the groves. Fixing the place up a bit had drained what little cash there was. Any profit would be poured right back into the operation, but Erica soon realized that it wouldn't be enough. She needed more capital.

She was sitting in her study one day, poring over her account books, trying to figure out a way to squeeze extra money out of the farm without having to sell part of the land, when Lupe interrupted her. "Señorita, Señora Miller is here to see you."

"Mrs. Miller?" Erica repeated blankly. "Jess's mother?"

"No, oh, no, I am sorry." Lupe almost smiled. "It is Señor Jess's wife, the one who used to be Judy Barton."

"Judy!" Erica exclaimed at the mention of her high school friend. "Heavens, I haven't seen her in years."

Erica jumped up and strode into the living room. Judy was plumper than she had been, and her blond hair had faded to a light brown, but there was still a merry twinkle in her brown eyes and her face was prettier in a soft way. "My, you look good!" Judy commented as she stepped forward to hug her old friend. "You've hardly changed. If anything, I think you're prettier than ever. It doesn't seem fair."

Erica smiled. "It's nice to see you. I didn't realize you still lived in Santa Clara. So you're married to Jess Miller now?"

"Yeah." Judy laughed. "Who'd have thought it? When we were in high school, I'd have said he was the *last* person I'd ever marry. But you know how it goes."

"Well, bring me up on the gossip of Santa Clara."

"Oh, you know this town. It never changes. Let me see. The bank had a facelift, and the club needs one, but it can't raise the money. So it's beginning to look seedy. Cat Benavides married a boy she met at college and they're living in Utah, of all places. Jeff Roberts still lives here. He's running his father's store. He and his wife were divorced about a year ago. The scoop was that she was running around with Lucio Cruz."

"Really?"

"Yeah, and you'll never guess what Lucio is doing now. He bought the Chevrolet dealership. Or at least his brother did. Antonio went to Houston and got filthy rich. Had you heard that?"

"Yes," Erica replied shortly, her heart beginning to knock.

"Well, Lucio's made a big success of it. Of course, the youngest one, Jorge, is still always in trouble. He's wild. Antonio could have given him all the money in the world, and it wouldn't have helped him. You should see Tonio. He's better-looking now than Lucio. I saw him in town about a year ago, and

he was absolutely yummy—the most beautiful body
in the world, and he was wearing tight-fitting jeans
and a gorgeous short-sleeved shirt that showed off
his muscles. He looked hard, you know, like someone you wouldn't want to tangle with, but
handsome. . . ." She trailed off with a sigh. "I told
Sylvie Harrison, if ever a man could make you forget
husband and family, Antonio Cruz is it!"

Erica dug her fingernails into her palms, trying to
maintain an expression of amused interest despite
the jealousy surging through her. She could clearly
envision Tonio from Judy's description, and she
hated the response he evoked in Judy—and every
other woman he met. No doubt Tonio had made
quite a few women forget everything for him. Erica
was sure she wasn't the only woman he had fooled.
Somehow that knowledge only made her pain more
bitter. She wanted to snap back sarcastically that she
was confident Tonio would be glad to oblige Judy,
but she realized she would make an idiot of herself
and reveal far too much of what she felt. So she
forced herself to sit calmly until Judy finally ran out
of things to say. After extracting a promise from
Erica that she would come to visit soon, Judy left.

Erica decided to take a walk to clear her head. She
drifted past the oleander bushes and the spill of
bright pink bougainvillaea against the side of the
house, wandering along the graveled road toward
the main highway. Before long she came upon the
old house, and for a moment she stood studying it.
On impulse she circled around to the side door and
felt for the key in its old hiding place. After all these
years it was still there, rusty with age. She tried it in
the lock. It turned resistingly, and the door creaked
open. It was dark inside the house, the curtains and
drapes closed. Erica found a candle and lit it, then

climbed the stairs to the bedroom she and Tonio had used. She paused in the doorway, and the pain of a time long past pierced her. She whirled away and scurried down the stairs, but as she reached the bottom step, she stopped, struck by a thought.

She could make a little extra money by renting this house. Her mother had done it several times. She wavered, reluctant to allow others into the house she and Tonio had shared. It seemed an invasion. She squared her shoulders and took firm hold of her emotions. It was ridiculous to regard the house as a sanctuary. It wasn't as if a great love affair had taken place there. To Tonio it had been nothing but a quick fling, a sordid little affair. There wasn't anything about it worth saving, and she refused to pander to her crazy sentimentality. She despised the man. Why keep any reminder of him?

Quickly she marched to the main house and called the town's real-estate agent, as though to ensure that she wouldn't break her resolution to rent. Frank Dolby, the agent, was pleased to hear from her, although his pleasure was muted somewhat when he realized that the purpose of her call was not to place the farm in his hands to sell. However, he assured her heartily that he would be happy to rent the old house for her, and suggested she drop by his office to sign papers designating him as her rental agent.

Taking Lupe with her, Erica walked back to the old house. While Lupe determined the amount of cleaning it would take and how much extra help would be needed, Erica strolled through it, examining the state of draperies, floors and furnishings. It was in surprisingly good shape. Grant had taken excellent care of it through the years, sending Lupe in to clean it periodically and always making the necessary repairs. The roof was good, the foundation firm and the furniture protected by dust covers. Erica was pleased to discover there was little to be done to it besides cleaning. It was a nice house, roomy and comfortable, although not grand. Her mother had modernized the kitchen and bathrooms. The quality of the furniture was good, although the style was several years out of date. All in all, it seemed to her that it shouldn't be too difficult to rent at a decent price.

Lupe and her sister-in-law cleaned it up in three days, and one of the multitudinous nephews cleared away the weeds and bushes that had overgrown the yard. By the time they were through, it was sparkling clean and rather attractive in a roomy, homespun way. Erica was pleased with her decision to rent it.

Erica stood at the stove, whipping up a quick breakfast of scrambled eggs for Danny. It was so early that the light outside was still muted, washing out the vivid colors of the yard. Danny bounded in and prepared his lunch pail while Erica dished up the eggs and added a slice of toast to his plate. Danny gulped down his breakfast, chattering between bites about the drawing project they were to start that day in school. Erica listened absently, now and then nodding or making an appropriate remark. Her mind was really on the old house. It had been almost three weeks since she had decided to rent it, and there hadn't yet been a nibble. Frank Dolby had pointed out pessimistically that only a large family would want a rambling old house like that, and what parents with a lot of kids could afford it? Erica had thought of lowering the rent to make it more accessible, but when she imagined four or five children and accompanying pets crashing through the place, she decided to keep the price where it was. Maybe there would be someone without a lot of kids who could afford it and just happened to like comfortable old houses.

"Gotta go." Danny jumped up and Erica leaned down so he could plant a kiss on her cheek. Then he grabbed his lunch box and schoolbooks and made a mad dash to the front door. Erica sighed and poured herself a cup of coffee. She sat down at the kitchen table and sipped it, enjoying her time alone before Lupe or the workers arrived, before she had to deal with any of the problems.

It had been almost two months now since her father had died. The work had helped her through her worst period of grief, had given her something to think about and fill up her days with. But now life was beginning to return. She found herself enjoying things—the morning quiet, a lovely sunset, a laughing romp with Danny. Anxiety was starting to weigh on her where once it had been unable to pierce the shell of her loss. What was she going to do? Even if she rented the old house, she still wouldn't have enough money. The other day Rafael had dropped the bad news on her that they needed a new underground drainage system for about forty acres of the groves. The old one was beginning to fail, and without drainage the trees would go bad. Erica sighed. She had to get a substantial loan. There was simply no other way to raise the necessary capital for repairs and improvements except by selling a portion of the land, and *that* she was determined not to do.

Propping her chin on her hand, Erica stared out the window into the side yard with its empty, cracking swimming pool and the high, shading hedge beyond. For Danny's sake she wished she had the money to repair the pool and fill it with water again. However, that was out of the question right now.

Maybe in a few years . . . Erica almost groaned aloud. The farm was going to be a burden on her for the rest of her life. Even if she could get it back on its feet and running smoothly, she didn't know if it would ever make enough profit to allow her to afford a manager for the place, so she could return to the line of work she really loved. Yet, she couldn't sell it. She simply couldn't—not when it had meant so much to her father. She had to keep it, no matter what.

Grimacing, Erica rose and put her half-finished coffee cup in the sink. She couldn't sit around worrying about the future. She had to get to work. As she crossed the hall to her study, there was a sharp knock on the side door, which lay at the end of the hall. She glanced at her watch. Who on earth would be here at this hour? Surely not a buyer. The next crop wasn't ready for purchasing yet. She strode down the hall and swung the door wide, then froze.

Slim and handsome in black slacks and a black shirt, he stood framed in the doorway, his thick straight hair as dark as his clothing, heavy, sensual lids drooping down to hide the black gaze. Tonio Cruz.

"What are you doing here?" Erica demanded.

"I can tell you're delighted to see me," he remarked dryly, moving past her through the hall and into the kitchen, where he took up a casual stance against the counter. Erica followed resentfully. Who was he to barge into her house and take over? And why did her mouth and throat go dry and her knees begin to quiver at the mere sight of him?

Tonio folded his arms across his chest, drawing Erica's eyes to them. She swallowed, very aware of the hard brown strength of his arms. She knew their touch well, just as she knew the mobility of his long, sinewy fingers, their toughness as well as their incredible gentleness. It took all her willpower to appear calm. "I asked you a question. Why do you keep turning up in my life?"

He shrugged. "I must be the proverbial bad penny."

"I'm not in the mood to stand around trading quips with you."

"I can see. Well, it doesn't matter. I came to talk business, anyway."

"You and I don't have anything to discuss. I am no longer in your employ."

"That isn't the business I'm concerned with at the moment. Erica, I want to buy the farm."

"Absolutely not." She remembered guiltily her earlier regrets that the farm would be a millstone around her neck forever.

"Don't be so stubborn. You won't get as good an offer anywhere else. Money's tight. Few people are interested in or can afford to buy a whole citrus farm. The best you'll get will be local offers to buy a parcel here or there. Even if there is a buyer somewhere, it'll take months of advertising in several newspapers and magazines to find him. This way you'll save time and expense—and make a lot of money."

"I don't care about making a lot of money. What I care about is this farm. Daddy loved it. I was raised here. It meant a lot to him and to me too." She moved farther away. His nearness was overwhelming and made her forget her decision regarding him. Instead of remembering that she hated him for what he'd done to her and that she'd decided his kindness to her had an ulterior motive, she found herself staring at the straight black hairs sprinkling his tanned arms and the slender fingers, with their callused tips.

"If you don't care about making money, you shouldn't be in the business. Erica, being the daughter of a citrus farmer does not automatically qualify you for farming. You have no experience."

"Don't I? Do you think that in living here for eighteen years, hearing Daddy talk about nothing but raising and selling a citrus crop, I didn't pick up any knowledge? I'm reasonably intelligent, and I paid attention. I used to ride Morning Star through the groves, watching what was going on. I saw the grafting, the planting, the irrigation, the picking. I even helped out sometimes when Daddy was short of workers."

"Do you think the industry hasn't changed since you left? Tell me quickly, which insecticides have been outlawed and which are still in use?"

Erica set her jaw. "Okay. I can't answer you. But Rafael could, and he's my foreman. And I can find out in the pamphlets from A & M that are in Daddy's study."

"There's more to successful farming than planting the trees and letting the fruit grow. You must manage men. You have to deal with contractors and shippers. You'll be bargaining with some pretty crafty buyers who'll be only too happy to outsmart an inexperienced girl."

"Woman," she corrected coldly. "You forget I'm not seventeen anymore, Tonio. I've had some experience in the business world. I managed a hotel, remember? I had to handle employees, wholesalers and salesmen. None of them were looking out for my interests, either. Besides, it's not your concern. It's mine. And if you're so sure I'm going to fall flat on my face, why not wait to buy the farm from me then? It'll be a lot cheaper."

Tonio made a disgusted sound and turned away. For a few moments there was silence as he stared out the window. Finally he swiveled back to her, his brown eyes boring into hers, hot and beckoning. "Do you really think what I'm concerned about is the farm? Damn it, there are lots of farms around here I could buy, and most of them in much better condition than this one, too."

"But this one is different, isn't it?" she blazed, crossing her arms defensively over her chest. It was so hard to think properly when he looked at her like that, his eyes offering her the whole world, and she hated the fact that he could so easily lead her astray. "You used to work for Grant Logan, and you resented the hell out of him for that. Humbling his daughter wasn't enough, was it? Now you want the satisfaction of owning his property, of knowing that I was forced to sell to you!"

The skin around Tonio's mouth whitened, and for an instant his eyes flamed. "Is that what it was for you? Humbling? What was so humiliating about it, Erica, feeling my dirty hands on your skin or aching to feel them there?" His nostrils flared. "I ought to have my head examined. For some crazy reason I thought you needed my help. I thought after a while you'd realize that this great crusade of yours to keep Grant Logan's land was only the aftermath of grief, a desire to assuage your guilt by offering yourself up as sacrifice to his land. I hated to see you sweat away your youth and beauty, struggling to make this farm profitable again."

His voice was raw, persuasive in its pain. Erica wanted to reach out and touch him, to smooth away the anguish. But she reminded herself sternly that there was no reason for him to be hurt. After all, she had every right not to sell her land if she didn't want to. And though he was very good at twisting words to make it sound as if he had been wronged, not she, they both knew the truth. She clenched her hands and sneered, "Such honorable motives."

"I don't know why I bother. You'll wrap the shippers around your little finger, and your workers as well. You won't sweat. Some poor dope will do the sweating for you. Where there are men involved, you always come out all right. Sorry I disturbed your morning." He whirled and slammed out of the kitchen and through the side door. Erica slumped into the nearest chair, feeling as though her legs wouldn't hold her up another second.

How did he always manage to get to her? He seemed to know exactly which buttons to push. Just seeing him threw her into an emotional state. She wanted to cling to him as she had when her father died. She wanted to move into his arms and let him bring her body alive. Erica was sure he knew exactly how she would respond to him. Then, when she had refused to sell, which was really none of his business anyway, he had looked so hurt that she longed to run after him and give him whatever he wanted.

She groaned and plunged her hands into her hair. Was she wronging Tonio? Did he really mean to be kind? Surely he wasn't that good an actor. Maybe he had a fondness for the girl whom he had made love to so long ago and, being wealthy, found it easy to help her out by buying the land. Or maybe he was sorry for his youthful callousness in leaving her and hoped to ease his conscience. Or maybe he was exactly what she thought he was—cold, scheming and seeking revenge for the Anglo contempt he'd known when he was a child.

Erica drew a long breath and stood up. Well, whatever it was, she wasn't going to waste any time worrying about it. She wouldn't sell him the farm, and that was all there was to it. Nor was she going to try to smooth things over between them. It was better this way, even if she had wronged him. If she let him back in her life for any reason, she would be walking on the edge and could teeter over into love for him at any time. Far wiser to simply stay away.

Two days later Erica returned from a day in the groves and headed immediately for the shower. She needed to wash away the grime before she drove into town to do some errands she had put off for too long already. She was halted by Lupe's voice from the kitchen. "Señorita, that Mr. Dolby called."

Erica started for the phone eagerly. Perhaps he had found a family interested in renting the house. She looked up his number and dialed it, then waited impatiently while his secretary transferred her call to him.

"Erica, I have great news. I can hardly believe it myself. I have a renter for you."

"Fantastic! When do they want to move in?"

"The sooner the better. He only wants the place for six months, but I figured, why look a gift horse in the mouth?"

"My sentiments exactly. Well, the house is ready for occupancy. I have some errands in town this afternoon. I could drop by your office in, say, twenty minutes, and sign. Would that seem too eager?"

"No, oh, no, he's anxious to move in."

"Great. See you in about twenty minutes."

Erica hung up the phone and wondered if she should change clothes. She was dressed for the fields in old jeans and a red and white T-shirt, with one of her father's flannel shirts thrown on like a jacket. She had worn a hat against the sun and had knotted her hair up under it. Not exactly the look of a well-dressed businesswoman.

She sighed. Frank Dolby would have to put up with her as she was. She didn't have time to shower, dry her hair and change into something smart if she hoped to complete her errands before the stores closed. She knotted the ends of the flannel shirt at her waist, ran a quick comb through her hair and tied it at the nape of her neck. Not too bad, particularly if she changed her muddy boots for clean sneakers. Grabbing her purse and keys, Erica bounded out of the house and into her car. The little blue Datsun sped along the main road to town, and Erica surprised herself by flipping on the radio and humming along. It had been several weeks since she had wanted to listen to music. Maybe it was a sign things were getting better.

When she reached Santa Clara she parked on the square and hopped out of the car. She strode briskly down the street, turned the corner and pushed open the door of the Dolby Real Estate offices. Inside she stopped dead still, letting the door go. It eased pneumatically closed behind her. Directly in front of Erica was the receptionist's desk, where an attractive, auburn-haired woman sat smiling up at Tonio Cruz. He lounged against the desk, flirting with her. Tonio Cruz! He turned up wherever she went.

At her entrance Tonio swiveled his head, then gracefully rose, his dark eyes fixed on Erica. The redhead, every hair in place and her makeup perfect, cast a speaking glance at Erica that moved from the bottom of her tennis shoes to the top of her thick, tousled hair, pulled back and held in a simple red yarn bow. Erica bit her lip, acutely aware of the

tightness of her faded jeans and the enbroidered
strawberry adorning one thigh. She wore no makeup
except a dab of lipstick, and she could feel the tiny
hairs that framed her face curling with dampness.
Next to the other woman, she knew she appeared
plain and all at loose ends. Tonio looked her up and
down, his eyes dancing with amusement.

Erica flushed. "What are you doing here?" she
snapped.

The secretary's jaw dropped at the bite in her
tone. Dolby, hurrying forward from his glass-
enclosed office, boomed merrily, "Miss Logan! I'm
so glad you're here. When I told Mr. Cruz you
would sign the lease this afternoon, he offered to
come in too. I take it you know each other?"

"Yes, I know Mr. Cruz," Erica replied dryly.
"Are you telling me *he* is the man who wants to rent
the old house?"

"Yes. Isn't it nice it's someone you know?"

"No! I won't let you live there," Erica told Tonio
fiercely.

"I'm not allowed to set foot on your sacred
property?" Tonio asked, an indulgent smile curving
his lips.

"But, Miss Logan, you've already agreed!" Dolby
expostulated, his meaty cheeks quivering with the
fear of losing a customer.

"I had no idea who wanted the place," Erica
retorted. "If you had said it was Tonio Cruz, I
wouldn't have consented."

"But Mr. Cruz is ready and willing, even eager, to
lease the old house. It could be weeks, months,
before another prospect comes along."

"That's true," Tonio added lightly. "Who would
want such a rambling old house except a large
family—and they don't usually have the money to

pay the rent. Face it, Erica, I'm a golden opportunity."

Erica's lips tightened, and she would have liked to snarl her fury at Tonio. It was impossible to explain to Frank Dolby why she didn't want Tonio living there. She couldn't reveal to a stranger the twisted strands of their relationship, couldn't admit that Tonio had once deserted her, much less that she had been fool enough to fall into his arms a second time, making him believe she'd be easy pickings again. No, that was something she could never tell anyone.

"Mr. Cruz has already given me a check for the deposit and the first month's rent." Mr. Dolby gripped her arm to lead her away from the others. Lowering his voice, he muttered, "You better grab this tenant. He didn't quibble about the rent, just paid it quick as a wink. You'll never find anyone else as good. Trust me, he's wealthy. You haven't been home in a long time, but he's—"

"I know, I know," Erica interrupted brusquely. "He's made good."

"Yes, he has. The best chance you'll get has just dropped into your lap. This is perfect, absolutely perfect, and I promise you'll regret it if you don't accept the offer." At Erica's unyielding silence, his voice rose in desperation. "He didn't even ask to see the inside of the place!"

"I used to work for Mr. Logan." Tonio entered their conversation. "I've been inside the old house several times." His eyes challenged Erica with their mutual knowledge of the reason for his visits. Then he turned back to Dolby, his rich voice inviting the others to share his amusement. "I have to confess, Mr. Dolby, that Erica has a longstanding grudge against me. I once made a pass at her when she was a teen-ager, and she's never forgiven me."

Rage bubbled up inside Erica and she wanted to take a swing at Tonio's smiling, complacent face. He had effectively blocked whatever excuse she might give for refusing his offer. No matter what Erica said, Dolby would believe she was nursing a petty grudge. What excuse could she give, anyway? Not the real one. And nothing else sounded believable or important enough to inspire her adamant dislike of Tonio. She glared at him and saw, beneath the light amusement, a rock-hard promise that he would eventually win their struggle.

Well, then, let him, she thought furiously. Give in and get it over with. Once he'd won, he'd be content and would probably go away. Let Tonio discover that he could force himself into her life, yet not beguile her into his bed again. He could stay at the old house as long as he wanted. She had so much work that she could avoid him for months. So she would hand him the victory and let him bask in self-congratulation. He'd learn soon enough that the house was all he'd won. And she'd be making money from his mistake for six months.

"All right," she spoke up suddenly. "Let's sign the thing and get it over with."

Chapter 9

IT TOOK A MOMENT FOR HER WORDS TO REGISTER ON Frank Dolby, but when they did he pounced on his secretary. "Diane, have you finished typing the lease?"

"Yes, I made two copies." She pulled open a drawer and bent over it, the smooth, chin-length cap of auburn hair swinging forward. Erica wondered irritably how anyone managed to tame her hair into such lustrous perfection. She herself had either to let her thick mane tumble free or restrain it in a harsh knot.

Diane found the file she sought and set it on her desk, spreading out the copies of the lease for inspection. Erica picked up a copy and skimmed through it, conscious of the other woman's blue gaze upon her. She was sure Diane was wondering why Tonio had once made a pass at someone who looked such a fright. Diane was assessing the competition— Erica was certain the girl had her eye on Tonio. After all, they had been flirting wildly when Erica had entered the office. Hastily Erica scrawled her signature on both copies and handed the pen to Mr. Dolby, carefully avoiding placing it in Tonio's hand herself. That effort won her a sardonic, knowing smile from Tonio, and she crossed her arms, bottling up her rage. When Tonio had finished signing and

Dolby held out Erica's copy, grinning like the Cheshire cat, she snatched it from his hands.

"Thank you, Mr. Dolby." She folded the copy and stuffed it into her purse, turning on her heel to leave.

"But wait," Dolby protested, "you forgot Mr. Cruz's check."

He bustled to his office and returned with a cream-colored check signed in Tonio's bold, flowing script. As she waited, she was fully aware of Tonio's eyes upon her, and assiduously avoided looking at him. She took the check and wrote one of her own to Dolby for his commission. Still ignoring Tonio, she handed the check to the real-estate agent and stalked out the front door.

She had taken only a few steps along the sidewalk before a firm hand gripped her arm and Tonio's husky voice sounded in her ear. "You must let me buy you a drink to celebrate our signing of the contract, Miss Logan."

Erica jerked her arm away and retorted without bothering to look at him, "I thought you were a pretty bright guy, Tonio. Why haven't you gotten the message? I don't want anything to do with you."

"Then why let me camp on your doorstep for the next six months?"

"You know perfectly well why!" Erica exploded, forgetting her resolution to not look at him or carry on a conversation. "After that idiotic story you made up to explain my not wanting to lease to you, anything I said would have looked foolish."

He shrugged. "What a straight line. But I won't comment—I'm too much of a gentleman."

"Look, I don't know what little game you're playing. But I'm not joining in."

"What game? I'm not in the habit of playing games."

"Leave me alone," she growled through gritted teeth.

"I will if you'll have dinner with me."

"It's too early for dinner."

"A drink, then? Cup of coffee? I understand the Pioneer Cafe is still in operation."

"And after that you'll leave me in peace?"

"Yes."

"All right." Again he gripped her arm and guided her across the square. In the middle of the block hung a familiar white sign lettered in green: Pioneer Cafe. Inside, there were a few renovations. The booths had been reupholstered and the chairs changed, but the Formica counter and tabletops were the same, as was the black-and-white tile on the floor.

"This place always reminded me of a big checkerboard," Tonio commented as his firm hand against the small of her back maneuvered her to one of the green vinyl booths.

Erica had to smile at his apt remark, involuntarily warmed and softened by his confident hand steering her along. She slid into a booth and Tonio sat down opposite her. For a moment she stared at him, but the sight of his molded face and dark, simmering eyes made her far too shaky inside, and she glanced down. "I'm sure you must have some reason for this," she commented.

"Hell if I know what it is."

"Then why do it?"

"Sometimes I like to play my hunches."

"Do your hunches turn out successfully?"

"Not always." He picked up a plastic-backed

menu and glanced through it. "What'll you have? Coffee? How about something sweet? They have pecan and apple pies. You look like you could use a little lift."

"Too fattening. Coffee will be fine."

He reached across the narrow table and touched her chin. "Your face is thinner. Have you been eating properly?"

"Yes, Mother," she retorted. "Now, will you kindly forget the pie *and* my weight?"

A grin broke across his face and he leaned back against the seat. "Okay. How's your little boy? Enrolled him in school here?"

"Yes. Why?"

"Don't glare. I'm simply making conversation. I thought your son's school might be a fairly safe topic."

"Sorry."

They lapsed into silence, broken by the waitress's demand for their orders. After the waitress left, Tonio sighed and ran a hand through his thick, dark hair. "Look, Erica, I'm sorry I lashed out at you the other day. I'd had a hard day the day before on the island, working out a structural problem on my design for the Breezes, and I'd gotten up early to drive over here to see you about the farm. I was irritable and sleepy, and I assumed you would have thought it over and decided to sell. So when you were resistant and antagonistic, I just blew up. I realize I was nasty to you and I apologize. Certainly there's no reason why you should sell to me if you want to keep the farm."

Erica, prepared for another attack on the subject of the farm, was thrown off guard by his apology. She stared, and suddenly her previous anger vanished. "Oh, Tonio, me too," she sighed.

He reached out and covered her hand on the table with his own. "Do you honestly believe I stayed with you when your father died because I wanted your land?"

The touch of his hand created a liquid heat in the area of her stomach. She concentrated with difficulty on his question and finally replied, "No, it doesn't really make sense. I was so emotional then that I wasn't thinking clearly. Obviously it would have been an excessive amount of trouble to buy a farm when all you'd have to do is offer the money. And I've looked at land prices since then. I know you're offering me top dollar, more than it's worth, really. So I have to accept that you're trying to help me."

Again he grinned, and an accompanying sparkle lit his dark brown eyes. "But it's hard, isn't it?" he teased. Erica hardly noticed what he said, for his thumb had started to draw a slow, hypnotic circle on the back of her hand. There seemed to be no feeling anywhere in her body except in that small circle of flesh, and there her sensitivity was almost painfully acute. She imagined she could feel each separate ridge and whorl of his thumb as it rasped over her skin. The area burned with a surface fire, ignited by the friction of flesh against flesh.

Their surly waitress broke the spell, slapping down their cups of coffee so hard that the dark liquid splashed over the sides of the cups and into the saucers. Erica jerked her hand out of Tonio's grasp and folded both her hands in her lap. "But that doesn't mean I trust you!" she blurted out. "I know your kindness must have some purpose."

"Oh, of course," Tonio snapped sarcastically. "Naturally *I* couldn't be honest."

"Well, it's true, isn't it?" Erica pressed. "You want something from me, don't you?"

"Yes!" he grated, frowning. "Yes, I want something." He paused and sighed. "Look, Erica, I don't care about the farm. What happened back at the hotel between us—frankly I don't want to lose it again. All those years since we—since I left Santa Clara, I've been searching for the passion we had. I never found it. Then I walked into the Breezes and saw you, and all the years in between seemed like nothing. I wanted you so badly I was shaking, inside and out. When we made love, it was still the same."

Erica bit her lip and glanced away, unable to bear the warmth in his eyes. Every word he spoke made her quiver inside and long to reach out to touch him. But she knew she must not believe his words. He had lied before, even pretending to love her. She must be cool and firm, or soon he would have her in his grip as surely as before. "Oh, no, Tonio, better." Her voice was sharp and jagged as glass. "You've obviously had a lot of experience since then."

Unexpectedly he chuckled. "Jealous?"

"Hardly. I had my fill of you ten years ago. I'm not going to risk it again. I won't have an affair with you. It's better if we avoid each other entirely."

"Why?"

"I don't have to explain myself to you!" Erica flared. "My life is my business. Can't you accept that and go find yourself some sweet young thing like Dolby's secretary? She's obviously panting to hop into bed with you."

Tonio grinned. "You *are* jealous."

Erica slammed down her cup. "You're insufferable. I'm not jealous. I don't care enough for that."

His mouth tightened. "All right. You're not jealous. But you can't deny what happens when we touch each other." She set her jaw stubbornly and gazed out the window, refusing to meet his eyes.

"Go ahead, Erica, ignore me as long as you can. But remember, I want you in my bed again." He rose abruptly and tossed money onto the table for their bill. "And I've changed since the old days. Now I'm used to getting what I want."

Erica continued to stare out the window, ignoring his departure. Her stomach tightened. She believed Tonio. It was obvious that he had become accustomed to winning. Everything around him was the finest, the best, the most expensive. Price didn't matter. And he was stubborn. Whatever rebuff she gave, he soon countered with a new attack. It would be hard enough handling the farm without having to fight Tonio too. What devil made him persist in pursuing her?

"Erica?" A man's voice interrupted her thoughts, and she glanced up, startled.

"Yes?" She stared at the man standing beside her table. He was tall, blond-haired, with a great, drooping mustache across his upper lip. There was something familiar about him—the gray-blue eyes, the blunt fingers, the long legs. "Jeff Roberts!"

He laughed. "Yeah. Gee, it's nice to see you."

"You too. Sit down." She waved toward the empty seat across from her.

"When I walked in and saw you sitting there, it was like jumping back in time. Then I remembered about your father—I'm sorry."

"Thank you."

They began to chat about old times and what each was doing now. Erica revealed that she intended to operate her father's farm and for the first time was met with approval. Jeff laughed at her almost comical surprise and explained that he had encountered the same resistance when he had taken over his father's business after Mr. Roberts's heart attack.

They edged into their personal lives a little, Erica telling him that she had a son.

"I don't have any family," Jeff said a little sadly. "I was married, but now I'm divorced. My wife, Diane, was too young when we married. I suppose I was too. She was nineteen and I was twenty-three. We lasted three years and then split."

"Does she still live here?"

"Oh, yeah. She didn't want to leave the area. She thought she had something going with Lucio Cruz. I could have told her differently. He dropped her a few weeks after we separated. Old Lucio isn't interested in long-term relationships." Like his brother, Erica thought bitterly. Jeff paused, then continued, "Anyway, now she's working for Frank Dolby."

"That was your ex-wife!" Erica stared.

"What do you mean?"

"I was just at Frank Dolby's office."

"Red-headed girl? Pretty? Looks like she stepped right out of a fashion magazine?" Erica nodded. "Yeah, that's Diane."

"Small world. I haven't gotten used to being back in a small town."

He smiled. "There's no getting away from anybody in Santa Clara."

Erica returned his smile, hoping grimly that his remark would not hold true where Tonio Cruz was concerned. They lingered for a few more minutes, then Erica rose. "I'm sorry, Jeff, but I have to run. I need to hit the hardware store before it closes. It was great seeing you again."

"Same here. Whenever you're downtown, stop by the store and we'll have a cup of coffee. Maybe sometime we could drive to McAllen for a movie."

"Sure. That sounds nice." Erica grabbed her

purse and hurried out the door. It had been nice talking to Jeff, but how flat and pale he seemed in comparison to Tonio. She could be with Jeff for hours and not feel a twinge of anger or desire. She could easily understand why his wife would prefer either of the Cruz brothers to Jeff. Thinking about Diane, Erica could barely suppress a snort. Apparently she would be more than happy to settle for Lucio's brother instead of Lucio. Little did she realize that Tonio was much harder than his younger sibling. He'd been getting out of entanglements with women for a long time now.

Erica got into her car and inserted the key, her movements sharp and irritated. Tonio was so confident of his ability that he planned a repeat performance with her. Well, this time Tonio would find out she wasn't so naive or easy. She'd simply stay far away from him. That way there'd be no chance of danger. Eventually he would be bound to give up and leave her alone.

The days and weeks passed quickly. They were approaching the holidays, the best market time for the grapefruit and oranges, and the picking crews were hard at work. Although Erica had nothing to do with that aspect of the operation, she was very busy. When she wasn't keeping the books, consulting with Rafael or dealing with buyers, she spent her time preparing a financial profile of the farm to present to the bank when she went to get the loan she needed to pay for the new subsurface drainage system.

She was constantly on the run, which made it easy to avoid Tonio. She saw him now and then at a distance as she drove down the driveway, but he kept to his house and didn't venture over to the main house to bother her, as she had been afraid he might. Half relieved, half piqued by his lack of interest, Erica was not as successful in avoiding him in her mind. Ironically the very fact that he stayed away made her think about him more. She was curious about what he did at the old house and where he went when he wasn't there. At first he spent only weekends at the house. During December he remained for longer periods of time, sometimes as much as four days at a stretch. Erica wondered how his business got along with him absent so much. And if he was doing all this to win her over, why did he never come to visit her?

Christmas sneaked up on her, and before Erica realized it, Danny was out of school for the holidays. She scurried around, buying his presents, thinking guiltily that she was hardly making it a merry Christmas for her son. She was too tired and hard-pressed to get into the holiday spirit. She noticed that Tonio came home for an entire week, and she often saw his mother, Lucio or his sister Olivia at his house. As always he made no attempt to speak to her, but the week after Christmas he came to the house to pay his January rent. When Lupe popped into the study and announced excitedly that Tonio wished to see her, Erica clenched her hands, fighting the sudden rapid pounding of her heart. "You can accept the rent for me, Lupe," she told her coolly.

"Oh, but, señorita, he wants to give it directly to you," Lupe protested with rounded eyes, obviously astounded by Erica's lack of interest in Tonio. "He wouldn't give so much money to me."

"Why? Does he think you aren't trustworthy?"

"No, of course not, but it wouldn't be right."

Erica glared at her housekeeper. "Lupe, can't you

see I'm busy? Tell Mr. Cruz he'll have to give *you* the check."

"He said he'd come back tomorrow if now wasn't convenient."

Erica grimaced. "Oh, all right." She rose and marched stiffly into the front room, where Tonio stood, gazing out the front windows. He turned at the sound of her heels against the tiles of the hall, his face unsmiling, cool and devastatingly handsome. "Hello, Tonio."

"Erica. How are you?"

"Fine, thank you. I understand you brought the rent check?" Her voice went up on a note of polite inquiry.

"Yes." He extended the check, and Erica pulled it from his fingers without touching them.

"Why didn't you mail it, the way you did last month?"

"I was out of town last month when the rent was due, but it seemed a waste of postage to mail it this time when I could so easily bring it. Besides, I wanted to find out how you're getting along. I haven't seen you drive by the past few days."

"I've been busy," Erica replied shortly, sticking the check into a pocket of her jeans. Tonio was as immaculate as ever in tan corduroy slacks, a pale green shirt and a forest-green pullover sweater. Erica felt at a distinct disadvantage in her casual jeans and navy-blue turtleneck. It didn't seem fair that one man should be so handsome, so at ease. Whenever she saw him she felt as if her bones would melt, while he remained as calm and cool as an autumn day. Of course, he probably found that easy to do around her since she always seemed to be sloppily dressed and lacking makeup whenever he met her. Surreptitiously she wiped an ink-stained hand against her trouser leg and wished she were wearing one of her trim business suits. However, jeans were the only feasible thing to wear when she was constantly in and out of the groves or the dusty barn.

"Thank you for the check," Erica told him coolly. "Now, if you'll excuse me, I must return to work."

"You shouldn't work so hard. Believe me, the farm won't run off. It doesn't all have to be done immediately." He kept his eyes on her, his husky voice making the mundane words warm and special. Erica found herself wanting to tell him all her problems and seek his help, which was ridiculous. He'd use her weakness to get into her bed—or start in again about selling him the farm. She wasn't going to rely on his help. She couldn't, not if she wanted to keep any self-respect.

She forced herself to answer calmly, "Irrigation begins in February, and I have to get the drainage system repaired before then. After that we start planting. I won't have time to delay anything." Which was why, she added silently, she was going to talk to a banker on Monday. If she didn't borrow the money soon, it would be too late for the improvements.

"There's something wrong with the drainage system?"

"You needn't concern yourself about it." Erica realized that she had already revealed too much.

His mouth twisted. "Sorry I expressed any interest."

Erica remained silent. She refused to let herself be drawn into any further conversation with Tonio. He lingered for a moment, his eyes steady on her. Then he sighed as if giving up, murmured a polite goodbye and left. Erica followed him to the door and closed it behind him. She stayed at the door, watching Tonio through the etched glass side panel as he walked away. His long stride quickly took him past the oleander hedge and out of her line of vision. Erica turned away, in her mind's eye still seeing his lithe walk and the lean, smooth line of his legs.

Chapter 10

ON THE FIRST MONDAY OF THE NEW YEAR ERICA dressed in one of her most attractive suits, a slim-lined brown skirt and jacket with a shimmering rust blouse beneath. The skirt and jacket were tailored and very businesslike, but the sheen of the blouse and the dainty ruffle around the high neck and cuffs gave the outfit warmth and beauty. Brushing her hair back, she curled it up in a low roll that was smooth and no-nonsense yet possessed an old-fashioned femininity. Her only adornment was an old ivory cameo at the throat of her blouse.

Anxiously she made a final inspection of herself in the mirror, rechecked her file on the farm's financial picture and ventured forth to face the loan officer at the bank in Santa Clara. As she drove past the old house, Erica saw Tonio standing on the porch. Diane Roberts was beside him, her auburn hair gleaming in the sunlight. She gazed up at Tonio, her face glowing, her mouth slightly parted in laughter at his last remark. Tonio raised a casual hand to Erica in greeting.

Erica's lips twitched with irritation. How dare Tonio wave at her as if nothing lay between them, as if they were friends! And what was Diane doing at his house this early in the morning? Why, it wasn't even nine o'clock yet! Was she leaving after spending the night there? Erica knew Diane had been chasing Tonio from the first. Perhaps her chase had been successful. Erica's fingers clenched around the steering wheel. She told herself that whom Tonio slept with meant nothing to her. She was through with Tonio Cruz. Absolutely through.

By the time Erica arrived at the bank, she had managed to smooth the frown from her forehead and put Tonio out of her mind. The loan officer who came forward to greet her was a short, rotund man in his forties. She barely knew him, for he was too young to be in her father's age bracket, yet too old to be a contemporary of hers. Erica wished she could have presented her plea to one of her father's friends. However, the man was friendly and shook her hand warmly as he introduced himself as Jason Smith, then asked if she'd like a cup of coffee. The bank still operated on a small-town basis, one of the centers of the community, where customers as often as not came to sit and chat rather than conduct business.

Erica refused the coffee and laid out her file on Smith's desk. Carefully she explained the sales figures for the last five years and the projected numbers for this year and the next, which she had spent several agonizing hours over. Proud of her handiwork, she sat back, smiling.

"Very nice," he commented. "Yes, very nice work." He paused and cleared his throat, braced his elbows on the desk in front of him and carefully positioned the tips of his fingers together. Watching his hands rather than her, he began, "Miss Logan, these are very tight times in the financial world. It's difficult to obtain a loan these days, as I'm sure you're aware."

"Of course, but not when you have the kind of collateral I do. The farm has only one small existing mortgage."

"Naturally, but we don't make a loan solely on the basis of security. Bankers work with money. We aren't in the business of farming or selling farms. Say you don't make your payments and we have to foreclose. The only way we can recover our money is to sell the land. That takes time, money and effort, and all the while we're sitting there with a producing farm on our hands. We want good security, but our first consideration is whether or not you can repay the loan. If it was your father asking, or some other farmer, it would be different, but frankly speaking, Miss Logan, we can't afford to take the risk on you."

"But you can see the figures right there," Erica protested, pointing to the file. "It's obvious I'll be able to meet the payments."

"Yes, if everything goes exactly right. You're cutting it too close. If something unforeseen happens, you won't be able to make the payments. Ma'am, I'm sorry as can be, but it's impossible to lend you the money at the present time. Our holding company wouldn't approve it. They're always on our backs because we lend money on the basis of character without sufficient proof that it will be repaid."

Erica clenched her jaw, anger and frustration surging through her. She managed to thank Smith politely and leave the bank without her rage bursting through, but all the way home she reargued her case with the loan officer in her mind. Imagine not lending her the money with that kind of security backing it up! It was crazy. Fuming, Erica made a sharp turn into her driveway, kicking up gravel. Tonio was still on his porch, although Diane was gone. He sat with his feet up on the banister, lazily leaning back in a chair, a sketch pad on his lap. He glanced up at her loud entry into the driveway and again raised his hand in friendly greeting.

Without thinking Erica slammed on her brakes and skidded to a halt. After cutting off the engine, she jumped out and strode toward the porch, her anger boiling up in her, aching to be released. It seemed that Tonio sitting in cool possession of the old house was the last straw in a terrible morning. "All right, Tonio, this has gone on long enough," she snapped as she mounted the shallow steps. "What do you hope to accomplish by camping on my doorstep?"

His eyebrows sailed upward in reproachful surprise. "Apparently what I've accomplished is to get on your nerves."

"Is that what you want? To know that your presence here makes me furious? That I hate driving past this house? That you annoy me terribly? Why didn't you tell me before? I'd have admitted those things gladly, and you wouldn't have had to rent the house to find out!"

He studied her, an errant grin tugging at the corners of his mouth. Finally he remarked, eyes gleaming, "Damn! You're beautiful." Erica clenched her fists, arms rigid at her side, barely restraining herself from stamping and shrieking with frustration. Tonio rose, laughingly apologetic. "I'm sorry. Did I make the wrong response? Should I have shouted back and given you a chance to display your splendid fury? Go ahead and scream if you want. I won't mind."

"I'm tired of this cat-and-mouse game you're playing!"

"What game?" He opened the door and motioned for her to precede him. "Won't you come in? You might like to inspect what I've done to the place and drink a cup of coffee while you vent your anger."

Erica glared at him and stalked through the open door. Inside, she stopped stock-still and gazed around her. The old house had been transformed. The walls had been repainted a soft, creamy white. The wooden floors were waxed until they shone, and were warmed by vivid Navajo rugs. A large Indian sand painting in muted colors adorned one wall. Tonio had imprinted it with his own personality without changing the appeal of the rambling house and old furniture. Erica realized that she would love to throw herself on the large sofa and indulge in a good cry, then snuggle up before the fireplace with a book. Despising the traitorous yearning within herself, Erica swung on Tonio. "You've painted it."

"Yes, the walls needed it. Surely you don't object to my sprucing the place up a bit—I didn't deduct the expenses from my rent."

"You had no right. This is *my* house."

He cocked his head quizzically. "Do you want me to restore the house to its former grandeur? I could paint the walls a dingy beige."

"No. It looks lovely, and you know I wouldn't repaint it to look old and tacky. But you should have asked me first."

"How could I? You wouldn't see me or answer my calls."

"You didn't call me!"

He grinned. "So you've been keeping track."

"This is pointless. I don't know why I stopped." She started for the front door, but Tonio grabbed her arm.

"Wait. You must see the rest of the house. Who knows what other horrors I might have perpetrated? Aren't you afraid I painted a wall somewhere turquoise or purple?"

"I wouldn't put anything past you if you thought it would get under my skin. Why do you try so hard to make me mad?"

"I don't *try*. It comes naturally."

"Why did you rent my house? Why is it so important that you somehow obtain a piece of this farm?"

"The reason isn't quite as dramatic as you believe. I need peace and quiet to draw my designs, and it's hard to find such commodities in Houston. Plus, I've begun construction on the hotel on Padre. I'm close enough here to check on the work often while I clean up my backlog of work. And I can fly to Houston whenever I need to."

"Why not live on South Padre? That's where the construction will actually take place."

"Ah, but there I'd be forced to be constantly involved in the construction. I merely want to check on it periodically. I need time for my plans. Besides, my mother and family live here. I wanted a place near them."

"Why this one? There are lots of other places to stay in Santa Clara."

"Give me an example. The El Sombrero Motel perhaps? Santa Clara is not the rental property capital of the state, you know. Finding a nice, roomy house to rent isn't easy. Yours fitted my needs exactly. I've turned the den, which is sunny, into my workroom. Come look at it." He led her down the hall and into the small den, now dominated by his drafting table. He had covered one wall with corkboard and tacked up several of his sketches. Erica stepped closer, drawn against her will to the drawings of a multistory glass and concrete structure.

"Like it?"

"It looks . . . very elegant."

"Thank you. That's what I was hoping to achieve. It's a hotel on an island off the coast of Georgia. I plan to begin construction this spring. Here's an overview of the whole complex." He pointed to another sketch. "This L-shape is the hotel, and this is the pool. Over here, a small wading pool. See how the pool thins out? I'm going to give it the appearance of a stream, trees branching across it and flowers growing beside it. I'll build a couple of walkways over it as it curves back into the main swimming pool. Then here in the center I'll set the pool bar on an island. There are tennis courts inside and out. It sits, as you can see, on the edge of the golf course. In the future I plan to add a string of condominiums along the perimeter of the course."

"Quite a development."

"Yes, it's one of my biggest projects. The worst problem was obtaining the backing. That's why I'm doing it in stages. The hotel will bring in the cash and prove its potential. Then I'll be able to find the backing for the condos."

"Do you get loans, or do other people buy a piece of it?"

"For this one I obtained a loan—or, rather, several loans. I'm developing it in partnership with a couple of moneymen. Cross will run the development and they'll get a percentage of the profits."

"Is that the way you build all your hotels?"

"No. We design and build some for other corporations for a fee. Others we build and sell to a chain. And then we keep some and run them ourselves."

"How do you decide?"

"In some cases money decides. I need quick cash flow for another project, so I require a short-term money-maker. We'll sell. Longer-term profits mean we keep it. We're more likely to keep condominiums, which involve less management that a hotel."

"Will you keep the Breezes, then?"

"Possibly. Most of the hotels Cross owns and operates are in Texas or Louisiana. I want to keep the chain small and close to home. Operation is not my specialty." Suddenly he grinned. "That's your area."

"My area?"

"Yeah. Isn't that what you're trained for, hotel management, not running a citrus farm?"

"Are we back to that again?" Erica swung away, the friendly mood broken.

"Don't you miss it?"

Erica sighed and leaned back against the wall beside the sketches. Miss it? Oh, yes, she missed it. Particularly after her disappointment with the banker. What was she to do? For a second she was tempted to tell Tonio about her meeting with Jason Smith and his refusal of a loan. Tonio was a far more experienced businessperson than she. Perhaps he could help her, could show her how to draw up a profile that would have a bank jumping to loan her money. He obviously could get people to loan him millions of dollars for his projects. She bit her lip and looked up at him.

He sucked in his breath and came toward her. "God, when you look at me like that, I could . . ." He stopped before her and placed his hands on either side of her face, forcing her to turn her face up to him. Erica's stomach turned uneasily, as if she were looking into a bottomless black pit. She knew she could fall into the depths of his eyes and be lost forever. "I want you."

She began to tremble violently. Why did she let Tonio do this to her? Where was her cool, her resolve? Why had she stopped to talk to him, after all her vows to keep away? Sternly she tried to control herself, to summon up a sharp comeback. But, embarrassingly, when she spoke, her voice came out tiny, almost pleadingly, "For the moment?"

"For ten years." His hands slid down the wall to her waist, brushing her arms with a feather-light touch that set off shivers along her spine. "Do you know what you look like in that suit? A very expensive, very creamy, very delicious chocolate candy." He pulled her forward, and limply Erica made no resistance. His hand caressed her hair. "You're so tempting with your hair up all prim and proper." Softly, slowly, he kissed first her upper lip, then the lower one, tugging it gently between his lips. One finger moved to trace the convolutions of her ear. His mouth came down fully on hers, and he wrapped his arms around her. The touch of his lips, the velvet of his tongue roaming her mouth, shook Erica to the core. She wanted to give herself up to the magic of his lovemaking, to forget both her cares and the past and drown in the trembling glory of his hands and mouth on her body.

His hands slid under her suit jacket, caressing the satin softness of her blouse, and came to rest on her breasts. Mindlessly Erica responded, molding her body to his, the nipples of her breasts thrusting forward for the touch of his hands. He answered their need, his thumbs circling the hard buds through her blouse, using the material to arouse them further. His mouth ground into hers, the hard nipping of his teeth highlighting the incredible softness of his lips and tongue. His ragged breath seared her cheeks as his mouth sought her earlobe and feasted on it. He fumbled with the buttons of her blouse, opening it to his roaming hands. Expertly he unfastened her brassiere, all the while driving her further and further into mindless passion with the movements of his mouth on her skin. He kissed her throat, his tongue making wet designs and traveling across the thin skin of her chest to the trembling lushness of her breasts. He pulled back and for one long moment gazed at Erica, his hot eyes caressing the blue-veined globes with their eager, swollen tips. When she felt as though she could stand it no longer, he came back, bending to reverently take one nipple into the hot, moist cavern of his mouth. He sucked gently, his teeth barely grazing the tender skin and his tongue slowly stroking the button of her engorged nipple.

Tonio slid his hands down and up, pushing up her skirt as he caressed her silky legs. The lacy panties she wore were little protection against his hard reality as he pulled her ever tighter against him. He groaned deep in his throat, mumbling, "Erica." He raised his head from his delightful work and breathed huskily, "Come to bed with me. Upstairs in our old room." He nuzzled her neck. *"Querida. Mi amada."*

Erica did not hear the gentle love words he murmured. The reminder of their earlier love affair had shattered her haze of mindless pleasure. Tonio desired her as he had before—and he would break her heart again just as carelessly. She wasn't a person to him but a prize. He was determined to win her over. He'd told her so. No doubt it was a challenge to reconquer the woman he'd hurt so badly years before. And how easy she made it for him! Here she was in the middle of the day in his workroom, her blouse gaping open and her skirt pushed up above her hips like some cheap hooker, panting and yearning for his expert touch. Humiliation coursed through her, and she jerked away, tugging down her skirt and pulling her blouse closed, her arms wrapped defensively around her. "No!" Tonio took a step after her, then stopped, his breath harsh and heavy. "No, Tonio, not again. I refuse to be a few weeks entertainment for you."

"Erica, don't—not now—come back." He extended his hands and started toward her. Erica broke and ran, darting out of the room and down the hallway. Tonio didn't try to follow her as she escaped to her car. He crashed a fist into the wall, then turned away, plunging his hands into his thick, black hair and pacing until his breathing slowed. Finally he slumped into a chair. "Cruz, you're insane," he whispered.

Erica carefully avoided Tonio's house after that, although she found it far harder to avoid the shameful memories of how she had almost yielded to him again. She used her work as a shield, driving herself harder than ever. She applied to other banks in the area—McAllen, Harlingen, even as far away as Brownsville—but she received the same negative answer everywhere. Erica hadn't thought she was naive in money matters, but she realized her hopes for getting a loan had been overly sanguine. After the sixth straight refusal in two weeks, Erica dragged herself home disconsolately. It appeared that she would be unable to improve the land unless she sold part of it to some local farmer. She hated to do it, but she couldn't allow the farm to sink into a gradual decline, either. She poured a cup of coffee from the old percolator and ambled into the den. Kicking off her shoes, she plopped into a chair and propped her feet up on the edge of the coffee table. She exhaled wearily and rubbed a hand across her eyes.

Danny spoke up from his reclining position on the floor beyond the coffee table. "What's the matter?"

"Oh!" Erica's eyes flew open. "I'm sorry, honey. I didn't see you when I came in."

"I was reading." He indicated the book spread open on the floor before him.

"The light's not good enough there," Erica lectured automatically. "You ought to sit on the couch and turn on the table lamp. You could see much better."

Danny ignored her warning with the ease of long habit. "What's the matter?"

"Nothing. Why?"

"You went like this when you came in," he retorted, imitating her. "Like you were tired or upset."

"I suppose I'm both. I've been trying to get a loan to improve the farm, but the banks turned me down. I need a new drainage system for a few acres. Plus, I'm having to hire extra help to repair the damage Goodson did."

"Why won't they lend you the money?"

"Because I don't have any experience. They're afraid I won't be able to pay them back."

Danny's forehead creased into a frown. "I could get a job," he offered earnestly.

Erica smiled. "That's very sweet of you, but I'm

afraid you're under the legal age to work. Besides, it wouldn't be enough. I need a big chunk of money immediately."

"Maybe Tonio would buy the old house. He likes it a lot. Would that be enough?"

Erica sat up straight, her whole body tensing. "You sound on awfully familiar terms with him. Danny, have you been visiting Tonio? I specifically told you not to bother him."

"But I didn't! I was just playing on the driveway one day and he was sitting on his porch. He asked me how come I never came to see him and I told him you wouldn't let me 'cause I'd bother him. He said he wouldn't mind and I could come anytime I wanted to."

Erica laced her fingers together tightly. She mustn't make a big deal out of his visiting Tonio, or it would seem suspicious. If she refused to permit Danny to visit Tonio after he had given him permission, it might make Tonio curious, even cause him to delve into Danny's background. He obviously hadn't recognized Danny's resemblance to himself. After all, people rarely were aware of how they looked or saw others' similarities to themselves. It was a risk to let Danny visit him, but a worse one to insist on keeping him at home. Reluctantly Erica admitted, "Well, I guess it's all right then, as long as you don't go so often you wear out your welcome."

"I won't. Well, what do you think? Would he buy the old house? He must be rich, 'cause he drives a Mercedes. And I know he likes you."

"What?"

"Well, he asks about you all the time, what you're doing and how you feel and whether you're still upset about Granddaddy."

"He's just curious," Erica protested.

"Nope, I don't think so. You know, when we were all at the hospital, he looked at you funny, like guys do in the movies. You know, right before the big kiss." He jumped up and demonstrated a movie clinch, wrapping his arms around his thin body and smooching an invisible partner.

Erica had to laugh. "You nut. Well, whatever you think about Tonio's liking me, I don't want you to talk to him about buying the house. He doesn't need it, and I won't put him on the spot. I'll handle it, I promise."

Danny shrugged so innocently that Erica would have been suspicious if she hadn't been preoccupied with her own thoughts. "Okay." In his head Danny noted that he hadn't promised not to tell Tonio about the turned-down loans.

Erica's fingers tapped the keys of the calculator, figuring the profits from the last month. The front doorbell rang and she punched up a partial total, sighing. She had to answer the door because Lupe was cleaning the old house, a task Tonio had charmed the dour woman into doing weekly. Erica strode to the door and swung it open briskly. When she saw who stood outside, she gasped, her cheeks flaming with embarrassment. Instinctively she moved to slam the door in his face, but Tonio was quicker than she and caught it with his forearm. "Hello, Erica, it's always to nice to receive a warm welcome."

Erica's throat tightened, though whether it was from humiliation or his nearness, she wasn't sure. She looked away. "What do you want? I'm trying to work."

"I'm here on business—and I think my offer will prove more profitable than whatever you're doing at the moment."

"All right." Grudgingly she stood aside to let him enter, then walked down the hall to her office without glancing back at him. In her office she pointed in the general direction of the red leather chair opposite her desk. "Sit down. Now, what do you want?"

"I understand you're in need of a loan."

"How did you know?" She stared, then narrowed her eyes suspiciously. "Has Danny been talking to you?"

"Relax, Erica, I don't usually discuss financial matters with children," he lied, as he had promised Danny he would. "Bankers talk, you know. One hears rumors eventually."

"Okay. You're right. I've been trying to get a loan to fix up the farm. What of it?"

"How much do you need?"

"Fifty thousand, not that it's any of your business."

"But it *is* my business. I intend to loan you the money."

"You're crazy."

"Maybe. But I told you once that I built my business by following hunches."

"*Sound* hunches."

Tonio chuckled, a rich, throaty sound that tickled at her abdomen. "Are you trying to persuade me that you aren't a sound investment? I think you have that backwards."

"No, of course not. I'll repay the loan. But I don't understand why you're so anxious to lend to me when no one else thinks I'm a safe bet."

"I'm willing to make a loan based on personal

knowledge of your character." His eyes suddenly gleamed, and Erica's cheeks reddened again. "Do I have to beg you to take my money? How about if I promise not to charge interest?"

"No! It's just that I—I don't want to be beholden to you." There was no way to explain her fear of loving him again and being crushed by him. She couldn't tell him that each thing he did for her bound her ever more securely to him, was another strand in the web he was spinning around her.

"Is it so terrible to be in my debt?"

"I don't know what you'll want in return. I'm not for sale, Tonio."

He growled inarticulately and rose, slapping his hands down on her desk and leaning over her. By sheer strength of will he forced her to look up at him. "Do you think I'm going to demand your virtue, like some villain out of a melodrama? Don't worry. I don't enjoy coerced sex. There are plenty of women out there who are willing."

"I'm sure you've sampled a few, too," Erica retorted hotly. "Was Diane Roberts first on your list?"

"That sticks in your craw, doesn't it? What's the deal, Erica? You don't want me, but it wounds your pride to think I might settle for someone else? Would you rather I wasted away with feverish longing?"

"The only thing I'd rather you do is leave town. Whom you choose to sleep with is no concern of mine. Maybe you enjoy sharing women with your brother."

His face paled and he clenched his fists. "What the hell does that mean?"

Erica stared. Did it bother him so much that Diane had had an affair with Lucio? Was his feeling for the woman that intense? An icy pain pierced her chest. "I—I'm sorry. Weren't you aware that Diane and Lucio were once—I mean, that's the rumor."

He rolled his eyes. "I don't give a damn about Diane Roberts's sex life!" he roared. "For your information I haven't slept with her and I don't intend to." Visibly he forced himself to speak calmly. "Look, I think we're getting rather far afield here. As I recall, we were discussing your loan. Now, if I promise not to take my interest out of your delectable body, will you accept the money?"

"I don't want to have to be grateful to you!" Erica exclaimed honestly.

"Meaning it's easier for you to believe I'm mean through and through? Well, if it will help you any, I'll require a lien on your property. If you can't make a go of it, I'll get the land I want. Is that self-interested enough for you?"

"Oh, I see." It made more sense that way. It was still humiliating to take Tonio's money, but with the land as collateral, it wouldn't bind her to him in quite the same way. That made it a business deal, not a personal favor. She couldn't stand to be dependent on him in any way. "If you'll charge interest and accept a lien on the farm, I would . . . appreciate the loan."

"Careful, you might choke on words like that," he teased. "You drive a hard bargain. I'll take eight percent. What do you want, a ten-year loan?"

"Actually I was thinking of five."

He raised his eyebrows. "Sure you can make it? Let me see your figures."

She dug among the files on her desk and handed him the projections. He studied the papers, one finger running thoughtfully over his lips. With his attention elsewhere, Erica could study him freely. She took in the smooth fit of his slacks and the well-cut navy-blue shirt, the strong line of his jaw, the shadow of his thick, black lashes, the finger sliding across his chiseled lips. A warm glow started in her abdomen and spread. She couldn't tear her eyes away from his hard face, and she knew she wanted to pull the papers from him, to place her own fingers against his lips and feel their velvet warmth, to know the touch of his hand upon her flesh.

"Let's try a ten-year time period with no prepayment penalty. That way you can pay earlier if you want." He glanced up and his voice trailed off. Erica knew he had read the desire in her eyes. She looked away, blushing. What must he think of her? How humiliating for Tonio to know she had no control, that she hungered for him and would probably leap into his bed if he so much as crooked a finger. "Erica." His low voice was a tangible caress. A shiver snaked through Erica.

Desperately she shoved herself away from the desk and strode to the window. "If that's what you want, it's fine."

"You know that's not what I want," he replied huskily.

"Oh, then what do you want?" she asked bravely, turning to face him. His eyes were dark and smoldering, sinking into her heart and soul and trapping her.

"You—willingly—in my bed."

"Tonight? Or until you tire of me?"

"Tonight and every night . . . until you want to leave."

"Tonio, please, don't."

"Don't what? Don't desire you? Don't tempt you? I haven't touched another woman since I met you again on the island. That's a long time, Erica." His mouth curved sensually. "I've developed a huge hunger."

Erica's mouth went dry as sand, and she forced a swallow. Using all her willpower, she managed to shake her head no. A fire flamed for an instant in the dark eyes, but he lowered his lids, and when he reopened them, his eyes were their usual slate. Tonio rose and tossed the file onto the desk. "Have your attorney draw up the note and deed of trust. I'll have the money whenever you want."

Trying to maintain a light tone, Erica quipped, "I hope Cross Corporation won't regret the investment."

"It's not from Cross Corporation. It's a private loan from Antonio Cruz."

She stared. "You have that much money lying around?"

"I can get it. I think you ought to raise the amount to sixty thousand. I suspect fifty will be short."

"But I . . . thank you." She flushed and glanced away.

"Hard words for you to say, aren't they?" He crossed to the door. "Oh, by the way, I have one further stipulation. Invite me to supper when the papers are drawn up. I'm tired of my own cooking."

"Yes, of course."

He opened the door, then swung around suddenly and returned to Erica in two swift strides. His sinewy fingers dug into Erica's shoulders and pulled her to him. His lips sank onto hers. For a long moment neither moved, their mouths clinging desperately. His teeth were sharp against her lips, his tongue demanding, possessive. Finally he tore his mouth away, his face contorted with passion and anger.

"Damn it, Erica, how long are you going to keep us from what we both want?"

It was a rhetorical question and he didn't wait for an answer, but almost flung her from him and walked rapidly through the door. Erica stared at the empty doorway, her arms wrapped tightly around her to still the shudders coursing through her body. She knew she had done the wrong thing. Why, oh, why, had she let him become involved in her life again? He would suck all the life and love from her and leave her an empty shell, just as he had before.

Chapter 11

THE PROMISSORY NOTE AND DEED OF TRUST WERE standard forms. Bill Matson finished them in two days. After Erica picked up the legal papers, she returned home and dialed Tonio's number. When he answered, her stomach knotted and for a second she couldn't get out a sound.

"Hello?" he repeated impatiently.

"Uh, Tonio, this is Erica."

There was a fractional hesitation. "Yes?"

"I have the note and second lien ready. You do understand that the bank has first lien on the property?"

"Yes. It's negligible. I'm not backing out on that account."

"Would you . . . care to come over this evening? I'll give you the papers."

"All right." His voice turned teasing. "And do I get that dinner?"

"Yes." Erica bitterly regretted agreeing to his dinner deal. The more she saw Tonio, the less she was able to hang on to her good sense. "What would you like?"

"Whatever. It doesn't matter."

"I'll ask Lupe to prepare enchiladas. It's her best dinner."

"No! I don't want Lupe to fix supper for me. I want you to."

"What difference does it make?" Her voice rose in amazement.

Tonio hesitated. He felt stupid, now that he'd said it. She was right. Why should it make any difference? But he wanted to know that Erica had prepared the food for him with her own hands. As if she cared for him. As if she were his wife and Danny his son, a happy family scene. "Indulge me. I want you to cook it."

"Okay," she replied in the tone of someone humoring a crazy man. "But I warn you, it won't be nearly as good. I'm not much of a cook."

"I'll suffer the consequences. I'll be there, say, six?"

"Fine." Erica hung up and began a search of the kitchen. Lupe followed her movements suspiciously. Erica almost giggled. Why, she believed Lupe was actually jealous of her invading the housekeeper's domain. "I thought I'd cook supper tonight, Lupe, if it's all right with you."

"Whatever you want," Lupe replied coldly.

"You see, someone's coming over for supper at six, and if you had it ready before you left at five, it would be either cold or dried out by the time he got here."

Lupe was diverted. "You have a man coming for dinner? Who?"

"Tonio Cruz."

A smile cracked Lupe's dour face. "Mmm. He's a good man for you, that one. Very—I don't know the word, very much a man."

"Virile?" Erica suggested dryly. "Honestly, Lupe, I didn't figure you'd be swayed by his sex appeal."

"You think I'm dead?" Lupe retorted.

"Lucio's handsomer," Erica teased, amused at discovering a weakness in the solemn woman.

Lupe made a face. "A pretty boy. There's not enough man in him. Ever see his children? He's married five years and only two children, both girls. But Antonio—a son every year, just like that." She snapped her fingers three times to emphasize her point.

"I don't want a son every year!" Erica protested, but her insides warmed.

"You wouldn't want him to give you fine sons, brothers for Danny?" Lupe queried. Erica's eyes narrowed. Did Lupe suspect or was her remark meaningless? Lupe shook her head despairingly. "You think I don't know?"

"Know what?"

"That Danny is his son."

Erica glanced around sharply to make sure Danny wasn't within hearing distance. "Lupe, how could you know? No one does, not even Tonio."

"He's a man." Lupe dismissed him. "What man can see what's right in front of his eyes? No, he'd be too blind with jealousy, wondering if this man or that was the father. But I'm not. I see Tonio in Danny's face."

"Lupe, please, don't say anything about this. I don't want Tonio to know. Or Danny."

"Whatever you say. I won't go against you. But it will come out."

"Not if I can help it," Erica replied grimly. "Now, what shall I fix for supper?"

Since she was preparing a dinner for the man of Lupe's choice, Lupe apparently had no objection to Erica's using the kitchen. She reeled off a list of possible dishes.

"No, no," Erica objected. "Nothing fancy. I don't know how to make any of those."

"I will show you."

"No. If Tonio wants me to make supper, he'll have to eat what I know how to cook. Do we have any steaks?"

Sighing, Lupe surrendered and pulled three steaks from the freezer. Erica thawed the meat in the microwave. Giving in to Lupe's pleas, Erica allowed her to dictate instructions for a chocolate cake and then spent the rest of the afternoon putting together the ingredients and baking it. Danny wandered in, drawn by the delicious aroma of the baking cake. He was thrilled to learn that Tonio would be their guest at supper and insisted on helping to ice the cake, anxious to be included in preparing the treat for his friend.

The cake took longer than Erica had expected, and by the time it was iced, it was almost six o'clock. Erica glanced down at her worn jeans and loose red shirt, both splattered by flour and drops of icing, and muttered a terse expletive. She couldn't meet Tonio looking like this, she thought, remembering her sloppy appearance at the real-estate office, the awful contrast to Diane's careful style. But she had little time to change. For a moment she hesitated, wondering defiantly why she should care how she appeared when Tonio came to dine. She hadn't wanted him to eat with them in the first place.

Erica bolted for the stairs, calling to Danny, "Honey, I'm going to bathe and dress. If Tonio arrives before I'm through, stall him."

"Okay," Danny shouted back cheerfully, and took up watch at the living room window.

Pinning up her hair, Erica dumped powdered bubble bath into the tub and ran the water while she searched her meager wardrobe for the proper outfit. Everything she pulled out seemed dreadfully tame or far too suggestive. Finally she compromised on dark purple slacks with a matching jacket, collarless and perfectly plain except for the piping down the front and on the two slanted slash pockets. Underneath the jacket she would wear a thin lavender blouse, very understated and feminine, with a low oval neckline that dropped almost to the tops of her breasts. One large, soft ruffle adorned the neckline. Erica tossed the clothes onto the bed, returned to the bath and quickly stripped to step into the tub. She scrubbed until her skin was rosy from the heat and friction. She would have liked to soak lazily for a while, but there wasn't enough time. Tonio would tease her all night about her feminine tardiness if she wasn't on time; in fact, she wouldn't put it past him to barge right into her room while she dressed.

That thought inspired her to towel-dry at top speed and jump into her waiting clothes. After slipping on earrings that resembled gold lace, she pawed through her jewelry box for the matching necklace. As she searched, her fingers brushed a small, round metal object and halted. Slowly she pulled it from the box. Tonio's medal. Holding it in her palm, she traced the raised figure on the front. She replaced it gently and closed the lid, deciding not to wear the necklace that matched her earrings. Hearing the doorbell ring downstairs, she dabbed on makeup and mascaraed her eyelashes. Then she brushed out her thick hair, pulled it back and caught it on one side with a dainty barrette covered with tiny lavender flowers. A quick splash of perfume was the final touch. She hurried down the stairs to the den, from which came the sound of Tonio's and Danny's voices.

The tableau in the room stopped her in her tracks. Her breath caught harshly in her throat. Danny was instructing Tonio in the use of an electronic game and they were laughing over Tonio's mistakes, their dark heads close together. How could anyone not realize they were father and son? she thought. And how much longer could she keep it from Tonio? Someone would see the resemblance and mention it to Tonio, and then—what? She didn't know, but the idea frightened her. "Hello," she exclaimed brightly, a little too loudly, to break the intimacy before her.

They raised their heads. Danny whistled boyishly and Tonio stood, his face a silent tribute to her looks. "Erica."

"I hope Danny's been keeping you entertained," she continued in a hostessy voice.

"Very," he answered gravely. His hand rested on the boy's head.

"Could I get you a drink?"

He shrugged. "If you like."

Her question had been the first thing that popped into her nervous mind. Erica regretted it immediately. Her liquor cabinet was poorly stocked, as she rarely drank, and so didn't bother to buy any liquor. "What'll you have?"

"Scotch and water," he replied carelessly.

Erica crossed to her father's liquor cabinet and opened it. "Sorry," she apologized, blushing, after a fast search. "No Scotch."

"Bourbon, then."

"None of that, either." Erica bit her lip.

A grin flickered across Tonio's mouth. "Gin and tonic?" Erica shook her head, her face flaming now. Tonio laughed. "I'm sorry. I didn't realize this was a quiz game. I give up. What's the answer?"

Erica turned back to the cabinet. "Well, I have rum and vodka."

"A screwdriver would be fine. A small one." He hesitated, then added with a teasing smile, "I trust you *do* have orange juice."

Erica cast him a fulminating glance and stalked away to the kitchen to fill the ice bucket and get the orange juice. Returning to the den, she mixed the drinks, poured Danny a glass of orange juice and carried the glasses to the coffee table. Then she realized she had no cocktail napkins. She hurried back to the kitchen for coasters. "I'm sorry." She was completely flustered now. "I'm not used to company, I'm afraid. I also forgot to get nuts or mints or anything like that." She brightened a little. "I do have some cheese."

Tonio chuckled and reached out to take her hand. He brought it to his lips, forcing her to move closer, and grazed her knuckles with his soft, warm mouth. Erica's stomach quivered at the velvety touch. "It's all right. I never expect the amenities from citrus farmers." Erica snatched away her hand and took a large gulp of her drink, which she instantly regretted. She had made it far too strong. Tonio grinned at her wry face. "Next time *I'll* make the drinks."

"When do we eat?" Danny questioned, not one to lose sight of the important things in life.

"Right now." Erica rose quickly. "I'll put on the steaks. How do you like yours cooked, Tonio?"

"Medium rare." He stood also, slipping out of his tan jacket. Erica couldn't help running her eyes down the smooth line of his body in the eggshell-colored silk shirt and tan slacks. His stomach was flat and hard, flowing into graceful, muscular thighs. Tonio rolled up his sleeves. "I'll grill the steaks. Why don't you get the rest of the meal on the table?"

Erica's mouth thinned irritably. How dare he take over like that! She started to voice her indignation, but he was already gone, Danny on his heels. With a low, wordless growl, she followed them. What an abominable evening this promised to be. She found Danny rummaging through the drawers for the long barbeque tongs while Tonio seasoned the steaks. "I thought you wanted this prepared by my own lily-white hands," she told Tonio sarcastically.

His eyes danced. He nodded toward the oven, in which the foil-wrapped potatoes were visible. "You've made the potatoes. That's adequate taxing of your culinary skills."

"What's culinary?"

"Cooking," Tonio replied, having become used to Danny's style of conversation.

"Oh, she did more than the baked potatoes," Danny assured him with pride. "Look." He skipped to the opposite counter and lifted the lid from the cake plate.

"You made that yourself?" Tonio queried Erica, his eyebrows rising.

"Yes," she retorted. "Don't look so amazed."

"She didn't even get it out of a box. She made it from a recipe," Danny informed him with pride. "And I helped her put on the icing. We fixed it especially for you."

"Danny, why don't you go set the table?" Erica asked through tight lips.

"A chocolate cake especially for me?" Tonio teased after the boy had gone, a flame glowing briefly in his eyes. "Erica, I'm honored. Are you trying to seduce me?"

She whirled to escape his gaze and opened the refrigerator, staring blindly at its contents. His arms

stole around her from behind, and Erica jumped.
"You won't find it in there."

"What?"

"What you're looking for." His lips feathered
across the back of her neck, sending shivers racing
down her spine.

"And what is that?" Erica could hardly think. She
wanted only to lean back against the steel of his
chest and give herself up to his caress.

"This." His hands slid up under the jacket and
over the silk of her blouse, crossing to cup her
breasts. He nuzzled her neck.

"Tonio," she breathed. Her mind was a swirl of
sensory perceptions far removed from thoughts. She
trembled beneath his touch, aching for him.

Danny's high voice called from the dining room,
piercing the haze of desire. "Mom? Do the spoons
go after the knife or before?"

A soft groan of frustration escaped her at the
interruption. One of Tonio's hands slipped down
between her trousered legs and pressed her to him.
She could feel the rigid expression of his desire
against her buttocks. "Tonight," Tonio whispered in
her ear. "I promise you. Tonight." He dropped a
final kiss on her bare neck and released her. "I'll get
the steaks going."

"Mom!" Danny repeated impatiently. Erica en-
vied Tonio his escape to the gas grill outside. She
could go nowhere to hide her hot cheeks and sparkling eyes.

"Yes, honey, I hear you. The knife goes to the
right of the plate and the teaspoon to the right of the
knife."

"Okay."

Erica took the salad bowl from the refrigerator
and set it on the dining table, added the dressing and

condiments, then brewed a pot of coffee. She steamed fresh broccoli, put it in a bowl and sprinkled it with lemon butter while Danny finished setting the table and plunked down the baked potatoes. By the time Tonio returned with the grilled steaks, the rest of the meal was ready. It was absurdly like an ordinary family meal, Erica thought. Unconsciously she had placed Tonio at the head of the table, and she and Danny sat on either side. It was an intimate grouping at the large, formal dining table, and a natural way to arrange them, but it also put Tonio in the position of father to the family, head of the household. He assumed the role with ease, dishing out the sizzling steaks, joking with Danny, reaching over to ruffle the boy's hair. Although his eyes touched Erica with a scorching intensity now and again, reminding her of his promise for the night to come, he kept the conversation on a normal plane. They discussed the weather, which was unusually warm for January, even in the valley, and talked about her crops and the progress she was making on the farm. Danny asked about the renovation of the Breezes, and Tonio described it in detail. "Tell you what, one day soon I'll take you to the island and let you see what they're doing. Would you like that?"

"Oh, yeah!" Danny responded enthusiastically. "That'd be super. When?"

"Danny, don't push," Erica admonished softly.

"It's all right. I don't mind. I'll be going over next week. How about then?"

"Sure!" Danny smiled and turned to his mother. "Can I, Mom?"

"Of course, as long as it isn't on a school day. Now, are you ready for some chocolate cake?"

Danny answered with a wide grin and Erica went into the kitchen to cut the cake and set it onto dessert plates. "Tonio, you want some coffee?" she called.

"Yeah. Black."

She carried in two plates of cake, then returned for the coffee. By the time she set the cups and saucers down and splashed a dollop of cream into hers, Danny was almost through with his dessert. "What did you do, inhale it?" she asked, laughing.

"It's good," he replied by way of explanation. "Especially the icing."

"You would say that."

Tonio looked at her. "Aren't you having any cake?"

"Nope. Too fattening."

He grimaced. "You worry too much. You're thin enough. A man wants more in his arms than bones."

A treacherous warmth seeped through her at his words. To cover her reaction, Erica joked, "What do you want, for me to be *gorda?*" She puffed out her cheeks.

Tonio chuckled. "Here, just try a bite." He cut a piece of moist cake dripping with icing and extended it to her on his fork. Somehow he managed to make the gesture intimate, suggestive. Erica clenched her hands beneath the table. How did he manage to be so damn sexy even about offering her a bite of cake? She leaned forward to eat the piece of cake, but it was awkward, and a bit of the gooey icing slid off and landed on her chin. Danny giggled. Erica reached for her napkin, but Tonio was quicker than she. He scraped the icing from her skin with his forefinger and held it to her mouth. With an instinct deeper and faster than thought, Erica opened her lips and caught his finger between them, the tip of her tongue raking the icing from his skin. His eyes smoldered at her sensual action. The roughness of his skin against her sensitive lips and the salty taste of his flesh mingling with the sweet icing stirred her.

"Mom, could I have another piece?" Danny's voice broke the moment and Tonio's hand dropped. Erica dabbed at her lips and chin with her napkin.

"Later, maybe, before you go to bed."

"I'm through, then. Can I go outside and play?"

"Sure." Danny was gone in a flash, the front door banging behind him.

Erica wet her lips and looked around nervously, unable to meet Tonio's eyes. Why did she possess so little control around him? He knew exactly what bells to ring, and she responded like one of Pavlov's dogs, hot and eager. It must give him a lot of amusement to toy with her, to watch her melt wantonly whenever he chose to make her respond. "Erica, look at me." His voice was velvet, husky and caressing.

She jumped up, seizing the first excuse she could think of. "Let me warm your coffee." She almost ran into the kitchen, unplugged the percolator and returned with the pot to refill both their cups. When she started back to the kitchen, Tonio pulled the pot from her hands and set it on the table.

"I've had enough coffee for the evening," he told her firmly. His warm hand clasped one of hers and pulled her closer until she stood right beside him, close enough to feel the heat of his body. Erica stared down at his hand, still avoiding his eyes. He rubbed the back of her hand with his thumb. His voice was low and resonant. "I enjoy having you serve me." He lifted her hand to his mouth, kissing it slowly, softly, then rubbed it against his cheek. He mumbled a string of Spanish words against her skin, his breath searing her.

"What did you say?" she asked shakily.

He raised his eyes and grinned. "Probably nothing you'd like to hear. I was, uh . . . eulogizing your physical attributes."

Erica flushed and jerked her hand from his grasp. She sank into her chair, her knees suddenly turning to water. She began to pleat the tablecloth between her fingers. He placed two fingers beneath her chin and tilted up her face.

"Look at me. I want to see your lovely eyes." She gazed into the black depths of his eyes, bracing herself against their glittering intensity. "I've been sitting here all evening, talking like an idiot, no idea what I'm saying. All I could think about was you. Your hair, your eyes, your mouth. I could have been eating cardboard for all I cared. What I tasted was your skin on my tongue."

"Tonio, please."

"Erica, come here." His tone was soft, but brooked no disobedience. Erica rose, almost without effort, and took two small steps to his side. His arms slid around her waist and he buried his head between her breasts. Erica leaned against him weakly. Tonio tugged her down onto his lap, and her head lolled back against his steely arm. His lips covered her throat, nipping, sucking, massaging the soft flesh. One arm curled around her, supporting her torso, and the hand of that arm cupped her full breast. The other hand roamed freely over her open body, exploring and arousing her through her clothes. Erica's nipples tingled and pressed against the cloth of her blouse, turgid and aching for his touch. She twisted on his lap and he groaned at the movement. His mouth moved to hers and she strained against him eagerly, her tongue sliding out to lock with his in a contest of pleasure. His hand spread into her hair, holding her head immobile, and his lips worked over hers, his breath searing her cheek.

Finally Tonio wrenched away, his fingers digging into Erica's hair and pulling her head back. He closed his eyes and sucked in a chestful of air. "God, I want you," he rasped.

Erica's tongue traced her bruised lips. "Then take me," she whispered.

He shuddered violently. "Don't tempt me." He lifted her onto her feet. "I could use a cold shower about now." Kissing one ear lightly, he stepped away. "Later," he promised huskily. "When Danny goes to bed, we'll have the whole night before us."

Erica swallowed. She would have liked to retort that she wouldn't succumb to him later, but she knew it wasn't true. She would melt as soon as he kissed her, just as she had now. Shakily she picked up the small dessert plates and carried them to the kitchen. Tonio helped her clear the table and stack the dishes in the sink. "I'll do them later," she suggested. "Just leave them there."

He smiled, his eyes twinkling. "I have plans for later. Let's clean up now. I'll help." He began to scrape and rinse the dishes and Erica placed them in the dishwasher. It was odd to stand beside the man who had just swept her away in passion and engage in such a mundane task as cleaning the dishes.

"What's the smile for?"

"Oh, nothing. Just thinking that you aren't exactly dressed for dishwashing."

He glanced down at his immaculate shirt and tailored trousers and shrugged. "My clothes adjust to me, not me to them." He nodded toward the chocolate cake remaining on the counter. "What inspired the dessert?"

"What makes you think I don't usually do such

things?" she inquired loftily. He cast her a speaking glance and she giggled. "Okay. I've never made a cake from scratch in my life. Lupe told me how to do it, then stood over me to be sure I did it correctly. She was absolutely horrified because I was going to cook such a simple dinner."

"So you fixed it to appease Lupe?"

She hesitated. "I'm sorry. That doesn't sound very polite, does it?"

"You're worried about being polite to me? The evil genius who plots to destroy you?" He raised one eyebrow in exaggerated amazement.

Erica flushed and quickly bent to drop a fork into the basket in the dishwasher. She felt unbearably stupid and awkward. She wanted—oh, so desperately —to hate Tonio. Then she wouldn't have to fear loving him again and being broken on the rack of his loveless passion. But it was so *hard* to resist his charm, to continue to believe he was wicked. His constant hounding of her seemed to have had no purpose except to help her despite her rejection. Erica grabbed a dish towel to dry her hands and stood twisting it. "I'm sorry. Have I been an ogre?"

"A very pretty ogre." He brushed a finger along the line of her jaw.

Tears sprang into her eyes. "Tonio, I don't understand you! How can you be so kind, so gentle sometimes, and yet . . . ?"

"And yet what?"

She shook her head, unwilling to reveal her hurt from the past. "Nothing. I'm confused."

His hand slipped behind her neck, massaging the tightness. His voice was soothing, seductive. "Let me help you, Erica. You have too much to bear alone—a son to raise, your father's death, this farm." She raised her head and his face tightened at the sight of her tears. Putting his hands on either side of her face, he wiped away the tears with his thumbs. He wanted to ask her to give herself to him wholly, to put her heart and soul in his safekeeping, to let him shoulder her burdens, but he was afraid she might pop back into the protective shell from which she had been shyly emerging all night. Don't move too fast, an inner voice warned. Tonio forced himself to be content with asking, "Will you let me help you? If you need anything, will you call me?" She nodded mutely, feeling weak but warmed and comforted. "Good." He smiled and released her. "Now, let's join Danny outside. It's a beautiful night."

He closed the dishwasher and turned it on, then led her to the side porch and the old wooden swing. It was a warm night for January, and with her jacket on, Erica was quite comfortable outside. The stars blazed white above them, and the moon was large and round, flooding the yard with a pale light. When he heard them step outside, Danny dashed around from the front yard to greet them, then charged off, returning to his game. They settled into the swing, and Tonio curved his arm around Erica, pulling her close. His hand drifted gently downward, cupping her breast in the dark, his thumb now and then tracing a lazy circle around her nipple.

"Tonio," Erica whispered, unable to raise her voice any louder. "Your hand—Danny."

He smiled faintly. "It's dark. Besides, he's gone back to the front yard. The only harm I'm doing is driving myself wild."

"You're not the only one," she retorted without thinking, then blushed at her admission.

Tonio chuckled. "Don't tell me you're affected too." His free hand slid beneath her jacket, roaming freely in its concealment, stroking the soft curves of her body, slipping lower to caress her thighs, while the first one kept up its slow, steady caress of her nipple. His fingers were adept, creating a pulsating warmth even through her clothes. Finally he traveled up her inner thighs, to the juncture of her legs, and stopped. He held her firmly, not moving, but the heat radiating from him spread insidiously through her. Erica felt heavy and weak, malleable, yet itching, aching, for more.

"Tonio! Please." She wriggled her bottom as though to escape his trapping hand, but the movement served only to create a delicious friction. She almost gasped at the sudden pleasure. Slanting her eyes up at him naughtily, Erica smiled. "Two can play at that game, Mr. Cruz." Slowly, deliberately, her tongue edged out and traced her lips. Tonio's eyes were fixed on her, and though his expression did not change, she could feel the surge of heat in his body.

Erica looked away from him, for all the world as if she were studying the darkened yard, but her hand went to his leg and began to move up and down it, making lazy patterns on the tight cloth of his slacks. She teased with her fingertips, drawing away, then returning. Tonio groaned and took her ear in his mouth, his teeth and tongue fiercely demanding. "Oh, baby," he growled softly. "Stop. I yield. I can't take any more." He removed his hands and she shifted slightly away from him. Tonio grinned at her. "Doesn't that kid ever go to bed?"

Erica glanced at her watch, but it was too dark to read the dial. Tonio's explorations had left her mind in some never-never land of the senses, and she found it difficult to think. It was insane to succumb to him, she knew. It would mean only heartbreak for her. Yet, she wanted him so badly, longed to feel the touch of his hands on her skin. She realized despairingly that she wanted to belong to him, would not be satisfied unless she did. And Tonio? She wouldn't let herself think about what Tonio wanted. Hastily she rose and went to the edge of the porch. "Danny! Honey, it's time for bed."

"Ah, Mom," he responded with automatic disgust, but came without any further fuss. With a smiling good-night to Tonio and an unexpected hug, he bounded through the door and down the hall to the stairs. Erica turned to Tonio a little shyly. "I—uh, I have to go tuck him in."

"I'll wait for you in the den," he promised, his voice rasping with suppressed desire.

Erica left without looking back and climbed the stairs to Danny's room. It seemed to take him forever to finish his bath and brush his teeth, which he usually did with lightning speed. Finally, however, wearing his crisp pajamas and smelling delicious, as only a child can, he ran into his bedroom, where Erica waited on the bed. He popped into bed and settled against his pillows for their nightly chat. "I like Tonio," he told her.

"Do you?" Erica sighed. "I do, too, I'm afraid."

"That doesn't make sense."

"Sometimes things don't."

Danny shrugged her comment aside as the vagary of an adult. "He told me he'd take me to see the hotel next weekend. Is that okay?"

"Sure." Erica carefully curbed her impatience as Danny continued to chat until she decided he had reached the stalling point in his dialogue. Then, with a firm "Good night," she rose and left the room, pulling the door to behind her. Her knees were shaking as she went down the stairs and into the den.

Chapter 12

TONIO WAS SLUMPED ON THE COUCH, HIS HANDS locked behind his head, staring up at the ceiling. Lithely he rose, his dark eyes glowing at her. "I finally gave up trying to read your magazines."

Erica didn't know quite what to do. She didn't want to seem too bold, but neither did she want to stall. It was time to quit denying that she wanted him. She was fooling no one, not even herself. Perhaps it was the absolutely wrong thing to do, but it was inevitable that she do it. "Shall we—" Her voice squeaked and she had to stop and try again. "Shall we go upstairs?"

He came forward without a word, extending one hand to clasp hers. Erica was grateful that he didn't tease or gloat. She led him up the staircase to her bedroom. He glanced around it briefly as he closed the door behind them. It was still a teen-age girl's room. Erica had never been the frilly type, so there were no ruffles or yards of eyelet. But there was a fresh, young quality to the yellow curtains and patterned bedspread, a confusion and searching for style. The furniture was white French provincial, too dainty and fussy for the adult Erica. He suspected that now she would choose strong, simple furnishings, coordinated but not perfect, with subtle tones and shadings.

His eyes returned to Erica, who stood a little uncertainly in the middle of the room. He came forward slowly, luxuriating in the moment. "I've waited a long time for this," he told her in a soft, almost dreamy voice. He grasped the lapels of her jacket and peeled it back and off her arms. "You have no idea how I've lain awake at nights, imagining it." He tossed the jacket on a nearby chair, then started on the buttons of her blouse.

"If I live to be a million years old, I won't understand you. You're tough, brave, hardworking, vulnerable. Beautiful. Callous. Cruel. But a good mother. And a true artist in bed." He placed his hands flat on her chest above her breasts and slid them beneath her opened blouse, pushing the material off her shoulders and down her arms until it fell in a crumpled heap of purple silk on the floor.

With the same slow, almost reflective gentleness, he continued to undress her, letting her other clothes join the pile at her feet. At last she stood completely naked before him, and for a long moment he simply viewed her exposed body, taking in the heavy, thrusting breasts, the nipples pointing under his gaze, the slender waist that flowed out into softly curving hips. Erica scarcely breathed, captured by his smoldering eyes. His look was as tangible as teasing fingers, setting her aflame and turning her insides to wax. She raised her hands to him and he caught them between his own, lifting them to his lips. The skin of her fingers was sensitized, alive, vibrating to the barest touch of his moist tongue, the tender nip of his teeth.

"Tonio," she breathed, and he bent to kiss her

ear, her cheek, her throat and finally her mouth. His lips fitted hers naturally, satisfying a deep primitive ache within Erica. His tongue entered the moist cave of her mouth, and Erica pressed herself into him, yearning to feel him inside her, to meld into his flesh. He kissed her again and again, ardent, molten kisses that shot sparks along her nerves. Erica moaned and moved against him, pleading wordlessly for the fulfillment only he could provide.

Tonio kissed her throat, his lips sliding to the delicate, pulsing hollow at the base of her neck. Lightly his fingertips caressed the hard line of her collarbone. He bent his head, moving downward to the soft crests of her breasts, making a slow circumnavigation of each with lips and tongue. Erica curved over him, nestling her cheek against his head, nuzzling the thick black hair, kissing it, while her hands played across his back. He smelled faintly of cologne and the pungent sweat of excitement. Erica felt for the hem of his shirt and rolled it up, her fingers seeking his sleek skin.

Tonio groaned and sucked at the peaks of her breasts. The pink-brown flesh darkened with desire under his expert massage, the points swelling and hardening even more. When she thought she couldn't stand it any longer he slipped farther down her white, lustrous body until he knelt before her, his head buried in the flat plane of her abdomen. He rolled his face against her skin, tickling, arousing, demanding. Erica clutched his hair, her fingers digging heedlessly into the thick mass. Gently Tonio parted her legs, and his tongue went to work. She writhed under the delightful torture, and he gripped her buttocks with his firm hands to hold her captive to his masterfully teasing mouth.

Erica quivered, panting mindlessly, as Tonio propelled her body to the heights over and over, drawing back just as she reached the summit so he could catapult her upward yet again. Her legs felt too weak and shaky to stand, but she couldn't break away, could only trust that he wouldn't let her fall, just as she trusted that he wouldn't leave her trembling on the brink, but would at last thrust her into the shattering pleasure she craved.

His tongue was moist, silken fire, rhythmically lashing her to a higher and higher frenzy. Erica sobbed his name and his fingers dug into her hips, pressing her against the hot seal of his mouth. At last he hurled her to the zenith and glory burst in her, sending rippling waves of electric joy throughout her body. Erica twisted and jerked under the onslaught until at last it subsided. She sagged, weak with dreamy satisfaction.

Tonio released her and Erica sank into the bed, filled with sweet lassitude and a swelling tenderness. Tonio had been so kind, so giving. Erica opened her eyes to look at him. He stood beside the bed, watching her, a faint smile playing across his lips. Her eyes were wide and glowing as she studied him, her expression so speaking of love that Tonio's heart flip-flopped in his chest. He wanted to crush Erica to him. He leaned over the bed, bracing himself with his hands on either side of her relaxed form.

"No." Erica smiled, her hands going to his chest to hold him off. "Can't I serve you now?"

"Whatever you want." His voice was husky, throbbing. Erica pushed him up, rising to her feet. Slowly she unbutttoned his flannel shirt and slipped it off his shoulders. Next her hands went to the buckle of his belt, undoing it at the same leisurely pace. She caressed his hard, flat chest, tracing his ribs and the line of hair that crept down his stomach.

Her hands slid over the taut material of his slacks, exploring thigh and buttock, floating with feather lightness as she led him ever deeper into desire. She heard his sucked-in breath and smiled, glancing up to watch his face, eyes closed, skin stretched tightly across the bones, nostrils flared.

She opened the snap of his trousers and pulled down the zipper, then tugged them off his hips and down his thighs. They fell at his feet and he stepped out of them, his hands going out to draw her to him. "Not yet," she whispered. "Wouldn't you like a bath first?"

"A bath?" he repeated blankly, and she nodded, a giggle threatening to break through at his frustrated expression. Wrapping a robe around her, she led him out into the hall to the bathroom. Quickly she ran water in the tub and removed his underwear and socks, teasingly massaging and caressing as she did. He swallowed hard, obviously fighting for control, and sat down in the warm water as she instructed him. He rested his head against the rim of the tub, watching Erica as she soaped a cloth and leaned forward to bathe him. Her robe gaped open, revealing the pink-crowned globes of her breasts, her slim waist, and it was somehow more exciting to merely glimpse her riches than if she had knelt beside the tub fully naked.

With the soapy cloth she roamed his body, scrubbing, stroking, slickly arousing him, all the while her breasts jiggling tantalizingly with her movements. She didn't miss an inch of his skin, proceeding at a snail's pace to wash his hair and lather his body all over. Then, with the same precision, she rinsed him clean. By the time she finished, Tonio was flushed and bursting with desire. "Enough," he growled low in his throat. "God, Erica, I'm going to explode."

He moved to get out. She pushed him back and he groaned. But before he could protest, Erica dropped her robe and stepped fluidly into the tub, sinking onto her knees astride him. Tonio swallowed, his glittering eyes intent upon her as she began to move. The water vibrated around them, repeating Erica's movements, enveloping them in a warm caress. Tonio's breath was ragged and harsh as he lay acquiescently, luxuriating in the supreme pleasure she gave him. Erica leaned forward and took his mouth and his arms went around her fiercely, his fingers digging into her sweet flesh. Their lips ground together, tongues flickering in imitation of his hard thrusts inside her, and their breath mingled. Tonio's cry was muffled as he arched, his passion engulfing them both. Then he relaxed, gulping for air, and Erica buried her face in his shoulder. It was a long time before either of them could speak. With a shaky chuckle Tonio whispered, "I never knew a bath could be quite so exciting."

She smiled, snuggling against him, eyes closed in lazy contentment. "Just takes a woman's touch," she murmured.

Erica opened her eyes, disoriented for a moment. Her head was pillowed on hard brown flesh. She remembered what had happened and closed her eyes, savoring the memories. After they had left the tub and toweled each other dry, she had massaged his muscles, warming lotion in her hands and then spreading it over his body. When she was through, Tonio had returned the favor. By then they were once again breathless with passion and had retired to bed to make love with the same wild fervor.

Smiling, Erica stretched and slid carefully out from beneath the sheets. Trying to move quietly so as not to wake Tonio, she pulled clothes from her closet and dresser, wrapped her old robe around her and tiptoed out of the room. She knocked on Danny's door to make sure he was up and getting ready for school. Then she went into the bathroom for a quick shower. As the water beat down her in a hot, hypnotic rhythm, Erica tried to put her life into perspective. But it seemed too jumbled up for that. She found that she wanted to think only about Tonio, to daydream like a schoolgirl about his face and voice, to recall everything he had said and done the night before.

She stepped out of the shower and dried off, then dressed in warm oatmeal-colored slacks and a shirt of various colors in a thin pinstripe design. She finished the ensemble with a pink pullover sweater that added a flush of color to her cheeks. After tying her long hair back with a barrette, she applied makeup, mascara and lipstick. Erica knew she was dressing better and spending more time on her makeup than usual because Tonio was there. However, she was too happy to try to fit into the rigid mold she had invented for dealing with him.

She raced lightly down the stairs, then began to make breakfast. She might as well face it, she thought. She still loved Tonio. She had vowed when she met him again not to let him come close. But she couldn't seem to keep from falling for him all over again. Or perhaps her original love had never died, but had simply remained dormant all these years. His handsome, sensitive face, his lithe body, his soul-shattering lovemaking, made her pulse with desire. Despite everything he'd done to her, he continued to hold her heart in his hand. She guessed some people just never learned.

But what if—what if Tonio had changed? He had

been a young man then, probably driven by little but his sexual desire, as young men so often were. Maybe now, after years of bachelorhood, after success, maybe he was ready to settle down, ready to love and be loved in return. Certainly she had seen none of his former callousness. Of course, she reminded herself sourly, she hadn't noticed it then, either—until he had left her. Still, she couldn't stifle the bright hope suddenly glowing in her chest.

Danny dashed into the kitchen with his usual vitality and plopped down his schoolbooks and jacket. He went to the refrigerator and pulled out the makings of a sandwich. After carefully building his sandwich, he slid it into a plastic bag and sealed it. Then he returned to the refrigerator and dug in the crisper drawer. "Mom, do you think this apple's okay?" he questioned, holding it up and studying it dubiously. "The last one I got was all brown and icky inside."

"I just got them a couple of days ago," Erica replied absently. "They should be all right."

"I think I'll take a tangerine," he decided, and dropped the apple into the drawer with a solid plunk.

"That's probably the way your last apple got 'all brown and icky inside,'" Tonio commented from the doorway. "From your shooting baskets with it."

Danny whirled to stare at the man lounging gracefully in the doorway, and his mouth dropped open. Erica turned from the stove, a crazy mixture of shyness and excitement boiling inside her. Tonio smiled across the room at her, and her heart set up an idiotic pounding. She loved him so much. Oh, please, she thought prayerfully, this time don't let it end badly.

Her son let out a yelp and rushed to greet Tonio.

Tonio swung him up in the air and Danny shrieked with happiness. Watching them, Erica felt a lump form in her throat. They looked so good together, so right. When Tonio set him down, Danny danced excitedly from one foot to the other. "I didn't know you were here!"

Erica flushed and turned back to the stove. It was an awkward situation, to say the least, one she hadn't really considered. How was she to explain Tonio's presence?

"Did you spend the night here so you wouldn't have to walk home?" Danny went on innocently.

"Uh, yeah, something like that." Tonio glanced over at Erica. He wanted to go to her and kiss her, but he didn't know how she'd react to that in front of Danny, particularly after the child's question. He wondered why Danny so easily accepted his sleeping over. Was it simply the natural innocence of a child interpreting a situation according to his world? Or was it because Danny was used to men staying with Erica? Tonio's eyes darkened with jealousy.

"Okay, Danny, you better sit down and eat your food. Would you like something, Tonio?"

His warm glance told her exactly what he'd like, but he answered mundanely, "Eggs and toast are fine, thank you."

Her knees watery, Erica turned back to the stove to cook an omelet. It was one thing she knew how to cook fairly well, and she felt the need to counter the poor impression she had given the night before. Danny chattered as he ate, now and then laughing at some remark of Tonio's. Erica paid little attention, so she didn't see when Tonio, gazing at the boy, suddenly frowned.

There was something familiar about Danny, he

thought. It had just occurred to him when Danny smiled. There was something sweet and charming about the way his dimple bounced in and out that looked like . . . Lucio. His heart began to pound in huge thuds. No! Erica's lover couldn't have been his brother.

But why not? Lucio hadn't known about Tonio and Erica until a few weeks ago. He wouldn't have known he was making love to the woman his brother loved. And when Tonio had told him about his affair with Erica, Lucio wouldn't have told him, not wanting to hurt him. No, no, it couldn't be. Lucio wouldn't have been so crazy as to leave a woman like Erica. He pushed the thought away, but it returned, wiping out all the elation he had felt that morning.

"Danny, you better hurry or you'll miss your bus," Erica warned as she set the omelet down in front of Tonio. Danny groaned comically, but picked up his lunch pail and books and hustled out of the house. Erica sat down across the table from Tonio and an awkward silence fell over them.

Tonio found himself suddenly without appetite, and though the cheese and mushroom omelet was delicious, he could only toy with it. The jealous thought of Lucio with Erica was driving everything else from his mind. He cleared his throat, knowing he shouldn't start this conversation, yet somehow unable to stop himself. "Erica, Danny's father . . ."

Erica stiffened. "Yes?"

"Who is he?"

She swallowed, fear and pride battling with her softened feelings for Tonio. She couldn't tell him. At least not yet, when she wasn't sure how he felt about her. "Please, let's not discuss this right now."

"Was he Hispanic too?"

"Why does it matter?" Erica asked fiercely.

"Because I want to know what son of—" he began in a low, explosive voice, then broke off abruptly.

"What? Handled your property?" Erica jumped up, anger surging in her. "God save me from the Latin ego! Or is it simply the male ego?"

Tonio's nostrils flared and color flamed in his cheeks. He rose to face her. "I'm sorry if the 'Latin ego' is such a trial to you. Does it cramp your style that he demands fidelity from his woman?"

"Fidelity! That's a laugh, coming from you. And I am not your woman! I don't have to answer to you."

"You *were* my woman. And last night—" He closed his eyes, visibly controlling his emotions. When he opened them again, his face was cold, expressionless, the fury drained from it. "I'm sorry. I have no rights over you."

"Well, I'm glad to hear you admit it," Erica retorted, feeling no triumph at all.

"Just tell me one thing. I have to know. Once you said something about sharing women with my brother. You said you were speaking of Diane. But—is he Lucio's? Did you sleep with my brother?"

Erica stared, then burst into almost hysterical laughter. "Lucio's! You think I'd go after your brother because I couldn't have you? Of all the obtuse, stupid . . . can't you even see what's right under your nose?" She stopped and sucked in her lower lip, fear springing into her eyes. She'd gone too far.

Tonio gaped, his face going slack; then light dawned in his eyes. "You mean . . . *Dios!* Danny is *my* son?"

Erica's frozen face was answer enough to Tonio's question. She clasped her hands tightly together, frightened of the storm about to burst around her head.

"You bore my son and didn't even tell me? For nine months you carried him in your belly and didn't bother to inform me? My God, what kind of mother are you, that you would allow your own son to be born illegitimate rather than let me know!"

Erica whitened under his attack. His rage was fierce and vicious. She had never seen him like this. She took a cautious step backward. He followed her, his lithe movements fearfully similar to those of a jungle cat. His fingers dug into her shoulders, and she could feel the sizzling current of anger surging through him. He backed her against the wall, his black eyes boring into hers. "It would give me great pleasure to snap that lovely neck of yours. You arrogant, heartless bitch! You kept me from my son, stole his childhood from me—and deprived him of a father. How deep is your selfishness? I'd told myself that the vanity and spoiled behavior were things of the past, yet even now you've refused to reveal his identity to me. Why, Erica? Did it give you some kind of kick to see me with him, unaware of our relationship?"

Erica swallowed and struggled to summon up a false front of bravery. "I never dreamed you'd care."

"Not care!" he thundered. "My son, and you think I wouldn't want to know? You'll have to come up with something better than that. What's the real reason? Was the idea of marrying me too awful, even to give a name to your boy? No doubt you didn't think Cruz a good enough name for him. Better to have a bastard Logan than a legitimate Cruz." He laughed bitterly. "I knew you were ashamed of me, even when you moaned in my arms and begged me to love you, but I didn't realize you thought that little of me. Even if you wouldn't marry me, at least you could have let me know I had a child. I could have seen him, held him. But then, I suppose I wasn't worth considering, was I?"

"How could I let you know?" Erica cried, goaded past fear by his unfairness. "You ran away and I didn't have the slightest idea where you lived! I'd have given anything to keep Danny from being illegitimate, even married you."

He snorted. "Then I guess the joke was on you for sending me away."

"What? How can you say that? What warped reasoning did you use to arrive at that conclusion?"

His lips curled into a sneer. "Erica, I was there. I remember what happened. I'm not some stranger you can fabricate a romantic story for."

"No, there really wasn't any romance, was there?" Erica replied coldly. "And you're right, I wouldn't have married you. I could have found you if I'd tried. I knew you'd gone to Houston. I even remembered the name of the firm you worked for. But I wasn't about to debase myself that way, to go to you and beg for a wedding ring."

"Heavens, no," he mocked. "Such degradation, to marry me."

"You're very good at twisting everything I say. But there's no way to misinterpret this: I didn't come to you because I hated you with every fiber of my being." She half turned from him. "I think you'd better leave."

There was a moment of silence, then he agreed coldly, "Yes, you're right." His lids fluttered down to mask the pain in his eyes. He strode rapidly along the hall, turned down the intersecting hallway to the front door and walked out, closing the door behind him with a solid click.

Erica wrapped her arms tightly around herself, forcing back the sobs boiling inside. Mechanically she placed one foot in front of the other and walked into the study. Closing the door behind her, she looked around almost blankly. Her mind seemed unable to focus on what she should do. There were so many things that needed her attention. She knew she ought to buckle down and get to them. Personal pain would have to wait. Immersing herself in her work would help ease it. She'd had plenty of experience in that.

She walked over to the desk and sat down, picking up a file with trembling fingers. Then a bleak wave of memory engulfed her. She wouldn't see Tonio again, at least not in a loving way. It was as if her life had ended once more. The only difference between the love she felt for him now and the love she had known as a teen-ager, she realized, was that now the hurt was even worse. She crossed her arms on her desk and laid her head on them, and no longer fought her tears.

Chapter 13

THE NEXT MORNING, AS ERICA SAT IN HER STUDY, trying to work on the farm's books, there was a sharp, peremptory knock on the side door. She went to open it and was taken aback to find Tonio outside. She stared, unable to find anything to say after their bitter parting the day before. His face was cold and tight, his eyes hard marbles, and when he spoke, his words were clipped. "Erica, I didn't give you your check yesterday."

He extended a small piece of paper. Erica had a momentary urge to fling it back in his face, but she resisted. No, she was determined not to be emotional. The relationship between them now would be strictly business. She must remember that. She reached out and took it, saying coolly, "I have the note and deed of trust in my office. Let me sign them and give them to you."

For a moment Tonio hesitated, then gave a brief nod and stepped inside. Erica realized with a flash of hurt that he was reluctant to even come under her roof. Resentment helped her walk into the study, pull the papers from her desk drawer and sign them. She handed them to Tonio without a word, and he received them in the same chill silence. Erica's stomach curled and she folded the check nervously.

Tonio started toward the door, then paused. "By the way, I'd like to take Danny to the island with me this Saturday."

He hadn't really asked permission, but Erica gave it anyway. She must not let him assume rights to her son. "Yes, Danny told me. It's all right with me. It'll be good for him to have male companionship."

Tonio's mouth twisted. "It's too bad you didn't think of that nine years ago." He swung and stalked through the door, taking the porch steps in a single stride and hurrying away across the yard. Erica shut the door, her spirits sagging even lower, if that was possible. Returning to her study, she laid the check on the desk and pulled out a deposit slip. Why was it that Tonio was so willing to give her financial help, yet tried so hard to break her emotionally?

Erica saw nothing more of Tonio until he came on Saturday morning to pick up Danny for their trip. Danny had barely been able to contain his excitement, and after breakfast he sat by the front window, watching for Tonio. As Erica was washing the morning dishes, she heard her son shout, "Here he is!"

Erica dried her hands and strolled down the hall, her heart knocking against her ribs. The front door was open. Danny was bounding down the steps and racing across the yard. When he reached Tonio, Tonio swung the boy high in the air, his impassive face suddenly radiant. He continued walking to the front porch, carrying Danny on one hip, Danny's legs twined around his waist. Erica swallowed the tears that sprang to her eyes at the sight of her son's shining face.

"Can I go now, Mom?" Danny asked.

Erica smiled. "Of course. But get a jacket. The sea breeze can be pretty cool."

"Okay," he agreed readily and darted up the stairs.

Erica glanced back at Tonio. He had remained on the porch. He still hated to enter her tainted house, she thought bitterly. "Please don't bring him home too late," Erica said stiffly.

Tonio agreed with an abrupt nod. Erica didn't know what to do. It seemed rude to walk away, yet he obviously hated to be near her. It was a relief when Danny came pounding back down the stairs. Erica bent to give him a kiss. "Have fun."

"I will." Danny skipped out the door and jumped off the porch, his enthusiasm causing him to run around in circles before he ran to the passenger side of the car. Tonio followed him without looking back or speaking to Erica.

She closed the door, biting her lips to repress the tears. She was simply *not* going to cry over Tonio Cruz anymore! Erica returned to the kitchen and finished the dishes without enthusiasm. Somehow she managed to stumble through the lonely day. The hours dragged, and she missed Danny as she hadn't done since he was a baby. She refused to admit that her loneliness was tinged with jealousy that Tonio hadn't asked her along on the outing.

She tried to work, but found she couldn't keep her mind on it, so finally she decided to give herself a treat and take the day off. She started to call Judy Miller, but realized that Saturday would probably be a day she'd prefer to spend with her family. After a few more minutes of restless pacing, Erica decided to drive into town and do some window-shopping. When she passed the furniture store that the Roberts family owned, she recalled Jeff's offer of a cup of coffee and a visit whenever she was in town. Impulsively she decided to take him up on it.

Walking straight back through the store, she found Jeff hunched over a desk in a tiny cubicle. She knocked lightly. He glanced up and a smile spread across his face. "Erica! I was beginning to think you were avoiding me."

Erica smiled and shook her head. "Just too much work."

"Same here. Well, come on in, sit down. I apologize for the surroundings. Could I get you a cup of coffee?"

Erica agreed, glad she had decided to come in. He brought her a cup of bitter coffee and they chatted for a few minutes. He was obviously lonely in this small town, where so few of his friends still lived. And he was just as obviously not interested in her romantically, but merely looking for friendship, living with a postdivorce fear of intimacy. When she rose to leave, he looked disappointed and suggested that they continue their talk later over dinner in McAllen.

Erica hesitated. She had no desire to spend the evening alone, but she didn't want to be away from home when Tonio returned with Danny. "Why don't I fix supper?" she compromised. Jeff agreed readily, pleased at the idea of home-cooking. She stopped by the aging food store on her way out of town and strolled along the aisles, her mind running over the problem of which of her limited repertoire of dishes she should prepare. She paused at the steak counter. That was easiest, but she was suddenly seized with the distinct desire not to have Jeff Roberts grilling their steaks. Hastily she grabbed a package of chicken.

When Jeff arrived, they ate and talked companionably. Jeff wolfed down the simple chicken-in-wine dish she had cooked, praising it as if it were the finest cuisine. They ate in the kitchen, stacked the dishes in the sink and left them there while they retired to the den to talk. Erica did her best to stifle comparisons to her meal with Tonio, but she met them at every turn. She remembered their shared amusement over her drinks, the quiet, competent way Tonio had taken charge of the meal, the tenderly sensual love play in the kitchen that had left her weak and molten.

She kept one eye on the clock, a fear so horrifying she couldn't admit it swelling within her. It was late, and still they hadn't arrived. Didn't Tonio know that Danny needed his rest? It was a petty anxiety, unworthy of the fear, but beneath it lay a larger, more basic terror: What if Tonio didn't bring Danny home at all? When at last the front door opened, then slammed, and Danny's familiar steps bounded down the hall, Erica released a pent-up sigh of relief.

"Mama, you should have seen it," he called, rounding the corner boisterously. He skidded to a halt at the sight of a stranger in the den.

Erica smiled and enveloped him in a hug. Danny shrugged her away boyishly. "Danny, this is an old friend of mine, Jeff Roberts."

Danny's loud entrance had covered the sound of footsteps behind him, but now Tonio entered the room, his hair ruffled from the day spent outdoors. He wore soft denim trousers, boots and a light-blue T-shirt, with a navy-blue Windbreaker thrown over it. His face was softer than it had been that morning, his dark eyes content, and he looked so good, so relaxed, that Erica had to fight a sudden urge to go to him and curl her arms around his neck. Tonio glanced at her; then his gaze moved across the room to Jeff. His face tightened, the pleasant glow vanishing. "Hello, Erica. Jeff." He nodded briefly at the other man.

Jeff rose, his face as stiff as Tonio's. It occurred to Erica that it must be awkward for Jeff to have to meet Lucio's brother. "Hello, Tonio."

Tonio's obsidian eyes slid back to Erica. "Sorry if I'm interrupting anything." His tone implied the opposite of his words.

"It's all right," Jeff hastened to assure him. "Erica and I were just talking, old-friends kind of stuff."

"Yes, you two go back a long way, don't you?"

"Yeah, since grade school, I guess," Jeff replied, either not hearing or choosing to ignore the underlying sarcasm.

Danny, tired of holding back his story, jumped into the moment of silence. "Mom, you should have seen the hotel. It doesn't look the same at all!" He went on to describe the new construction with great enthusiasm and detail. When he finally wound down a little, Jeff interposed quickly that it was time for him to go.

Erica walked him to the door politely, conscious all the time of Tonio's watchful gaze on her back. He even trailed them into the hall like a stern parent. Erica was tempted to kiss Jeff just to show Tonio, but she didn't want to scare the poor guy. When he had gone, she closed the door and marched purposefully to the den. Tonio had discarded his Windbreaker. He stood waiting for her, arms crossed, his face glowering. Danny had flopped down on the couch on his stomach, chattering away to the oblivious Tonio.

"Danny," Erica began as she walked in, "it's past your bedtime. He's used to going to bed at nine o'clock, Tonio."

"I'll remember that," he returned dryly.

"Run upstairs, brush your teeth and hop into bed," she commanded Danny, and after only a token protest he obeyed her. Erica swung back to Tonio. "Exactly what do you think you're doing, coming in here and glaring at my guest as if he were an intruder? And following me out into the hall to watch us! What's the matter with you? Your relationship to Danny gives you no rights over me, you know."

"I'm fully aware of that. How can I not be, when you're so cozy with me one day and Jeff Roberts a few days later?"

Her cheeks blazed. "How dare you imply that I—that I was sleeping with him!"

He raised one eyebrow. "You're hardly a nun."

"I never professed to be. But neither am I a slut. Even if I were, it's none of *your* business!"

His well-cut nostrils flared. "Perhaps not. But Danny is my business. I want him with me."

"No!" The adrenaline of terror coursed through her. It was happening, what she had feared most; Tonio wanted to take Danny from her. "Absolutely not. You have no rights to him."

"I'm his father! What more do you need?" His brows contracted. "You've kept him from me for nine years, but no longer. I intend to be a father to Danny now."

"He thinks his father is dead. It's better that way. Danny believes him to be a hero, someone larger than life. I won't let you spoil that."

"He needs an actual father a lot more than he needs a bunch of wild dreams. Erica, I want to tell Danny I'm his father."

"No!"

"I deserve at least that much."

"You deserve nothing!" she spat at him. "Nothing! I am not going to tell Danny that you're his father. It would be far too upsetting and to no purpose. You'd probably be interested in him for a few weeks, while it's still a novel experience being a father, but when you got bored you'd drop him too. I won't let my son be hurt that way." Everything inside her screamed that she would protect Danny from him, even though she was incapable of protecting herself. "I won't allow you to see him anymore."

"You won't allow it?" he repeated sarcastically. "I'm sorry, my dear, but you won't have anything to say about it. I'll go to court to get my rights established." His face was as still and cold as a glacier. "He is *my* son and I want to be with him. I'll never drop Danny. You don't know a damn thing about me and never did."

Erica paled. "You aren't serious, are you? Surely you wouldn't expose yourself to the embarrassment of going to court."

"Watch me."

"Well, you can't prove Danny is your son. Only my testimony will do that. I'll say he's not yours. I'd claim a relationship with every man in town before I'd let you take Danny."

His upper lip curled. "I'll recite in detail every time we made love, where we met, what we did. I can describe it all perfectly, right down to the color blouse you wore."

"I'll deny it." Her voice rose hysterically. "I'll say that at the same time I was sleeping with Jeff Roberts or Bill Cunningham. Chuck Wilson. Any- and everybody, whenever you weren't there."

His face was taut and blank, a skull with skin stretched over it. His eyes glittered ferally. "Are you really the kind of mother who would do that to her son? You don't deserve to have him." He turned on his heel and stalked from the room.

Erica raised trembling hands to her face. He was right, of course. She wouldn't do any of the things she had threatened. Of course, a court usually gave custody to a mother. Surely, if the parents weren't married, they would be even more likely to do so. But Tonio had money and could hire a stupendous attorney. He could have all kinds of evidence manufactured so that it would appear that she was having affairs with several men, that she wasn't a fit mother.

She wrapped her arms around her body, choking back the tears. Oh, God, he couldn't do that. But then, she had no idea what Tonio might be capable of in order to get what he wanted. He hated her for not informing him of Danny's birth. As if she should have realized that he would want to see his illegitimate son when he didn't care about the mother. Tears battered at her eyelids. It was all too much: the farm, the work, her father's death, the need to mother Danny, the pressure Tonio had put on her to sleep with him, then his abrupt rejection when he found out about Danny. This was the final straw. What if he managed to take Danny from her? How would she live?

She stared at the dark-blue jacket he had taken off and discarded on the couch, gulping down the sobs tearing at her throat. Tonio . . . how could he do this to her? How could she stop him? She must. She must. Erica knew she was allowing her fears to run away with her. She was hysterical. She cautioned herself to be calm, but it was as if a violent storm hammered at her, sweeping away all rationality. Fear controlled her, drove her.

Suddenly she grabbed the Windbreaker and ran to the front door. Tonio was out of sight. She pelted down the sidewalk to the drive. Far ahead of her, Erica could see his slim, straight figure, and she ran after him, not daring to call out lest Danny hear and come down to investigate. Her breath was rasping in her throat, joining the unshed tears in ripping it to rawness. Tonio whirled at the sound of her frantic approach, frowning when he saw it was she. She slowed to a halt and approached warily, holding out his jacket as if it were a peace offering. "You left this."

He almost jerked it from her grasp. "You ran after me to give me this?"

"No. I—I—" She drew in a deep breath, fighting for control. In a low voice she continued, "Tonio, I came to ask you—*beg* you—not to do this. Danny loves me; he's happy with me. He's all I have." The panic was rising now, taking over her voice, cracking it with sobs. "Oh, God, Tonio, don't take him away. Please! Please! I'll do anything, sell you the farm if you want. Anything. But don't take Danny from me. Don't put him through a custody hearing."

Tonio stared at her for a long moment, his face unreadable in the dim light of the half-moon. When he spoke his voice was laced with anger. "Is that what you think of me? That I would jerk my son from the only parent he's known for ten years and force him to live with me? Do you think I'm so cruel, so unfeeling?" He shook his head and ran a hand through his hair, sighing.

"I don't know what you are. I only know what you said."

"I said I want my rights to my son. I want to visit him, to see him, to be able to take him out as I did today. The kind of thing a divorced father does. I never meant to steal him from you. That was your warped idea."

Tears of relief suddenly gushed from her eyes. "I'm sorry. I'm so mixed up. It's all so crazy. You've been so—so *hard* about Danny."

"Lord, Erica, what did you expect me to be? Happy? I was so low in your eyes, you wouldn't even let me know I had a son."

"Well, of course you were low in my eyes!" she lashed back, stung by his words. "What else could you have been after you deserted me? I was only seventeen, Tonio!"

"You have a very convenient memory. If you'll recall, you were the one who gave me my walking papers. I didn't leave you."

Erica stared. "Do you actually believe that? Have you managed to mentally change what really. happened in order to justify yourself?"

"Change! What are you talking about? Ten years ago you tricked me into thinking you loved me, then dropped me flat. I wanted to die. Didn't you realize how it would kill me, having Grant tell me you didn't really love me, that you didn't want to see me anymore, not even facing me yourself. Or did you just not care how much pain you caused me?"

"What are you talking about?" Erica almost shrieked, fear suddenly seizing her stomach. "I never asked Daddy to tell you anything. He didn't know about us. I kept it a secret from him. That's why I sneaked out every night to meet you. Do you think after all that I would have told him?"

"But you did," he argued, confused. "You asked him to get rid of me for you. You didn't have the guts to do it yourself."

"I just told you! I never let Daddy know about us.

I certainly didn't ask him to talk to you. Where did you get such a crazy idea?"

"He *told* me! He drove to my house one afternoon and called me out to the car. He said you'd informed him about us because you were tired of me. You didn't want to see me again, so he had come to warn me off."

"You're lying."

His eyes flashed. "Damn it, I'm not lying! Why should I lie? Would I make up something like that just to tear my heart out? Believe me, I'm not in the habit of inventing conversations to destroy my world."

"Oh, my God," Erica whispered. Suddenly the world seemed distorted, unfamiliar. Her mind went to her father's words on his deathbed. He had mentioned Tonio, then in fragmented sentences had said that he never knew and that he was sorry. She had assumed that his mind was wandering, that he was talking about Danny. Had he meant he was sorry for lying to Tonio and breaking up their romance?

Tonio watched her, concerned. She had paled, and her eyes were huge and staring, her lips colorless. What was the matter? What was she doing? Why insist she hadn't told her father about them when he knew it wasn't true? He strode to her and gripped her arms firmly. "Erica, for God's sake, tell me what's wrong. Do you swear you didn't send him that afternoon? Did Grant lie to me?"

Tears formed in her eyes. "If he said I'd told him about us and sent him to get rid of you, yes, he lied. I never breathed a word about you, even after I discovered I was pregnant." She uttered a brief, mirthless laugh. "No wonder he didn't question me about the father. He knew all along it was you."

Tonio's hands trembled on her arms. The truth was staring him in the face, but it was too awful to accept. He whirled away violently. "But I went to your house that night, and he was right. He said you were going out with Jeff Roberts, and you did." He faced her, searching her features for the truth. "Grant told me you had been dating Anglo boys all the time you were sleeping with me. He said you were ashamed of me, wouldn't be seen in public with me. You'd never marry me because I was a Mexican. You'd love and marry only an Anglo."

"That's not true!" Erica cried. "How could you believe it? I'd just told you the night before how much I loved you. Didn't you have any faith in me?"

"Oh, yeah, I had faith in you. I told Grant it wasn't true, that he was lying. I was going to ask you to marry me. But he said he could prove it. Jeff Roberts would be there that evening to pick you up for a date. You were going out, as always, with an Anglo. So I went to your house and, sure enough, there was Roberts."

"I had made that date with him weeks and weeks before. I didn't think it was fair to break it at the last minute. It was a big dance at the club, one of those times when it was important to have a date. I'd promised to go with him before anything happened between us. I didn't feel I should back out. That's all. I had no interest in Jeff Roberts. I was bored stiff all evening and kept wishing I was with you. Except for that one time, I didn't date anyone from the moment I saw you. I wasn't ashamed of you. I loved you, and I'd have dated you publicly, but I was underage, and I knew Daddy wouldn't approve. Sneaking out was the only way I could continue to see you until I reached eighteen. I hoped that after you went to Houston and became an architect,

Daddy wouldn't object any longer, that he'd regard you as something besides one of his workers. Then we could have brought it out in the open. But you disappeared. I waited and waited for you at the old house. I was worried something had happened to you. Finally I worked up the courage to ask Daddy about you. He said you'd left town. I couldn't believe you didn't love me, that you'd deserted me. But eventually I had to. I couldn't continue to fool myself. Then I found out I was pregnant. Is it any wonder I didn't seek you out in Houston to let you know? I was too proud. And I hated you, despised you, for deserting me."

Tonio backed away, the full horror of her words creeping through him. "No, Erica. No. I didn't know. I thought—I thought you didn't love me, that you were playing with me. I loved you."

"Then why did you believe my father?" Erica lashed out. Rage was boiling in her now, rage for all the wasted years, the heartache, the loneliness. "Why did you take his word over mine? I'd said I loved you only the night before, yet when he came to you, you automatically assumed that he was telling the truth and I was lying!"

"I told you, I saw you with Jeff and I thought—"

"The worst, naturally," Erica finished with contempt. "It's what you always thought of me. You must have been so pleased to have your doubts confirmed. You *wanted* to cast me as the villainess."

"That's not true. I loved you," he retorted.

"Oh, yeah, sure. You loved me," she mocked. "No doubt that's why you assumed I was running around on you. You could have asked me, you know! You could have told me what Daddy said. Why didn't you say, 'Erica, I love you and want to marry you. Will you marry you. Do you love me too? Or is what your father said true?' I could have shown you it was all a lie. But no, you were so anxious to think I was a cruel, conniving bitch, so eager to believe I didn't love you, that you lit out without a word to me. What did you care if I suffered? All you worried about was *you!* Because I was an Anglo, I was constantly under suspicion. I had to prove myself over and over, and it still wasn't enough."

Tonio sighed and shoved his hands through his thick hair. Erica made a sound of disgust at his silence and whirled away. "You threw away both our lives. I can't forgive that. I'm going home. Don't call me. Don't come by. Just leave me alone!"

Chapter 14

ERICA HARDLY SLEPT THAT NIGHT, TOSSING AND TURN-ing in her bed, bombarded by conflicting emotions. She was swept with incredulous horror and a deep, bitter regret when she thought about the mistake. It seemed such a shattering waste of time, such bleak, unnecessary pain. And she burned with rage that Tonio had condemned her without even hearing her side of the story. He hadn't had a speck of trust. There could never be anything between them if he mistrusted her so.

Then she would stop and ask herself why she would consider anything between them. She didn't know if Tonio loved her now. A lot of time had passed. They were changed people. It wasn't simply a matter of picking up where they had left off. Yet, a thrill raced through her when she thought that Tonio had loved her and hadn't purposely deserted her. He still wanted her. He loved Danny. His love might rekindle easily.

In this manner she passed the middle hours of the night, dropping to sleep just before dawn. She awoke late and dragged herself downstairs. The sleep hadn't improved her mind, she found. She struggled to get some work done and finally gave it up to play with Danny, but she couldn't keep her mind on that, either. She teetered between highs and lows, loving Tonio, filled to bursting with the knowledge of his past love, then furious with him and certain nothing could ever be worked out.

Late in the afternoon Danny decided to visit Tonio. Erica waited impatiently for his return. When he came back a couple of hours later, she tried to maintain a casual air as she asked about Tonio. When Danny told her that Tonio had packed a bag and left for Houston, her breath caught painfully in her throat. Tonio was gone. True, she hadn't wanted to see him. She was in too much turmoil to face him. But a small voice within her cried: She hadn't meant for him to leave completely! What if he didn't return? If he didn't, it was all her fault, because she had sent him away.

His departure jolted Erica from her confused, angry state. She realized how much she loved him and how foolish she had been to lash out at him when she discovered her father's treachery. In the first fraction of an instant when it had dawned on her what had happened, she had been shaken by a hatred of Grant and of herself, hatred that she immediately transferred to Tonio. Tonio had been at fault, certainly, for not talking to her, but she had been to blame too. She had been stupid not to realize that her father had probably found out about her affair with Tonio. The glow of love must have shown plainly in her youthful countenance. Grant's lack of interest in the identity of Danny's father would have given her a clue, if she hadn't been thinking only of herself. But she had been blind and willful and proud.

Looking back on it, Erica could see how her flirtatious pursuit of Tonio would have encouraged him to think her vain and heartless. She hadn't given her love to him freely, but had tried to lure him into extending his love first. And when Tonio had left without a word, she could have written or called him to find out why he had left so abruptly after declaring his love. But her pride had held her back. Her pride, as much as his mistrust, had kept them apart.

Though the events and the years in between had been painful, Erica knew they had been valuable too. She had been too immature at seventeen to handle the problems and responsibilities of love. The heartbreak and her struggle to raise Danny by herself had forced her to grow up, developed her into a thinking, caring person. If she had gotten Tonio as easily as she had everything else in her life, Erica suspected she might have wrecked their marriage with her selfish, willful ways. Now she was mature, and so was Tonio. They had borne their troubles and learned to conquer them. They would be more careful this time to nurture their love. So the pain and years apart had not been merely a devastating waste. It wasn't often a person learned from his or her mistakes and then was given a second chance to try out the new knowledge. She would tell Tonio so and apologize for her anger when he returned—*if* he returned.

But before that she would make a start on correcting the past by talking to her son. On Monday after supper Erica joined Danny in the den. He lay crosswise on an old easy chair, his heels drumming a soft tattoo on the side as he read a children's mystery book. Erica sat down on the couch across from him, her hands placed nervously on her knees. Where did one start with a story like this? "Danny, I—uh, I need to talk to you."

He let the book flop down and raised his eyes to

hers, startled by the seriousness of her tone. "About what?"

"Well, about telling stories." His forehead wrinkled in a puzzled frown. "See, I've been telling you stories about your father for years, things that weren't true. I did it with the best intentions. I wanted you to love him, even though you'd never seen him. I wanted you to think he loved you and had been forced to leave you."

Danny cocked his head, hurt beginning to show in his eyes. "And that's not true?"

"Not exactly. He does love you, and I'm sure he would have loved you all these years, but he didn't know you were alive. Now that he knows, he loves you very much. A couple of days ago I found out that my father lied to me because he wanted what he thought was best for me. But it was the worst possible thing he could have done. So I decided that no matter what happens, I need to tell you the truth." She drew a long breath as though about to plunge into cold water. "Danny, Tonio is your father."

For a long moment he stared at her, then jumped up to throw himself into her arms and launch into a joyful babble of questions. Erica laughed and hugged him. "If you'll calm down enough to let me get a word in edgewise, I'll tell you." She related the story of her youthful love for Tonio and of Grant's deception. Wide-eyed, Danny took it all in, and at the end let out a shrill yelp.

"I'm glad," he told her earnestly. "It's nice my dad turned out to be Tonio. It'd be terrible if he'd been a real jerk, wouldn't it? Some dads are, you know."

"I know," she agreed, smiling.

"Now he'll be around a lot, won't he? Will he

move in with us? Or will we go down to his house? Do you think we'll move to Houston with him?"

Erica tensed. "Danny," she began cautiously, "we might not live with Tonio. Not all fathers and mothers live together."

"I know. They don't when they're divorced," he replied knowledgeably. "But you and Tonio will, won't you? I mean, you still love him, don't you?"

"Yes."

"Then what's the problem?" He backed off, a new thought obviously occurring to him. "He's not already married to somebody else, is he?"

"No, I don't think so." Erica hid a grin. Danny was such a funny, charming mixture of innocence and sophistication. "But, darling, sometimes after such a long separation two people don't click anymore. They don't feel the same way. People change a lot in ten years."

"But Tonio likes you. I can tell," Danny argued.

Erica smiled and teased softly, "Mr. Know-it-all strikes again."

"Well, he does. Besides, even if he didn't, you could get him to," Danny assured her confidently.

"Danny, I can't make Tonio love me. He went to Houston the other day without saying a word to me, and I'm afraid that means he doesn't want to see me anymore."

"Why don't you ask him?"

"I couldn't . . ." Erica stopped short. She was doing it again: assuming what Tonio thought or felt, interpreting his actions without checking them out. Why shouldn't she call Tonio, as Danny suggested? Better yet, she could visit him and talk it out face to face. She'd take off work tomorrow and fly to Houston. The worst that could happen would be that he'd tell her he wasn't interested anymore. It might be embarrassing and painful, but this time she wasn't about to stand back and lose her chance for a happy, loving relationship. Her pride had already cost her too much.

With that firm resolve she made a reservation on a morning flight from Harlingen and went to bed early. Her sleep that night was undisturbed, and she awoke the next morning refreshed and in bubbling spirits. Tackling life head-on was so much better than sitting around, waiting for things to happen to you. She switched on her radio as she dressed, humming merrily along.

A weather announcement came on and the nasal voice of the weather-service spokesman drew her up short. An unexpected cold front was moving toward the valley and a freeze warning was in effect for that night. Erica slumped onto her bed and listened despairingly. A freeze was one of the worst things that could happen to a citrus farm. Although much of her crop for the year was already harvested, the freeze would damage the remaining crop and, far worse, would hurt the trees, affecting future crops. With a sigh Erica stood up and began to skin off the clothes she had just put on and replace them with worn, warm clothing. There was no question of her going to Tonio now. She had to help prepare the groves for a hard freeze.

After a quick breakfast with Danny, she walked out to the equipment shed, where her foreman and crew were loading heaters onto the backs of several pickup trucks. Rafael called to her, "Did you hear?"

"Yeah," she responded glumly. "They're predicting it will drop to nineteen degrees."

Rafael shook his head sadly. "It could hurt. We don't have enough heaters for the whole grove. We'll have to protect just the best trees." Freezes were rare in the valley, which made it economically unfeasible to provide much cold protection for the trees.

Erica donned thick work gloves to protect her hands and helped the men lift the tall, cylindrical heaters onto the pickup. When they were all loaded, she drove the farm's truck to the groves while Rafael drove his own truck also loaded with heaters. When they reached the groves, they placed the heaters in niches between the trees. The hedgerow planting of the trees would help keep the heat in and protect them. Erica's arms soon ached from pulling the metal heaters and from controlling the steering wheel of the pickup as she sped over the bumpy earth. However, she couldn't stop to rest, for the temperature was dropping fast. By noon a wind had sprung up and the cold sliced through her jeans and flannel shirt and jacket. Inside her boots and heavy gloves her hands and feet were numb.

Shortly after one she drove the truck back to the shed for another load. She parked and leaped out, followed by two workers. Glancing across the yard, she stopped, her heart suddenly pounding. Tonio was loping up the driveway. He was dressed in old jeans, a flannel shirt and down vest, and was pulling on a pair of work gloves as he came. Erica bit her lower lip, her worries about the freeze vanishing at the sight of Tonio. She wondered why he had returned and what she would say to him in front of the men. She turned quickly and disappeared into the shed. Tonio followed and took a frim grip on the heater beside her.

"Thought you could use some help," he told her shortly.

"Yes, thank you." What else could she say? The urgency of the situation overshadowed their personal problems. They worked side-by-side, silently and quickly. By four o'clock Erica was dragging with exhaustion and chilled to the bone. When they returned to the yard, Tonio grasped her firmly by the shoulders and propelled her toward the house.

"You're through for the day."

"I'm not tired. We aren't finished yet," Erica protested.

"*You* are." His voice was firm and final. "No matter what your inflated opinion of yourself, you are not capable of doing a man's share of manual labor." Erica started to argue, but he plowed on. "Isn't it possible for you to simply shut your mouth and do as you're told?"

"You have no right to tell me what to do. It's my farm and I intend to see this through to the bitter end."

"I have every right," he replied, and the look in his eyes warmed her even in the brisk cold. But he explained prosaically, "I loaned you the money and have a lien on your farm, remember? I have a vested interest in it. Besides, I'm more experienced than you. Don't you think Rafael and I are capable of lighting the heaters without your supervision?"

"Of course, but I should be there."

"You haven't a single logical reason. Believe me, no one will think any less of you. Your workers admire you for what you've already done. Please, go home and take a long, hot bath. You're no use any longer. You're too tired. You'll merely slow down the rest of us."

Erica grimaced. He was right, of course. She could barely drag one foot in front of the other. It seemed disloyal, like a captain leaving a sinking ship, but she no longer had the energy to argue. "All right."

She plodded to the house and up the stairs to her room. There she stripped, wrapped an old, dingy bathrobe around herself and ran a hot bath. She soaked for a long time, then climbed out, toweled dry, slipped into the robe again and padded to her bedroom. Sprawling across her bed, she was instantly asleep.

It was dark outside when Erica awoke. There was a light blanket spread over her. She sat up, yawning, and fumbled in the dark for the switch on her bedside lamp. The sudden glow revealed a hunched form in the chair across from the bed, and she jumped, her heart pounding, then let out her breath loudly. It was Tonio sitting there, fast asleep.

The noise she made awakened him and he stared at her blankly for a moment. "Oh." He sat up straighter and rolled his head, massaging his neck. Erica noticed that he held a small gold object in his hand. "You were asleep, so I put that blanket over you. I thought I'd wait for you to awaken, but I guess I fell asleep too." His eyes traveled over her and Erica was acutely aware of the old, unattractive robe she wore, as well as of the way it gaped at the top, revealing a great deal of her white throat and chest. She knew Tonio wouldn't miss a bit of it, either. A warm flush bathed her stomach and she rose nervously, tightening the sash. "I liked your other robe better," Tonio commented, referring to the short terry-cloth robe she had worn at the hotel. "But this one has its advantages."

Erica didn't know what to say. His words were melting, out of place with his businesslike attitude earlier in the day and with the anger of their parting. She wanted to tell him she loved him and ask for another chance, but her throat closed. Tonio rescued her by rising and coming toward her. She saw that the small gold object was a medallion on a chain. Then she recognized it as his St. Anthony medal.

"I found this lying on your dresser beside your jewelry box," he told her, extending the medal toward her. "You kept it all these years."

"Yes."

"Why?"

She chewed at her lip and glanced away. "I—it was special to me."

"I've been asking myself why a woman would keep something like that for so many years if she hated the man who'd given it to her. And why would that same woman tell her child—*his* child— wonderful, loving stories about his father? Erica, I know you said you hated me after my desertion, and the other night you told me to get out of your life."

"Tonio, I—"

"No, let me finish. I got a call from my secretary in Houston on Sunday, and I had to go there for an emergency meeting with the engineers on one of my projects. Otherwise I'd have been back sooner. When I got in this morning I heard about the freeze, so I came to help you. Circumstances seem to keep getting in my way and delaying the talk I planned to have with you."

"Talk?" Her heart was knocking against her ribs. Tonio was so close that she could have reached out to touch him. His clothes were stained with dirt and sweat from the day in the fields. She fixed her eyes on the still-damp cloth in the center of his chest, then realized that was as dangerous a place to look as any. There was no portion of his body that wasn't sexually inviting, from his thick black hair to the open collar of his shirt revealing the strong column of his throat to the glove-tight fit of his faded blue jeans.

Unconsciously she clenched her fists and took a small backward step.

"Yes," he continued. "I did a lot of thinking after the other night. You were right, of course. I acted like an idiot. I threw away both our lives for nothing. But it wasn't because I mistrusted you, Erica. It was because of how I felt about myself. I had an inferiority complex, or whatever you want to call it. I'd been treated like dirt all my life because of who and what I was. I expected to get kicked in the teeth, and it became a sort of self-fulfilling prophecy. It didn't take much to convince me you'd used me, because I didn't feel worthy of your love. I was hurt and angry, but I didn't question it."

"I'm sorry."

"It was a long time ago. I'm a different person now. I've made a success of myself and I've shoved it down everyone's throat. Along the way I found out that I always tried a lot harder than was necessary. I told you once that I'm not the same guy you knew before, and it's true. I believe in myself now, Erica. There won't be any more suspicion and distrust." He turned away slightly. "I want to marry you."

"What!" His words stunned her. "Why—what—"

"Danny needs a father. I want to be with my son. I want to be a real father to him, not merely a guy he sees on the weekends who takes him out for hamburgers or to the circus. We could hire a manager for the farm and move to Houston. You could join the operations side of Cross, do the work you really love."

"Are you trying to bribe me with that?" she asked, hurt surging through her. Not once had he said anything about loving her. He wanted to marry her for Danny's sake. "Well, it's not good enough."

"Erica, we could make it work this time, I promise. I'd be a good husband, a good father."

"I'm sure you would, but a good marriage isn't based on giving me a good job or loving Danny or providing us with a nice home. What is this? Do you want to support us because you feel guilty?"

He made a low growling noise. "Why are you thwarting me about this? Damn it, I know you still care. Tonight Danny told me you'd explained that I'm his father. And the stories you told him, your keeping my medal . . ."

"Yes, I still love you!" Erica almost shrieked. "But what about you? One-sided love is no good. Neither is marrying for a child or to make up for some past wrong. I won't marry for anything less than love."

Tonio stared, then began to laugh, a harsh, grating, almost uncontrollable laugh. Thrusting his fingers into his mop of hair, he pivoted and flopped back on the bed. "Oh, God, that's good. That's rich. You don't want to marry me because I don't love you? Why do you think I've been chasing you all these months when anybody with any sense would have been deterred by your constant rebuffs? Why do I live here and run myself ragged commuting to Houston and the island? Why did I give you a loan and try to buy your land for a hell of a lot more than it's worth? I'm not an idiot, Erica. Or at least I'm not with anyone except you." He drew in a shaky breath. "Yes, I love you. I never stopped loving you. No other woman has ever satisfied me. I've never felt the slightest urge to marry, or even to spend two months with the same girl. I wanted you. All the time I hated you, I wanted you. And when I saw you again on the island I knew it had all been wasted effort. I hadn't forgotten you. I loved you as much as ever. More. You're stronger, more beautiful—both inside and out. You're even more desirable." He sighed, resting one arm across his forehead. "Oh, Erica, you manage to make me feel like a bumbling, fumbling sixteen-year-old again. When I try to talk to you, it comes out all wrong." He held out his arms to her. "Come here. I love you and I want to marry you." He grinned. "I also want to kiss you and hold you and make love to you until neither one of us can move. Is that clear enough?"

Joy swelled in Erica and she rushed forward, flinging herself onto the bed so hard that the springs creaked in protest. "Oh, Tonio, Tonio, I love you." She rained kisses all over his face. His evening stubble was rough against her lips, exciting. She breathed in the pungent odor of his male sweat, stirred by a primitive longing. "Yes, yes, I'll marry you. Why did you keep rattling on about all that other stuff? I love you so much. I have for years and years. I was going to fly to Houston and tell you so this morning, but the freeze interfered."

His hands moved to either side of her face to hold her still and he kissed her deeply, lips and tongue claiming her mouth as his. His breath was harsh against her cheek, as hot as his seeking, moist tongue. Erica shivered, her desire shooting to the surface, and she murmured his name. It set up a soft ache within him, but he took her shoulders firmly and pulled her up, rising with her. Puzzled, she blinked at him. "Don't you think I ought to take a bath first?" he asked.

"I don't care." She snuggled against him.

"Ah, but I have a certain fondness for your baths." He grinned, merriment lighting his eyes wickedly.

Erica caught his meaning and chuckled. She

leaned against him and kissed him hard, her lips aggressive, sucking and nibbling at his until he groaned. Her fingers worked at his buttons, sliding down his chest until all were undone, and then beginning on the snap of his jeans. Tonio's skin was aflame, and his hands dug into her arms almost painfully. Erica drew away enough to whisper, "Shall I run your bathwater now?"

"Later," he growled. His arms wrapped around her and he pulled her back with him onto the bed. "Later. We have all the rest of our lives."

Genuine Silhouette
sterling silver bookmark
for only $15.95!

What a beautiful way to hold your place in your current romance! This genuine sterling silver bookmark, with the distinctive Silhouette symbol in elegant black, measures 1½" long and 1" wide. It makes a beautiful gift for yourself, and for every romantic you know! And, at only $15.95 each, including all postage and handling charges, you'll want to order several now, while supplies last.

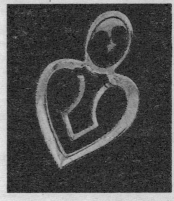

Send your name and address with check or money order for $15.95 per bookmark ordered to
Simon & Schuster Enterprises
120 Brighton Rd., P.O. Box 5020
Clifton, N.J. 07012
Attn: Bookmark

Bookmarks can be ordered pre-paid only. No charges will be accepted. Please allow 4-6 weeks for delivery.

N.Y. State Residents
Please Add Sales Tax

Silhouette
Intimate Moments

more romance, more excitement
$2.25 each

Silhouette Intimate Moments

more romance, more excitement

READERS' COMMENTS ON SILHOUETTE INTIMATE MOMENTS:

"About a month ago a friend loaned me my first Silhouette. I was thoroughly surprised as well as totally addicted. Last week I read a Silhouette Intimate Moments and I was even more pleased. They are the best romance series novels I have ever read. They give much more depth to the plot, characters, and the story is fundamentally realistic. They incorporate tasteful sex scenes, which is a must, especially in the 1980's. I only hope you can publish them fast enough."

S.B.*, Lees Summit, MO

"After noticing the attractive covers on the new line of Silhouette Intimate Moments, I decided to read the inside and discovered that this new line was more in the line of books that I like to read. I do want to say I enjoyed the books because they are so realistic and a lot more truthful than so many romance books today."

J.C., Onekama, MI

"I would like to compliment you on your new line of books. I will continue to purchase all of the Silhouette Intimate Moments. They are your best line of books that I have had the pleasure of reading."

S.M., Billings, MT

*names available on request

Love, passion and adventure will be yours FREE for 15 days... with Tapestry™ historical romances!

"Long before women could read and write, tapestries were used to record events and stories . . . especially the exploits of courageous knights and their ladies."

And now there's a new kind of tapestry...

In the pages of Tapestry™ romance novels, you'll find love, intrigue, and historical touches that really make the stories come alive!

You'll meet brave Guyon d'Arcy, a Norman knight . . . handsome Comte Andre de Crillon, a Huguenot royalist . . . rugged Branch Taggart, a feuding American rancher . . . and more. And on each journey back in time, you'll experience tender romance and searing passion . . . and learn about the way people lived and loved in earlier times than ours.

We think you'll be so delighted with Tapestry romances, you won't want to miss a single one! We'd like to send you 2 books each month, as soon as they are published, through our Tapestry Home Subscription Service.℠ Look them over for 15 days, free. If not delighted, simply return them and owe nothing. But if you enjoy them as much as we think you will, pay the invoice enclosed. There's never any additional charge for this convenient service — we pay all postage and handling costs.

To receive your Tapestry historical romances, fill out the coupon below and mail it to us today. You're on your way to all the love, passion, and adventure of times gone by!

HISTORICAL *Tapestry* ROMANCES

Tapestry™ is a trademark of Simon & Schuster.